THE ENDING IS EVERYTHING

AARON M. CARPENTER

THE ENDING IS EVERYTHING. Copyright © 2017 by Aaron M. Carpenter.
All rights reserved. No part of this book may be reproduced in any form by any electronic or mechanical means including photocopying, recording, or information storage and retrieval without permission in writing from the author.

Cover art, interior design and edited by Aaron M. Carpenter

www.aaronmcarpenter.com

Give feedback on the book at:
feedback@aaronmcarpenter.com

Twitter: @acmatthews04

Burnt Blue Publishing - First Edition

Printed in the U.S.A

ISBN-13: 978-0-9991175-0-7
ISBN-10: 0-9991175-0-5

To my parents, Chris and Tony. Thanks for your support.

" 'NOUGHT LOVES ANOTHER AS ITSELF,

NOR VENERATES ANOTHER SO,

NOR IS IT POSSIBLE TO THOUGHT

A GREATER THAN ITSELF TO KNOW. "

- WILLIAM BLAKE

CHAPTER ONE

11/9/2024

Twenty-four hours before the world as I knew it ended, I threw a party. Not just any party. It was my belated return party. You can't blame me for the timing, it was not my idea. I spent the last six months trying to avoid such interaction. My friends insisted. In fact, they forced me into it.

My home was filled with people I barely knew. The living room with its green and brown alternating walls and one hundred square feet swirled with loud, annoying, music from my expensive audio system. Unfortunately, what I enjoyed was not considered party music for the throng of attendees. My music was too punk without the pop, heavy without the frivolity. Music at parties needed to be in the background with an emphasis on beats and sing-able lyrics, not heavy, thoughtful and poetic. The vaulted ceilings carried the music (Thanks to Spotify. On the air: Lorde, *Green Light,* a favorite at my prom, seven years ago, or at least that's what I heard. I didn't go.) and various conversations floated into the tiny dining room, where I sat, drinking a beer, out of a standard red plastic cup.

I did my best to be a competent host. I greeted everyone at the door. Said, "Welcome." Plenty of "How you doings?" "How's life?" "Welcome backs." I smiled, thanked them for coming, then went back to my seat at the dining table and was left alone. The way I preferred it.

Throughout the night, my attention kept focused on the couple sitting on my red couch. The couple was of great discussion amongst the party-goers, due to the fact half the couple consisted of my ex-girlfriend, Kaitlyn. Three years estranged and with one party invite on a social media platform she appears like the ghost of Christmas past. Not just her, she had the audacity to bring along her husband. They were in town on business and saw the invite. And then decided to appear and surprise me. Surprise indeed. I did not despise her for this, nor did I hold some sort of grudge. It was just awkward. I wasn't sure what I would feel once the alcohol kicked in.

The next four hours flew by in a haze of ridiculous conversation, alcohol and a driving beat. The more I drank, the more it felt like I was time-traveling.

Outside, on the back patio in the cool November night, I was engulfed in a ridiculous conversation.

"His is more purple," Zero said, pointing at and referencing Ethan's penis. "I'm a thick dick motherfucker, so I know no one will be fucking with me. He's good, though. It looks like a baby fetus." The crowd laughs at this amusing, yet disturbing, metaphor.

"One night we were staying at the Flamingo," Jenna said as she turned to me, placing a delicate hand on my shoulder, as if we were best friends. We were introduced at the door when her, Drew, Zero and Ethan arrived together. "And I come into the room, and it's Marie and Ethan. Here's Ethan." Removing her hand from my shoulder Jenna imitates a sex act by dry humping the air. "And Ethan's all." More dry humping the air. "Then Marie's all, 'What's up cuz?' And I was like, I just wanna get my shit. She's all, 'Ethan man, he doesn't wanna finish.'"

"I'll tell ya. I'll fuck you for a long time," Ethan said.

"That's my story," Jenna said.

"Remember when I fucked her at her house, and Aaron had to leave?" Ethan said.

Jenna turns to address me once more, her red cup swaying dangerously in my direction. "I was at my friend's baby shower, and I was passed out after all day partying. And all of a sudden on the bed." She again goes into her sex pantomime, her beer held in the air like an Olympic torch. "And then I wake up. And who is it, Ethan and my cousin."

"I fucked her cousin," Ethan said as a boast.

"Yeah, who let Ethan out of the dog house!" Zero said.

"I've seen this guy work it," Jenna said.

"Small, but mighty, fuckers!" Ethan said.

"I don't know. I never saw anything," Jenna said.

My first friend was Ethan, he lived across the street, and when I was four, he came over and knocked on my door by himself and asked if I wanted to play. It was a ballsy move for a four-year-old. I did. And we immediately became best friends. Playing *Star Wars* was our constant, since both of our fathers, before we could talk, sat us in front of the TV and made us watch the original trilogy. We would constantly argue about who would be Han Solo and who would be Luke Skywalker. No one wanted to be Luke. He was boring. We all wanted to be Han.

"They call me Captain expando," Ethan said, which made Zero and Drew laugh hysterically.

"My cousin doesn't fake it either."

"The best was when you were fucking that chick and I walked in, doggy style in the kitchen," Zero said. "Ethan's like, 'Zero! Is this too big for my body?' I was like. 'No. Wow. That's purple.'"

"Perfect. Nice. I love it," Jenna said.

"All I heard that night was, screaming like a cat in heat. I've never heard that before," Zero said.

"Who needs another round?" Drew said. His long mop top, a relic from childhood and cheap trips to Supercuts, recalled the early sixties and Beatlemania. Another friend from my youth, I felt I barely knew. Married for the past five years and usually missed these types of shindigs. I wondered why his wife, Alicia, let him out of the house.

"I do," Zero said. In high school, he shared a Math class with Ethan, and after a pop quiz, Ethan asked him what he got, and Zero showed him the paper with a big, red, circle at the top right. Ethan yelled, "Zero!" and laughed for three days straight. The nickname was born. My mom, when introduced to Zero, assumed the nickname came from the ghost dog in the movie, *The Nightmare Before Christmas,* since Zero followed Drew, Ethan and I around like a lost dog. I never did get a chance to correct her assumption on the origin of the name.

The five of us went over to the keg and refilled our drinks.

I sat on the sagging outdoor couch. Jenna sat next to me, examining the liquid content inside her red cup. Her index finger, nails painted black, caressing the lip as she stared into the void. Dark hair. Blue eyes. Pale skin. Athletic build. She was wearing a tight white t-shirt and plain blue jeans. She had an air about her like she could care less about her looks, which made her even more attractive.

"So, why haven't I seen you before tonight?" Jenna asked, not looking in my direction. I wasn't even aware she had noticed the drunken host seated next to her.

"Well, I was in the Army-"

"That's so weird," she said, interrupting the story she asked to hear.

"What is?"

"You. In the Army," she said. "I don't see it."

I didn't see it either. Hell, while I was in the Army, I didn't see it. "Neither did I. So, when I got back, I just wanted to be left alone. Some time to re-acquaint myself with civilian life."

"Then you decided to re-enter the world, with a huge party?"

"Yeah. Pretty much," I said, as I lit up a cigarette using a cheap green lighter. Most kids my age (we were in our twenties) used electronic, vaping devices, to get their nicotine fix. But, I was still an analog kind of guy. There are no charge ports for your battery in the deserts of Syria.

Every now and then, the patio door would open, and a blast of music and noise would pierce the night. Then swiftly the door would shut. Leaving the quiet and low-frequency vibrations.

"So you gonna ask me?" Jenna breaks the silence.

"What?"

"About why you've never seen me before?"

"Why haven't I seen you before tonight?" I asked. Not seriously, but interested in the answer.

"You have."

"When?"

"In school. I was there, a couple of grades below you."

"Sorry, I can't... It's been six years."

"That's okay. It's not like we were best friends. And I was always with my boyfriend. I mainly knew Ethan. We had a math class together. I should've kept in touch more after school and besides the Vegas trip which you heard bits and pieces of," she said with a smile. "I never hung around much, just lived with my boyfriend." The word, boyfriend, was said with such spite it sliced through the air like a drunk with a samurai sword.

"That bad, huh?"

"Yeah, but it's over now, so that's good," she said without conviction. "Speaking of exes, is that really yours inside?"

"Yes."

She did not continue, just shook her head and nodded, as if she understood.

Back seated on my throne, at the dining room table, I began to count how many people were looking at their new Google phones. Twelve, so far. Half the party. The newest model is wholly transparent, except for a half-inch, black, square in the center. I thought the phones were ridiculous, you'd place them on a table, and they would disappear. But then someone showed me (don't remember their name) that you could set it up, so if it were lying still for an extended period, a pulsating LED would flash along the edge of the phone. It was impressive, in the drunken state I was in, that this transparent six-inch glass would come alive in your hand.

Ten minutes or an hour later, I could not tell, some guy bumped into me while I was standing in the kitchen. I turned around to see some kid (he was probably a year or two younger than I was) with those damn virtual reality glasses on. Glasses that a user wore that projected digital objects in the real world, a bizarre mixture of the virtual and the real. Apparently, the guy was watching some virtual object and couldn't see me, a real live human being.

"Sorry," he said. He wore a Guns N' Roses tour shirt from 1987. One he bought at Wal-Mart, no doubt. I doubt he was at said tour in 1987, as he would have been minus fourteen years old.

"Watch where you're going or get some real glasses," I said.

"Don't need to be an asshole about it."

"I can be an asshole all I want, this is my house. Why don't you get the fuck out of here, before I go and get my shotgun and end your reality for good."

The guy stood there for a moment sizing me up. I ignored him and went back to my spot and my drinking. He left without a word, along with two of his friends. Again, I had no idea who they were or how they even knew about the party.

Struggling, to not just tell everyone to get the hell out. I sat in the dining room, which was, to be frank, a small transition area between my living room and kitchen, observing the party. The music was pulsating. People gyrating back and forth. The smell of beer. The bass from the subwoofer shaking the table. It all seemed so surreal. As if I was a visitor from another planet observing some obscene native ritual. It was unnerving the contrast from what it's like in the Army. The strict structure and discipline. Compared to this wild, hedonistic free for all.

What were they doing here?

"Dude, a girl is passed out in the bathroom," a guy, with purple hair and a forked tongue, said. I got up, struggling to maintain my balance and stumbled into the guest bathroom. No one was there. "Not that one, the other bathroom," the purple-haired guy said, as he watched me stumble down the hall to the wrong bathroom. I spun around, maintaining my balance by extending my arms to the hallway walls and went to my master bedroom, which should have been locked and closed.

Lying cockeyed between the toilet and the shower was Jenna. "I'm sorry. I'm drunk," she said, her head leaning on the porcelain toilet.

"And honest," I said. "Looks like you have been sitting by the keg all night." I kneeled down next to her. "Are you okay?"

"I'm fffine. I wooon't member much anysays."

Trying to listen to someone who is intoxicated, and slurring their words, while excessively loud hip-hop is blaring throughout the house is difficult, especially when you need to keep one eye closed to see straight.

"What are you staring at?" she asked. I was probably staring.

"We need to get you to bed," I said, as I reach to grab her hand.

"What? No. I'm fine."

"Come on. You can sleep in here... I will sleep on the couch tonight." I added the last sentence because of the audience observing behind us.

"No. I'm fine," she said and tries to pull away from me. But her momentum carries her backward. Her arms flailing, a hand reaches out trying to grab the edge of the toilet, with no luck, her head barely misses the edge of the porcelain seat. Now she was wedged even further in the space between the toilet and shower, lying on her back.

"I am so sorry. I am so sorry," she said, as she grabs the edge of the toilet, pulls herself up and begins to scrub the linoleum with a towel, in the tiny bathroom, on her hands and knees.

I bend down to her level and saw there wasn't much to clean up. "It's okay. I will clean it up."

"What's going on?" Ethan said, from behind us.

"Trying to get Jenna here up and into bed so she can sleep it off," I said. He gives me a once over with his eyes. As if he was deciding if I was capable of such a task. Or, more disturbingly, questioning my motives. He just nods.

I struggled, but eventually, got her up and back down on my bed. As I grab the blanket and pull the covers over her, she says something unintelligible.

"What's that?" I asked.

"Was your name?"

"Blake," I said, while thinking, damn how much has she had to drink. We were outside in conversation just a few hours ago.

"Thanksyou. Bake."

"It's not a problem."

"Niceto mee you." Her head rolled to her side and her eyes closed. I took her shoes off. Tucked her in, as best I could. Turned off the light, locked the door and left the room.

Seated on the kitchen counter, at 12:15 a.m., with my head against the cabinets was not a comfortable way to sit. It was here that I found myself in a conversation with Zero. The party was bustling drunkenly, even though a few of the guest had left. My shotgun conversation had made the rounds. I am sure the story evolved and was now about the crazy host who threatened to get a bazooka.

From my perch on the kitchen counter, I could see through the kitchen window and seated on the couch outside were, Kaitlyn and her husband, having an animated conversation with Drew. It seemed throughout the night wherever they went, the opposite direction I headed. It wasn't conscious. Maybe subconscious.

"Why is she here?" Zero asked.

"She was in town with her husband for work and then blam... I send out an invitation to all my friends, thanks to your insistence, which she is one. On Facebook. And then she is here."

"That takes some nerve."

"I guess so. I don't really care. It's just weird."

"Bullshit. You care."

"I'm fine with it."

"Liar."

"Truly."

"Uh, huh." Zero did not believe me. It had been three years since we decided to go our separate ways. Now, she was there, with her husband. Of course, I wasn't feeling fine with her being here.

"You want me to kick his ass?"

"What?"

"The husband? Want me to kick his ass? You know me, I don't care."

"How would that help?"

"I don't know. Could be fun, though."

I knew he was just trying to cheer me up. But, there was a seriousness to his voice that made me believe that if I said yes, Zero would've walked right over there and punched him in the face. There was a strange sweetness to that knowledge.

"It's alright. I don't want to be that guy. You know? I'm glad she is happy."

"How do you know she is happy?"

"I don't. I'm just saying. Glad, she found someone."

"Blake," Zero said, shaking his head. "Always trying to be the good guy."

I don't believe I was a good guy. I just wanted to be left alone.

CHAPTER TWO

11/10/2024

The next morning, I awoke with a fright (bad dreams were a way of life since I came home) on the red couch, and now it felt like I was stuck. Not stuck, sticky. I must have passed out and spilled my beer on the sofa. The red plastic cup was still in my hand, curled up against my chest like a favorite stuffed animal. What happened? My head was pounding. I looked around as half my body hung off the sofa. The home appeared empty.

I stumbled off the couch, found my way to the kitchen, poured myself some stale coffee and placed the coffee mug in the microwave to reheat. The kitchen counters were concealed behind red plastic cups, with various amounts of stale beer floating in each. I stood still trying not to move (every time I did it felt like someone hammering my head with a boxing glove) and began to replay the previous night in my mind. It was a blur of images: on the back patio talking to Jenna, then Zero in the kitchen, sitting by myself, VR glasses, a shotgun and a transparent phone. I could've sworn I saw a police drone, associated with a complaint about noise. That was about it.

Not one for getting drunk, I surprised myself at the level obtained. Oh, I don't mind drinking, but getting blackout drunk was not something I did. Unless you count my twenty-first birthday. But that doesn't count. Now, I just had to hope the worst thing I did was pass out on the couch and some spilled beer.

Outside, I checked the backyard. The sun had just risen in the east and my eyes instantly closed against the bright, warm, light. More red plastic cups littered the yard, some on the outdoor coffee table, some on the sagging sofa, some on the grass, but no party-goers passed out in the bushes. I went back inside, grabbed my coffee from the beeping microwave, and three two hundred milligram ibuprofens. Took those and swigged them down with bitter coffee. I sighed and headed into my room to take a shower.

Jenna.

She slept awkwardly on my bed, at a diagonal, snoring loud for a person of her size. Still in her jeans and a white t-shirt. My black comforter had been pushed aside onto the floor, and the burnt blue linen sheets were wrapped around her body like a confused boa constrictor. I realized I had been staring which (sparkling vampire's excluded) is creepy, so I grabbed some change of clothes and quietly left the room.

An hour after I dressed and made a half-hearted effort at cleaning, I sat in the backyard and smoked a cigarette. I had a copy of my favorite book, *Brave New World* by Aldous Huxley and I was determined to re-read it. I made numerous attempts since I came home, but I just couldn't concentrate long enough to get past the first few pages. I used to love reading. Now, I struggled.

"Blake?" Jenna apparently awoke while I was staring at page one. She stood in the doorway, shielding the sunlight from her eyes, her unkempt hair moved mildly in the slight breeze.

"Hey. How you feeling?" I asked.

"Like shit."

"You want some aspirin or something?"

"Sure."

"Coffee?"

"Sure."

I got up, put the book down on the patio coffee table and was on my way to the kitchen.

"I really want to apologize," Jenna said.

"What?"

"About last night. I'm sorry."

"No need for an apology. We've all been there."

"Did we?" she asked with hesitation.

At first, I did not comprehend the question. Did we? What? ...Oh! There were numerous gaps in my time-travel festivities from the previous night, but I would not forget that.

"I don't think so," I said.

"Well, thanks anyways for not using your devilish charm to take advantage of me."

That statement threw me for a loop. She should never have to say thanks to anyone, for not taking advantage of her. "Devilish charm? Yeah, I'm full of that."

"Seriously. Thanks."

"For what? Being a decent person?"

"Yeah, well... The world could use more decent people."

With that... we just stood and stared awkwardly at each other. I knew some additional factors, unknown to me, accounted for her state of being. She never quite looked me directly in the eyes. But, I just met her and didn't want to pry further.

"Here." I placed my hands on her shoulders and guide her to a comfortable chair. "Sit down, and I will get you some coffee and aspirin. The breakfast of champions."

A few minutes later, I was back outside with coffee and aspirin in tow. The sun was slightly raised from the horizon in the east. Illuminated in the light sat Jenna, with her knees up and legs underneath her, staring off into the distance. She made no movement as if she heard me. I cleared my throat. She turned to me, her bright blue eyes flashing in the sun, as she turned in my direction.

I placed the cup of coffee and the bottle of ibuprofen on the side table next to her. "Here you go." I brought the whole bottle.

"Thanks." She took a few ibuprofen, swallowed and washed it down with some black coffee.

"No problem."

"What were you doing out here earlier? Reading?" Jenna asked, after an uncomfortable moment of silence.

"The book?" I asked. She nodded. "Not reading. More like staring at empty pages."

"Why?"

"Well, I'm not sure. I can't seem to concentrate long enough to get the words to stick." She gave me a look that appeared to question my sanity.

"What's the book?"

I held it up to her. "*Brave New World*, one of my favorites, since I was a kid."

"You've read it before?"

"Many times."

"Why don't you try something new? That could help. Maybe something simpler and newer. When was that written? A hundred years ago?"

"About that."

"So it's not considered an easy read."

"Not easy. But it's not difficult."

"Every time I want to do something I am struggling with. Like, say, going to the gym or back to school, start with something simple and easy. I walk the treadmill. Take an easy class, like Film Studies, just to get back into the routine."

"Maybe, your right. I've been trying to read this for the past three months," I said. "You going to school now?"

"No," she said and laughed.

"What are you doing today?" I said.

"Hmm... nothing much. Didn't really have any plans."

"You wanna go out and grab some breakfast?"

"You mean like out and about?"

"Yes."

"Sure. Why not? Can I use your shower to clean up?"

"Of course."

Hours later we found ourselves in my favorite bookstore. A small, independent, somehow still alive, bookstore. One of the few places that had not changed in the past three years. The bookstore in question was located in one of those strip malls that popped up and littered the landscape in the early nineties. Gray, one story, buildings and uniformly square. In big, cursive, red letters, written from the bottom left of the storefront window, to the top right, was the name of the store: *Book Me!* Not, exactly, the most clever title. But, I liked it.

Inside, books were everywhere. It was sorted well, but, from one glance, one would think the books were thrown around without order. The small desk at the front of the store housed the lone employee.

Always one there were. No more, no less. Facing the inside of the store from the entrance: left side, Non-Fiction; right, Fiction. The store only sorted into a few genres: Literary Fiction, Sc-Fi/Fantasy, Romance & Mystery. That was it.

"How did this go from, let's get breakfast? To buying me a book?" Jenna asked.

How we arrived here is quite clear. The conversation went something like this:

"What's the last book you read?" I asked Jenna.

"I haben't read a book in years," Jenna said, with a mouthful of pancakes.

"Well. After this, I am buying you a book and I will grab myself an easy one, like you suggested."

"I like this place. I used to know most of the people that work here," I said, while walking down a cluttered aisle of fantasy books.

Jenna continued walking right past me, saying only one thing. "Uh huh."

"So, what kind of books do you like?" I asked.

"Why, you really gonna buy me one?"

"I said I would."

"Well, it's been awhile since I read anything."

"Genres? Authors?"

"I don't know," she said. Putting a book she had in her hand back on the shelf. Then wiping the dust off her hands on her jeans. "You pick."

"You gotta give me something."

Quietly, she said, "I used to read fantasies when I was in high school."

"Sweet I knew there was something I liked about you. You were a D&D nerd."

"I only played a few times." This reply made me laugh out loud.

"Don't worry I don't think any less of you." I paused for dramatic effect. She kept looking at books on the shelf. "So... were you a thief, wizard, dwarf?"

She, without losing her gaze on the books, punched me in the arm. A no-look punch. Very sneaky. "It was a long time ago."

Meanwhile, the lone employee sat observing this terrible cat and mouse, mating ritual. Shaking his head, distracting himself for a moment from reading Stephen King's, *IT*. I am sure he thought for a second to intervene, so we didn't make a mess of the bookstore. But, after looking around at the current state of the store, decided instead to let the ritual continue.

I ended up with the first Lee Child, Jack Reacher novel, a series of books my mom used to love and looked like an easier read than Huxley. Jenna, at my suggestion, was taking home *Homeland*, by R.A. Salvatore, the story of a Dark Elf and his complicated relationship with his family and race of people. Not a bad haul. Especially, for the total cost of $9.75.

"So, where to now?" I asked as we left the store.

"I should probably head home," she said while looking at her phone. It was just before noon.

"Sure, no problem," I said, even though I was disappointed.

"I just promised Aaron I would meet up with him at one," she said.

"Aaron?"

"My boyfriend. Or ex," she said and laughed a hesitant laugh. "Sometimes I don't even know."

"Okay. Home it is," I said, as we approached my car. The wind was blowing the bag in my hand around until it became a twisted knot. The dreaded Santa Ana winds. Jenna's hair swirled around her face, she was pushing it away, when I asked, "Just do one thing for me?"

"What's that?"

"Let me know how the book is."

She smiled.

The drive home was silent. The car, a twenty-ten, small compact, Hyundai, that I purchased five years ago, droned along through the windy streets. The extended silence with Jenna was an odd feeling. Throughout the morning, we talked as if we've known each other for decades. But, once Aaron's name was brought up, it was like a power surge had blown a fuse out of the relationship. It was no fault of mine. It was no fault of hers. It was just the way it was.

She gave me directions to her apartment. She lived in an apartment complex that I believe every person in town lived in at least once in their twenties. She told me, how she got the place months ago after she and Aaron broke up the first time. I really wasn't listening.

I pulled into the apartment complex. She was still talking, when I interrupted. "Which one?"

"...Oh. Number two-twelve. On the right."

I drove up to her apartment. It was a small second story apartment. I never visited hers, but I had been in many like it. A six hundred square foot box, with white walls, a beige carpet, one bedroom and one bath.

"Want me to walk you up?" I asked.

"No. I'm fine." She got out of the car; book in hand. "Thanks for the ride and company."

"No problem."

"What are you doing tonight?"

"Not sure."

"Well, I think we were planning on meeting up with Ethan later. Maybe head to the Roadhouse."

"Okay."

"I will text you."

"Sure."

"Bye Blake."

"Bye Jenna."

With that, she shut the door and walked to the stairway leading to her apartment. The wind causing her hair to extend out behind her like a black flame. She stopped and looked back, smiled and went up the stairs and into her apartment. I sighed, put the car in drive and drove away thinking that was the last time I would see Jenna.

Alone at last, back home. This time it was with a hint of sadness. Being alone, was a concept I had grown familiar with and even relished. But, for the first time in a long while, it didn't seem as comforting. As I stepped inside and looked around the empty house, I was hit with a sudden realization that I needed to clean. The place smelled like a locker room mixed with a brewery. The hangover, while subsided, came roaring back to life at the smell and I almost wretched right there in the doorway. I wanted to curl up somewhere and sleep. Maybe read my new book. I did neither.

Cleaned my kitchen.

Made lunch. A turkey sandwich.

Cleaned the backyard.

Vacuumed the house.

Watched an episode of *Buffy*.

I did not sleep or read.

Around dinner time, I was preparing some chicken salad, still a little hungover, but I was beginning to feel alive again. The Television was on. The news was talking about an imminent terror attack. The news always talked about imminent terror attacks these days. Nothing ever came of them. At least not an attack from an outside entity. Not for the last twenty years anyway. Most terror attacks since 9/11 were homegrown radicals. Influenced by Islamic terrorist? Some.

Then my phone rang. It was Ethan. As I grabbed my cheap cell phone, with its flimsy plastic feel, from the kitchen counter, I realized I missed eight text messages.

"Hello," I answered.

"Blake. What's up man?" Ethan replied.

"Not much. You?"

"Pretty good," Ethan replied. Then he paused and mumbled something to someone else. "Hey, Jenna wanted to ask you something?"

"Sure," I said and began to wonder if we were back in junior high.

"Blake?" Jenna asked.

"Yes."

"What are you doing?"

"Cooking myself some dinner."

"Scratch that. Come out to the Roadhouse with us."

"Us?" I stared at the chicken that was half-cooked on the grill. "Who's us?"

"Ethan. Myself, obviously. Zero is supposed to meet us there and… Aaron." Aaron was said with a whisper.

"I don't know. I think I am just gonna stay in tonight. I gotta work tomorrow."

"Tomorrow's Veterans Day."

"Yes. Ironic isn't it," I said. I did have to work, but it was on a volunteer basis. No one was required to be in the office.

"Well. I'll guess I will see you later then."

It wasn't that I did not want to go. I just felt like I shouldn't. I liked Jenna, this I knew. It would just cause more problems if I were there with her boyfriend. Or ex-boyfriend. There was no good to come of it. I did the practical and rational thing. Take myself out of the equation. Of course, that could all be bullshit, and I was just being a selfish asshole who would rather spend time alone in his stuffy home than deal with the complex reality of having friends. That was an option as well.

Around 11p.m. I went to the stereo, a relic from my father and a bygone age. Put on a record, sat down on the red couch and lit up a cigarette. I tried not to smoke inside but felt this was a real exception. The couch was still sticky. I thought to myself, I would have to clean that more thoroughly, with no real desire to follow up. I kept trying to put the thought of Jenna out of my mind. But, when I did, my mind would then drift to Syria or Afghanistan. The violence, fear, and oppression. My thoughts, slowly drifting to a moment in time I would never forget. When Joe was killed by an IED. It was, as all of these cases are, out of nowhere. Just walking along a street then… The endless ringing in my ears. It could've been any of us. But, it was Joe. My only real friend during my time deployed. A crazy, smartass. A soldier through and through. While I always felt like I was wearing a costume. Joe and the others were soldiers from head to toe. Solid and fearless. Then again, they could've felt exactly the way I did. Everyone else seemed like real soldiers, while inside they felt like impostors.

I had to go to work tomorrow. Why did I volunteer? I worked a boring office job. Creating reports. Dashboards. Microsoft Excel. It was so insignificant and pointless I did not bring it up until now.

The music played. Fugazi, *The Argument*.

Half awake. Drifting between consciousness. The music flowing through me.

11:07 p.m. On a Sunday night in November.

Rancho Cucamonga, California.

Eyes fluttering between open and closed.

Ian Mackeye, singing about the argument.

Then.

Nothing.

The music stopped.

All the lights went out.

I came to my senses and sat up with slow movements in the darkness. Out the front window, I could see a glow on the horizon to the west. I walked with trepidation to the window, pulled up the blinds for an unobstructed view and saw a mushroom cloud rising to the heavens, lighting up the horizon. It seemed small from this distance, like the moon. A terrifying orange-red glow with billowing orange clouds. I blinked my eyes twice, just to verify it was still there. It was. I stumbled backward to my red couch, sat down with a plunk and lit up another cigarette. I knew right then, at that moment, that all the distractions and worrying these past days, months, years, meant absolutely nothing.

CHAPTER THREE

11/11/2024

A few minutes after I saw the mushroom cloud and after it had faded into the horizon, I was still sitting on the red couch, smoking a cigarette. The home was pitch black. The lights still out. I used my cell phone to brighten my local area. This isn't real. That didn't happen. The truth was too much for my mind to handle. I just sat there. The cigarette tasted amazing. So much for cancer concerns. I needed to worry about radiation. Radiation? I surveyed my house and saw windows, the window I used to see the mushroom cloud in the first place, and could just imagine little, invisible rays of radiation seeping between the cracks. Creeping. Slowly. Closer. Landing on my skin. Slowly, but surely, killing me.

STOP!

I shook my head. "Stop thinking about the radiation and worry about the next step," I said out loud. I put my cigarette out and stood up. As I stood up, I became dizzy and lightheaded. I braced myself on the couch arm and breathed. What did I learn in the military? What did they say about a nuclear explosion? "Stay in your bunker." Okay. So, I will stay inside. That part was easy. Nothing else came to me. I slowly walked to the kitchen. Where was the explosion? Los Angeles? Jesus. Thousands possibly dead in one horrible second. Los Angeles was fifty miles west of here. West? Wind direction? I almost screamed with revelation. The fallout would fall over the Pacific ocean thanks to the Santa Ana winds. It didn't mean there would be no radiation or fallout. But, that the immediate fallout would be pushed out toward the ocean. Not toward the east. Not toward my home.

With a sense of relief, I went to the kitchen sink and poured myself a glass of fresh tap water. Water? Oh shit. Water. I had plenty of food storage. I felt relatively content on that account, even if I didn't leave the house for a whole month. Water, though? No plans were made for water.

I opened my fridge and used my phone in flashlight mode to light the interior. Five bottles of water. Damn. In my guest bathroom, I began filling the bathtub with water. At least, I could create a tub of water, that can be boiled for drinking. I even had some toilet water if needed. I began to feel pretty good about my chances of survival.

Wait. My phone. Shouldn't I call someone? What if I was the only one to see it? Dialed Ethan's number... Busy signal. Zero's number... Busy signal. Damn, I haven't heard a busy signal in fifteen years. What happens when my phone dies, and the electricity never comes back on?

I found a real flashlight and batteries in a kitchen drawer along with some duct tape. Turned off my phone to save the battery, grabbed the duct tape and went to the front window of the house. The one that looks out onto the neighborhood. I began duct taping the edges of the window. It was likely a futile effort, but it gave me something to do.

I was half way around the top edge of the window when I saw my neighbor outside. He was a stocky, short, Mexican man, named Enrique. He moved in just over four months ago, with his wife and two little girls. We were friendly, but not friends. He told me about his old house in Irvine before he lost his job and was forced to rent this little home, next door to me, from his brother-in-law. He seemed like a good guy. Now? Now, he was throwing a bunch of suitcases and bags into the back of his late nineties SUV. The SUV was the bane of his existence, he had once told me. Always breaking down. Always trying to fix it himself. I once suggested he take it to a proper mechanic and he looked at me like I insulted his sister. He saw me staring at him. Me with duct tape in hand, him with a suitcase. He waved a quiet, normal wave and shrugged. As if to say, 'can you believe this weather?' I waved back and continued to duct tape my windows. I suppose I could've mentioned to him, not to stand outside for extended periods of time because of the possibility of radiation. But, he probably would've just shrugged me off and continued doing what he was doing. Fifteen minutes later, Enrique and his family sped off into the night, never to be seen again. At least not by me.

The question going through most people's mind, at least to those individuals who saw the explosion; To flee or hole up? I believe the biggest reward and risk, is to escape. If you can get on the road and get out of an area quickly, the better off. The problem is, you are not going to be the only one to make that decision, and you could be overrun by everyone else trying to get out of town. The more conservative option, especially if you have the food storage and the reasonable belief you don't have to leave your bunker for long periods, is to stay put. Find a comfortable place and dig in for the long haul. That's what I decided to do. The windows were duct taped. This included all the doors leading in and out. Even the attic opening was covered. Would this stop a direct hit of radiation fallout? No. Is it better than nothing? Yes.

Next up was to put on long sleeves and layers. If the radiation got inside the house, there was no need to allow it a nice wide area of skin to land on. I put on a t-shirt, under a long sleeve shirt, under a black Raiders raincoat; a beanie, pajama bottoms, under a loose fitting pair of jeans, a thick pair of socks and Rockport weatherproof boots. Thank the gods it was November, not July. I, also, put aside, gloves and ski goggles to wear, if I needed to go outside. But, while inside, there was no need to be that uncomfortable.

I checked the time on my phone: November 11, 2024. 2:15 a.m. 50% charged. No new messages or calls.

In my bedroom, I stripped the sheets, blankets, and pillows off my bed, grabbed the mattress and drug it into the hallway. I needed a place to sleep comfortably and feel safe. The best place for that was the hallway that ran the center of the home. It provided access to the bedrooms, bathrooms, living room and kitchen. More importantly, it was the most interior space in the house. No windows. I can close the doors to my guest bedroom, my office and my master bedroom. (This may sound like a large home, but it was quite small. The guest room was one hundred and twenty square feet. The office, smaller than that. I had a three-bedroom home that was only one thousand square feet. Visitors are always surprised there are three bedrooms inside.) While the house was small, that was a huge benefit at this particular time. No need to worry about monitoring a huge home. I can live in the hallway and be aware of the whole house. The queen size mattress did not fit comfortably with its sides creeping up the walls of the hall, but it would serve its purpose.

Next, organize the weapons. I had three guns. A shotgun, which I mentioned before. Along, with an assault rifle and a handgun. I spread them out on the red couch. Made sure each was loaded. Safety on. Then put the AR, shotgun, and the ammunition underneath the sink in the guest bathroom which was at the end of the hallway so I could guarantee the only access was through me. The handgun, I kept with me.

I sat down on my makeshift bed in the hallway and tried to fall asleep. I had water and taped up every crevice along windows and doors. Made a temporary shelter in the hallway. Enough batteries for my flashlight to last quite a while. I had moved my food storage to the bathroom at the end of the hall, along with the weapons. I was ready. Ready to bunker down for at least a month. Maybe I should get my new book.

Sitting on the mattress, head against a pillow propped along the hallway wall, I began to drift off to sleep.

I was going to survive this.

I checked my phone: 2:27 a.m. 49% charged. No new messages or calls. I closed my eyes...

I awoke suddenly, to a loud knock at the door. Then the doorbell chimed, which was right above my head in the hallway. That woke me up.

I immediately had my handgun ready and fully aware. I walked purposely to the front door. Flashlight and gun in hand. There was a knock again. At the door I looked through the peephole. That was useless. All I saw was a black blob, without the ability to turn on the porch light. But, it looked like a female. Long hair and a slender build. Jenna? Maybe? The doorbell rang again, this time with more urgency.

"Who is it?" I asked through the door.

"Kaitlyn." Kaitlyn? My ex? Who came to my party with her husband and sat on my red couch all night? Why was she here at three in the morning? I opened the door.

She burst through the door talking a mile a minute, pacing back and forth. "Do you know what's going on? There was an explosion. I was just sitting there after my friends left and I saw it. It looked like those explosions in movies from the fifties, a nuclear bomb, Jeff went back home yesterday, and I am stuck in a hotel, and I had nowhere else to go." She finally stops and looks me over. "Is that a gun?"

There was a time when being with Kaitlyn was all I ever wanted. At Cal State Santa Barbara, she was my world. The person who made me feel the most alive. Unfortunately, that all ended. Now, she was standing in my house at three in the morning, in the dark, looking at me like I was crazy. Of course, I did have on a large jacket, a beanie on my head, and bundled for sub-freezing temperatures in my own home. Oh, and I had a gun in my hand.

"What are you doing?" she asked.

"What am I doing? What are you doing?"

"I had nowhere else to go."

"So, you came here?"

"Look, I know after our fight on Saturday, you wouldn't be happy to see me, but I mean this is extraordinary circumstances."

Saturday? I don't remember talking to her at all. I remember Jenna. Staying up late with Zero, discussing all the stupid things one discusses at one in the morning. Then I woke up on the couch.

"You don't remember anything do you?" She must've seen the quizzical look on my face. "Jesus, Blake."

"What did I say?" I asked, not sure I wanted to hear the answer.

"It doesn't matter now does it?"

"I suppose not."

We both sat down on the couch, slowly letting the idea of our argument on a Saturday night, meant absolutely nothing, on a Monday morning.

"You drove here?" I asked. She nodded. "How was it?"

"Fine. Nothing out of the ordinary."

"Most people are asleep and will have no idea when they wake up in the morning." A sobering thought. She sat on the red couch; quiet. I did, as well. I put the gun on the side table and pulled out a cigarette from the interior pocket of my jacket and lit it. Four years ago, Kaitlyn would have admonished me for smoking, especially indoors. Now? She barely noticed.

"What's with the outfit?" she asked.

"Radiation."

Her face turned deadly white. "Oh, my God. I didn't even think about that."

"You should be all right," I said, in between drags. She had on a long sleeve t-shirt and jeans, paired with red Converse. I used to love it when she wore Chucks.

"Do you have anything I can wear?"

"It's okay. Most of the fallout will fall over the Pacific Ocean." This didn't seem to placate her. "If you want, take a shower. I have plenty of jackets you can wear."

She shook her head. "I've got my suitcase in the rental." I think the shock of everything was finally hitting her.

"To be safe, you might as well use the shower now. While the water is still on. I have a feeling that won't last."

She got up in a robotic manner and went to my bedroom. I showed her where the towels were and told her to look in the closet for a jacket she thought would be appropriate, so she wouldn't have to go out to her car to retrieve her clothes. Then I left the bedroom, sat down on the red couch, lit up another cigarette and tried not to listen to the screaming in my head. Instead, I concentrated on the water from the shower. The, never more welcome, Santa Ana winds. The silence mixed with the sound of the rushing water through the pipes in the home and I did my best to hold the voices and fear at bay. I closed my eyes, enjoying the cigarette.

Twenty minutes later she emerged from my bedroom wearing an old, purple, Los Angeles Kings sweatshirt and her thick brown hair tucked underneath a brown and red, *Superbad*, beanie. I was still awake, but my eyes kept closing by themselves. I checked my phone, and it was 3:30 a.m. Approximately four hours since the explosion. I looked at Kaitlyn and smiled. She always pulled off the casual style swell. The clothes hung on her like a child in an adult's costume. Kaitlyn was always short, maybe five feet tall, and cute as can be. She smiled sheepishly, holding out her arms, the sweatshirt sleeves pulled up to fit. Her green eyes, mixed with the dark brown hair, made me question my sanity for leaving her and joining the fuckin Army. Especially wearing that sweatshirt, which I had not worn in years.

"You look nice," I said.

"Thanks," Kaitlyn said. "You used to always wear this sweatshirt."

"I did. Not sure it even fits me now?" I said, and she paused and pulled out the sweater to get a better look at it.

"What's with the bed?"

"It was going to be where I crashed for the night. Hole up in the interior and protect all sides, extra layers and walls, from the radiation."

"Do you really think it will be that bad?"

"It really depends on the size of the bomb." I lit up another cigarette. "Since we could see the top of it from fifty miles away, is not good. But, I think with the Santa Ana winds, it should've pushed the fallout west. At least till the winds die down and switch to the standard ocean breeze. We should be okay and hopefully by the time that happens. Maybe Wednesday. It will have dissipated to a point where it won't cause any immediate issues... Hopefully."

"I still can't believe it."

"I know."

"How am I gonna get home? They probably grounded all the planes."

"We'll figure something out. And you can stay here as long as you want. I got plenty of emergency food supply. Water in the tub should suffice, for now. A couple of guns. We won't even need to leave the house until we know it's safe."

"Your mom inspire you to get the food supply?" I forgot how well she knew my mom. They always got along.

"Yep."

The next morning, we found ourselves spooning on a curled up mattress, in the middle of my hallway. The spooning was familiar, we slept like this for at least a year straight. Her head resting on my left arm, my right arm resting on her right hip. She curled up in a ball, with her hands in a prayer position out in front of her. She always liked to ball herself up. It may have seemed intimate, to an outsider, but after last night, it was hardly more than a fleeting connection. That and the fact we were still wearing outdoor wintry weather clothes. We both, even after awakening, just laid still, enjoying the company. The sun was shining from one of the front windows, allowing light to enter our hallway cave. Eventually, she stirred. My right hand moved to her head and combed through her hair. Another gesture, born out of instinct and familiarity than out of purpose.

"How am I going to get home?" she said.

"We will find you a way," I replied and meant it. She didn't respond and snuggled in deeper into my body. Kaitlyn currently resided in Ogden, Utah, a long way from Southern California. She was down, because Jeff was out here for work and she tagged along to visit friends from Cal State Santa Barbara and, coincidentally, was available to go to my return party. As I mentioned before and will again: I have terrible timing. She decided to delay her Sunday morning return flight to visit with her ex-roommates before heading back to Utah, Monday morning. Her husband, meanwhile, took the scheduled flight home. Their daughter, was with his parents for the weekend, he didn't want to leave them with that responsibility any longer than necessary. She was only staying in an Ontario hotel last night, instead of the one they had stayed at near Pasadena, so she could get to the Ontario airport early in the morning. Ontario is only a few miles from my house. These arbitrary decisions led her to my door.

"What time is it?" she asked. I turned my phone on. 9:41 a.m. 32%.

"Nine forty-five." I checked to see if I could get online. No such luck.

"I would've been arriving in Salt Lake by now. Possibly home." I didn't say anything.

KNOCK! KNOCK!

We nearly jumped ten feet in the air. I was immediately up and signaled to Kaitlyn to stay quiet and stay put. In the living room, the light was blinding after our time in the hallway cave. The gun was still on the side table.

KNOCK! KNOCK!

Slowly, gun drawn, I approached the front door and just as I am about to look through the peephole...

"Blake! Stop jerking off and let me in. The world's ending!"

Zero had arrived.

CHAPTER FOUR

11/11/2024

It took some time to decipher Zero's rambling story, but eventually, we learned what happened to him that morning. Evidently, he went to work just like everyone else and didn't notice anything unusual until he arrived at the work site where Zero was employed by a construction company. On this morning, when he arrived, half the crew were aimlessly wandering around, and none of the supervisors or project managers were seen. While they waited, Zero was sure it was a holiday that he forgot. "But, that wouldn't have made sense, cause half the crew wouldn't have forgotten the same holiday," he clarified.

"It is a holiday. Veteran's Day," I said.

"No shit? Damn. I don't think we get that off though."

After an hour of shit-talking and time-wasting, the crew decided to head home, and it was on his way home that Zero heard about what happened as he was refueling his truck. The line for the gas station stretched three cars deep out onto the right lane of the main boulevard. Since he had nothing else to do, he waited. I told him he was lucky to find a self-powered gas station, as most gas stations would be closed since the power was out. A half hour later, while pumping gas, he learned the truth, from a random guy at the pump next to his.

Or as Zero put it, "So there I was, minding my own business, getting gas. Finally. And this guy at the pump next to me starts staring at me funny. I was trying to ignore him. But, I accidentally looked him in the eye. Then he smiled at me and said, 'Crazy huh?'. And I thought he was talking about the long line for gas and I was like. 'Yeah.' He just looked at me, like I was insane. 'I can't believe a nuclear bomb went off.' At first, I thought what the fuck is this dude babbling about. But, then I looked around and saw everyone running around like a god damn chicken with their head chopped off, and everything started to make sense. Then the guy next to me said, 'I heard there was more than one.'"

"Wait. What?" I asked.

"He said he heard on the radio that more explosions happened at other places."

"The radio," I said. Kaitlyn, who barely knew Zero, except for a brief encounter at my return party and a Christmas party four years past, had a perplexed look on her face, like a dog looking at its master not sure of the command. "We should have checked the radio."

"What radio?" she asked.

"Yeah, I don't know if I even have one that works." I had an entertainment system, for MP3's, CD's, the internet and vinyl listening. I never bothered hooking up the antenna to the receiver.

"You could go out to the car and listen," Zero said. Now we both looked at him like a dog looking at its master not sure of the command.

Outside, it was a balmy seventy degrees on this day in November.

Wearing the outerwear Kaitlyn and I had on was absolute overkill. The heat was magnified near uncomfortable levels in my car. But, we all piled in, Kaitlyn and I up front, Zero in back, and I began scanning the A.M. stations. Nothing but static. None of the L.A. stations were broadcasting. A few had the annoying, emergency broadcast sound, but nothing else. Finally. 1140 A.M. Something could be heard despite the static. It was a live radio show, and the DJ seemed flustered and out of breath.

"We are definitely getting reports, that DC, New York, Dallas, Atlanta, Seattle, and Detroit, have all been hit with a nuclear explosion," the DJ said.

"Holy shit," Zero said. Not loudly. More as a sad statement.

The DJ continued. "All of this is conjecture and moving pieces. But for now, it appears everyone needs to stay in their homes and wait for updates. We have heard of some military activity out of San Diego. But, nothing is confirmed. So, please, everyone, stay inside. If you are near one of the blasts zones especially. Board up your house and hunker down. We will continue to provide information as we get it."

I turned off the radio and said, "Well. That's that then."

By two in the afternoon, not only were Kaitlyn, Zero and myself hanging out in my home, but Drew and his wife, Alicia, and their two daughters, Jane and Natalie, were present as well. The Welles family. They showed up a couple of minutes after we heard the radio broadcast. It was, of course, right after I resealed the door with duct tape, that the doorbell rang. They thought I might know what was going on and hoped I was home. Their immediate thought was to get out of town once they heard about the bomb. But, when they approached, close to the freeway, they could see the traffic back up and headed to my place.

We went through the entire process again with Drew and his family. The bomb. The possible radiation. Thankful for the Santa Ana winds. The sealing of the house with duct tape. The bedroom in the hallway, which would now have to be changed.

Natalie, age six, looked like her mother, with flaming red hair and pale skin. Jane, age five, looked like Drew with her thick, wild, jet black hair. They weren't very happy about the paper and crayons I gave them. They would much rather have a tablet. But, eventually, when they realized the electricity was out at my house and I didn't have a tablet, they accepted their fates and began scribbling incoherent images of homes and families with unknown origins, except in the minds of their creators.

"When I came home, Alicia was already there, and we both went to pick the kids up from daycare together. The place was mostly empty," Drew said. "Thankfully Mrs. Nash was waiting with all the children who had not been picked up yet. And it wasn't until after we left that we heard the news. You'd think they would've sent out a big bulletin or something."

"No channel to do so," I said. "Most of the electricity in the area is out."

"Why is that?" Kaitlyn asked. "We are pretty far from the blast site."

"An EMP?" Zero suggested. He probably saw it happen in a movie.

"No. Not an EMP. An EMP would've knocked out your phone, immediately. And every electronic device, including your car," I said. "If I had to guess, there was an electrical surge when the bomb went off, and then everyone panicked, and no one has gotten around to fix it... Yet."

"So, the power could be back soon?" Alicia asked.

"Yes. I would think so... Unless there is something else going on."

"Like what?" Kaitlyn asked.

"No idea. No one showing up to work. Maybe," I said.

"Well. What do we do now?" Alicia asked.

This was the question that needed to be answered. The only instructions from any sort of authority, was from some DJ in the high desert, telling us to stay put. We heard no official announcements from any government body. With the electricity and cell phones out, who knew what was going on in the government.

"The way I see it," I said. "We have a couple of options. Number one. We all hole up at our own places and wait till we hear something from any government officials. Number two. We try and brave the traffic and get out of town. Number three. We all combine our resources and hole up together and ride out whatever comes our way. I suggest number three."

They looked at me with a renewed sense of confidence. Drew seemed to turn to Alicia to say 'I told you we came to the right place.'

"Number Three," Drew said.

"Fuck. I got nowhere else to be, and my place is a shithole," Zero said.

"Can you watch the language?" Alicia said, as she looked at the children, who were giggling at Zero's unburdened, colorful language.

"Sorry. Ma'am."

"We need to gather some supplies and people." I went through a whole list of things we need to survive at least a month without leaving: boxed or canned food, bottled water, propane, gas, weapons, blankets, pillows, binoculars, weather-proof coats, boots, sleeping bags, flashlights, batteries and anything else that we could use.

"We also need to stop by Ethan's. He may be home and see if he wants to join us," Drew said. "And do you think this is the best place to stay? It's not very big, with all these people."

"I think that is why we should stay here. A small place is easier to keep an eye on, than a bigger one. And because it's tucked away in a cul-de-sac, I think we can avoid any unwanted attention," I said.

"What, like marauders or something?" Drew asked.

"Maybe."

"Do you think it will come to that?" Alicia asked.

"I don't know. I really don't," I said. Which was true. I was just making most of this stuff up, as we went. Obviously, based on some military training. But, not a lot of apocalypse training was provided by the Army.

Eventually, we decided that Zero and I would go out to his place, the Welles home (Drew gave me the key) and to stop by Ethan's, once the sun went down. Alicia found some crackers and fruit for dinner for the kids and the others who stayed behind. I showed Drew where I hid the guns in the bathroom. I believed everything was in order. We had our strange grocery list, and I was taking my handgun.

I turned to Kaitlyn who was sitting quietly on the red couch watching the kids color on my rug. "What do you think?"

"I don't think I have much of a choice," she said.

"I know, and I told you we would get you to Utah as soon as we can and we will."

CHAPTER FIVE

11/11/2024

It seems almost surreal to me now that everyone appeared to treat that night like any other. I remember reading a similar thought in the novel by H.G. Welles, *War of The Worlds*. I remember thinking as I read, how can people continue to live as if nothing happened? A giant meteor landed in a field directly from Mars, and the start of an alien invasion was imminent, yet people were just going about their daily lives. I, of course, was a little unfair to the citizens in *War Of The Worlds*. I knew it was an alien invasion. I read the description on the back of the book. Yet, while driving with Zero to pick up our survival supplies, I saw similar reactions. While Kaitlyn and I were bundled up and anxious about radiation, a man a few blocks down was washing his car at twilight, basking in the fresh air, drying his Ford Fusion, with a microfiber towel. They say there are two primary responses to a perceived harmful event; fight-or-flight. I would like to add a third;

ignore. A twenty-first-century human reaction to the unimaginable. I will ignore everything and pretend the world and myself are just fine.

As we drove the two miles to Zero's apartment, I observed nothing out of the ordinary. No speeding cars. No riots. Police sirens were nowhere to be heard. It was all too strange. Zero while driving, was also, quiet. Which, for him, was unusual. He seemed to be operating with a heightened sense of awareness as if the alien invasion of H.G. Welles' novel was going to burst out of the sky at any moment. Hands at ten and two, checking the mirrors repeatedly. He was, of course, anticipating more from this night, like myself, than the actuality of the situation.

It was curious these days that the person I would call my closest friend was Zero. We had never been close. It was always mutual friends who brought us together. Either, Ethan or Drew. It was never our first thought to call each other and see what we were doing. Yet, over the past six months, it was Zero I talked to on a regular basis. It was Zero who 'suggested' I host a party. He was the one, without question, since I've been back who has treated me like I was the same person. We met playing roller hockey as freshmen in high school. He let me borrow a pair of hockey gloves. Mine were worn through, and I could feel the stick in my bare hands. It was ideal for grip and a tactile feeling of the stick, not so ideal for my hand's safety. Zero, even at the time, was the life of the party. Always cracking jokes and being his imprudent, absurd, yet innocent, self. He offered the gloves to me without asking. "Fuck dude. Your gonna get a splinter with those gloves. Here try these." As he tossed the new pair over, I was laughing. A splinter? That is what made me laugh. Hockey sticks haven't been made of wood since the early nineties. Seated in his truck, I felt a sincere admiration for the man we all called, Zero.

After five minutes on the road, Zero still drove with that anticipating look on his face. I was staring at that face when he slammed on his brakes, jerking my neck sideways. Out the windshield, a block away, red taillights, contrasted with the sunset. It was the intersection of Baseline Street and Milliken Road. At that intersection; a grocery store and a gas station.

"Turn right up here into the neighborhood," I said and pointed at a turnoff to a side street twenty feet from where the car idled in the middle of the road.

"We need to go left, not right to my place."

"Yeah, but the next left turn is way up there."

"We don't need a turn," Zero said and turned left...over a medium separating the west and eastbound lanes. The medium, three feet across, comprised of grass, concrete, and brick, that created triangle patterns crisscrossing between the green grass. When he hit the curb, the whole truck creaked, and all his work equipment in the back trembled and threatened to eject from the truck bed. Thankfully, there stood no trees where Zero turned, and we were soon heading back east, the way we came. But, we saw our first sign that everything was not as serene as it first appeared.

Ten minutes later we arrived at Zero's apartment, and I had finally begun to process the significance of the past twenty-four hours. In a rush to figure out how to survive and the urgency of incoming friends, the impact of the previous twenty hours had eluded me. Standing in Zero's apartment, raiding his kitchen, it finally dawned on me how the world had irrevocably been altered. Even if the news we heard on the radio was not true, that other bombs had gone off throughout the country, even if that was the case, one nuclear explosion in Los Angeles was sufficient to alter everything. Tens of thousands of people had died in an instant. Nothing was going to be the same. Maybe in the rest of the country, watching in horror, they thought that everything would eventually return to normal. But, it dawned on me, in Zero's not so clean kitchen, that nothing would be the same.

"What are we looking for?" Zero said, interrupting my meditation.

"Look for anything that you would take on a camping trip."

"I usually take beer, and that's about it."

I didn't respond. I knew he was playing Zero, not himself, when he said absurd things like that. "Sleeping Bags, Barbecues, Charcoal, Lanterns, Canned food... Anything that you think we can use." He just nodded and went into his bedroom. I went back to scouring the kitchen.

By the time we reached Ethan's house, we had thoroughly extracted everything useful from not only Zero's home but Drew's as well. The Welles family home was a gold mine of supplies as they always took camping vacations. We grabbed everything we could need for an extended stay at Hotel Blake.

It was just after 8 p.m. My phone was down to ten percent. I was hungry and tired when we knocked on Ethan's door.

No answer.

We peered through his front window. Dark and gloomy. Zero shined a flashlight in the front window of the apartment. Not as dark, still gloomy.

"Should we break in?" Zero asked. I didn't think that was an option until he said it.

"If we can get in without making much noise," I said, and Zero went to the window and pushed on the pane of glass, to see if he could move the window enough to dislodge the locking mechanism. It was slightly alarming to see him do this so casually. It was evident he had performed this level of unlawful entry before.

The sound of Zero's movements echoed disconcertingly across the silent apartment complex. I looked across the park with its colorful playground, at the many beige stucco apartment's that sat in silence. No one moved. Three cars scattered between empty spaces in the parking lot. The apartment complex, single story, with buildings spread throughout the compound in a horseshoe around the common, sat still as a lion awaiting its prey. It was not one of the more pleasant apartment complexes in Rancho Cucamonga, but the ground level and cheap cost kept it perpetually occupied. Yet, on this strange November night, there was not a person in sight.

"I think I got in," Zero said. With one quick hard push, he had removed the window pane and laid it on the ground. He hopped into Ethan's apartment and opened the front door with a "Ta-da!"

Inside we found a mess. Trash accumulated on the kitchen counters. Dishes in the sink, which had not been washed for days, possibly weeks.

"Jesus, I thought my place was bad," Zero said. "It looks and smells like no one has been here in months."

"Yeah. Let's just see if we can find anything we can use and get out of here." It felt betraying to be in Ethan's apartment. As if we were gazing into a slice of a friend's life he didn't want us to see.

Ethan had been my closest friend throughout my youth. Yet, as I walked around his apartment, I honestly felt I did not know him at all. In his bedroom, I found dirty clothes strewn across the twin bed and piled on the beige floor. On a cheap IKEA dresser, buried underneath a pile of dirty clothes I found a framed photograph. It was of Drew, Ethan and myself, from our high school graduation, in our purple graduation robes and hats, smiling as if we just won the lottery. I had this same picture in a box somewhere in storage. The past eight years had flown by. I went off to college a few months after this photo was taken. Drew met Alicia that summer and married her a year later. Ethan? Ethan drifted from job to job. Taking college courses here and there, never with a plan of finishing.

"What's that?" Zero asked. I showed him the picture. "Cute. I don't think there is anything here we can use. No canned food. Water. Nothing."

I put the photograph back on the dresser, moving aside some dirty clothes. "Yeah. Let's get out of here."

On the way back to my place, by way of side streets, we passed a small business center, and an idea popped into my head.

"Pull into the business center." Zero did as I instructed. "One of the issues we are going to have is a contaminated water supply. At least, for a while." Zero looked at me with a blank expression. "What does every small business have?" Zero shrugged. He'd probably never been in a real office. "Water."

"We're going to break into the business center?" Zero said with a smile on his face.

"Yep."

There we were, two old friends standing in the dead of night, pitch black, dressed like we were in the heart of winter in Minnesota, about to commit our first felony together. Or at least it was the first for me. For Zero, I had no idea. The small business complex we stumbled upon was a perfect spot for our thievery. It was located on a commercial block full of warehouses, far away from residential housing and shopping centers. An ideal location, especially with the electricity out, which meant no alarms, unless the building had some sort of backup generator, which I doubted.

"So, how are we getting in?" Zero asked.

"Not sure." The doors were all made of glass. Each office had a separate door. But, the primary tenant, at the center of the compound appeared to take up half the space. That was our first prize, and then we would try the others. It was a real estate office and at the entrance was a double door made of glass, with garish gold handles. Locks located at the top, by the handle, and at the bottom.

"We can try around back and see if we can bust any windows," Zero said. Which seemed like a promising idea. But I had a better one. I grabbed the polished, gold, metal door handle, which ran horizontally and pulled. Nothing happened. Zero laughed. Then I pushed… And walked right in.

"Holy shit. Like a damn Jedi," Zero said. I was just as astonished myself. Bosses, supervisors, employees, in haste to leave, forgot to lock the door.

I said a slight prayer to the Powers That Be and turned to Zero. "Let's hope they still use the old school water dispensers and not the new ones. Grab the flashlights and the dolly, we're gonna need it."

Inside, darkness, except for an unnerving green glow emanating from all the exit signs. A few laptop computers were still on, with little lights blinking in flat black boxes on desks in various states of order.

At the front of the office we found the receptionist desk and behind the receptionist's ergonomic chair was our prize. A white, with hot and cold, water dispenser. Thankfully, it was the classic style, not the new water dispensers that tapped directly into the water line, like a refrigerator. The blue jug on top appeared to be two-thirds full of water. I motioned Zero over, and we both looked at each other and at the dispenser. Neither of us had filled or removed a three-gallon water jug from a water dispenser before.

"We need to take the jug off as quickly as possible, so we don't spill water everywhere," I said.

"Why don't we just lay the whole thing on its side, then take it off?" he said.

We lowered the entire dispenser down, with care not to let the jug dislodge from the opening at the top. Once it was on the floor, we lifted the jug from the dispenser not spilling a single drop. With a look at Zero, we both smiled. That was easy.

"Load the dispenser into the truck," I said, as I brought the dolly over. "And I will try and find the break room and see if we can get some foil, saran wrap or anything to cover the top of the jug and hopefully some more of these things." Zero nodded, and I went exploring.

I found four more water dispenser's throughout the building. The breakroom had the newer style, which was no use to us. The other three I found in various conference rooms with varying amounts of water. I also found, in a maintenance closet, two, untouched three-gallon jugs of water. Again, I thanked the Powers That Be. It took about fifteen minutes to get all the jugs into the truck. The hardest part was loading them onto the truck. In total, in that one office, we took six jugs of water, along with two dispensers.

Zero asked about the second dispenser, "Why do we need another one?" I told him I would explain later, once we got back to my place.

At a dentist office, we tried the door, with no such luck. I was looking at the hinges on the door when Zero grabbed a sledgehammer from the back of his truck. I saw him at the last minute as he raised it over his head to smash the glass to pieces.

"Wait," I yelled. He pulled back his swing at the last moment, missing the glass door by inches.

He gave me a cross-eyed look. "What? What's the difference?"

"It's one thing if things ever go back to normal, which still may happen, and finding their water stolen. It's another to come back and find their front door smashed to bits."

"Why?"

"One may spark an investigation, the other probably won't." That poor reasoning seemed to satisfy him momentarily. "Let's check the other offices for open doors, then we can come back here, and you can smash at will," I said, and a big grin spread across his face.

We found another office with an unlocked door and two more jugs of water. Bringing the total to eight.

"How many of these things do we need?" Zero asked.

"As many as we can fit in your truck." Which looked to be able to accept three or four more in the bed. We had moved all of Zero's work equipment and the supplies we procured from Drew's house into the cab and front passenger seat. I would take the return journey sitting in the back with our confiscated liquid passengers.

Back in front of the dentist office, Zero had his sledgehammer high above his head waiting for the go-ahead. I nodded. With one fast swoosh, the sledgehammer struck the door above the door handle. A deafening sound echoed across the pavement. I, on instinct, looked around. No movement. No light. Zero had managed to create a glass spider web, about twelve inches in diameter just above the handle. He raised the sledgehammer again, with a big smile plastered on his face, like a madman playing the strongman game at a carnival. This time the door had no chance as it instantly shattered. Zero's momentum almost sent him right into the falling glass shards, but he caught himself at the last minute and fell backward, landing on his backside.

Zero sat on the sidewalk, motionless, then looked up at me with a bemused, 'did I do that?', smile and laughed. Sometimes there was nothing else to do but laugh. Neither of us were traditional thieves. Yet, here we were.

Zero picked himself up, and we entered the dentist office, glass crackling under our feet. The waiting room had another water dispenser. We also found one in the small employees break room, but that one was of no use. Another jug was found in another utility room, that we had to persuade open. Two more to the count. I used a rubber band and saran wrap to cover the tops of the jugs, and we loaded them on the truck. Zero was about to leave when I went back into the dental office. I was not looking for more water jugs. When Zero asked, what I was looking for, I responded: Drugs.

In one of the back offices, we found a closet with all types of drugs. Mainly topical anesthesia and a variety of mouthwash. But, we grabbed all the pain medication we could in a plastic trash bag.

"We could get high as hell on some of this shit," Zero remarked. Yes, we could.

Back at the truck, we were ready to leave. I sat in the bed with my back to the cab and my knees to my chest. "Ready whenever you are," I said.

Zero opened the little window that separated the bed from the cab and handed me a bottle of Jack Daniels.

"I am now," he said.

"Where did you get this?"

"In one of the desk at the real estate office."

Off in the distance we heard multiple, loud, popping sounds, echoing from all directions, like a spontaneous fourth of July celebration

"What the hell is that?" Zero asked. All around us the lights sparked to life. Street lamps, lights in offices and then came a loud ringing, like a car alarm, except it wasn't coming from a car. It was coming from the dentist office.

"We better go," I said. Zero nodded, and we headed out.

CHAPTER SIX

11/11/2024

Seated in the bed of Zero's truck, I watched the familiar places, streets, and intersections, hurry past, and I was consumed with an immense feeling of nostalgia, for this town I called 'home.' With the electricity now coursing through its arteries, the city began returning to life, awakening from a deep slumber.

I was born in Rancho Cucamonga at the closing of the previous century. When I was a kid, the city had already boomed to a population of over one hundred and sixty thousand. My dad used to tell me that when he was a kid, there were huge trees that lined the main boulevard, of the grapevines and orange groves and how he used to walk three miles to school. I am sure that last part was made up, but as a kid, I used to imagine walking to school and having an adventure on the way, like in the movie, *Stand By Me*. I only took the bus.

My parents lived in a mobile home (trailer) park when they brought me home from the hospital. They moved in when my grandparents moved out the year before and into the house where I currently reside. A passing of the residential torch, so to speak. Maybe three generations from now my descendants will be living in a huge house at the top of the hill?

The mobile home park, or trailer park, was not as bad as others, who lived outside the park, made it out to be. Of course, I was a kid, and may not have been aware of some of the unsavory aspects. To me, it was a huge playground. A playing field that just expanded as I got older. Up until I was five I could only play on the street directly in front of the house. From five to eight, I could play on the road above and so on and so on until I had full reign of the whole park.

My parents would let me do whatever I wanted as long as I was home on time, which depended on the day. I suppose, we were a new generation of latchkey kids. Too poor to have the modern leashes, like cell phones, tablets, and computers. The computer was for homework or for my mom to play solitaire on, that was it. We were not allowed on the internet unless one of my parents was present. "Too many perverts," my mom used to say. I don't think Ethan had access to the internet until his thirteenth birthday.

I spent most of my time outside, especially at Ethan's. Ethan's mom was never home, and his dad left when he was five. Not before showing him *Star Wars*, so at least he had that. While Ethan's mom was never home, always working a shitty waitressing job, we had the run of the place. We would play video games, watch movies we had no business watching and enjoyed the freedom of no parents. But, the best thing about Ethan's, besides the freedom, were the snacks. The cupboards were always full of a variety of Hostess products. Cupcakes. Twinkies. Swiss Rolls. Every sugary, fantastic product you could think of. All of which were absent from my house. My parents were far too practical to buy such snacks. It was kid heaven.

When I was home, my dad was absent until after seven, when he would arrive home from his soul-sucking office job in a bad mood. Dinner was at seven-thirty. We ate, then watched some crappy TV for an hour and then went to bed. It was like this for most of my childhood. I would come home from school, drop my backpack off, and out I went.

I haven't mentioned my older brother, William. That's probably because he wasn't a part of my life when I was growing up. His main contribution to my life was to introduce me to the wonderful world of Punk Rock. He was five years older than me, was never home and if he was, he was in his room or should I say, our room. But, I never stayed in the room, except to go to sleep. It was HIS room, and I was just a tenant. When he left, after high school, I saw him only at Christmas. He was one of those dreamers. The guy who always had big plans and ideas, but they never quite worked out, because he never put in the work to achieve his goals. He drifted from place to place. He lived in Denver, for some time. Then Salt Lake City. Now? I believe he is in Oregon somewhere. We lost touch many years ago.

In my early teens, before high school, social media, and personal phones shattered everyone's private life. While the rest of my classmates all had mobile phones, always texting and commenting on whatever it was they were commenting on, Ethan and I were out of the loop. Even when I brought up the fact that my parents could always get a hold of me and locate me if I had a phone. My mom just said, "Are you gonna be in a place where I don't know where you are?" "No. But everyone else has one," I replied with purpose. "If everyone else has a phone, then just borrow one of theirs if you need me." My mom must've weighed the pros and cons of letting her twelve-year-old son have a phone and decided the cons were higher than the pros. Practical. Ethan never had a cell phone, because his mom couldn't afford one for him.

Both my parents were rational and practical. They always had an excessive amount of food storage, just in case. This would be an important trait, when they passed this, practicality, down to me. They never lived outside their means. While my dad made decent money at his office job, enough, I thought, to buy us a 'real' house, we still lived as though we were never financially stable. Christmas, our birthdays and Back To School, were the only times we received gifts or new clothes. If we went to the mall for its thirty-screen movie theater, we never went inside the mall. And I could never con my mom to buy me a video game, a movie, or a pair of sneakers, just because we were nearby and I wanted one. No matter how much I begged and cried. The money went into savings and I.R.A's, not for the latest video game or candy at the grocery store. Practical and rational.

As we approached middle school, another member had joined our little clique, Drew. He lived at the top of the mobile home park, while Ethan and I lived at the bottom, right along the main avenue. Drew lived in the enviable, triple-wide (a double-wide with an add-on), mobile home. It was just Drew and his mom, but she was more of an older sister than a mom. They had things like Netflix and a TV in every room. I watched some of the classic horror films in Drew's bedroom, during sleepover's. Drew loved his horror movies. He had an Apple phone and kept us in the loop, so we weren't too big of outcasts when we went to high school.

My high school was not the hell it was made out to be. It just was. The jocks didn't terrorize the nerds, the potheads were not pushers, and the band was not a bunch of nerds with terrible acne. It was just kids. I made some new friends, including the one and only Zero. But, besides doing homework and having a few bad teachers, to me it was boring, tedious, monotonous and every other synonym for excessive boredom. My teachers would say I under-achieved. I remember watching *Buffy the Vampire Slayer* with my mother (her favorite show) and its metaphor of high school being hell and thought that's nothing like my school. No vampires or demons here. Not that I was an expert on what everyone's experience was like at my school. I am sure some students had a terrible time. But, to me, it was a big bag of nothing.

I didn't play sports. The only team sport I ever played was roller hockey, and that was because Zero conned all of us into playing. My mom approved and bought used hockey equipment because it would keep me active. Zero, while hanging out with us, was one of the "rich" kids. He lived closer to the mountains, which in Rancho is how one deciphers who has money and who doesn't. I think he wanted us to play so he could use the mobile home parks empty tennis courts as a hockey rink. And play we did. It was a lot of fun. It probably looked like slow motion to someone who played more seriously. But to us, it was the fastest game, on a mobile home parks unused tennis court, in the world.

At sixteen my parents divorced. They calmly came into my room one night and said my dad was leaving. Moving to Ohio, for a job opportunity that he couldn't pass up. My mom didn't want to move out of Southern California, so we stayed. I was calmly told, dad would keep in touch and send money. A lot more money than he was making now. That meant more money for the household. That was good. A few weeks later he was gone. No muss. No fuss. Practical and rational. I never saw him alive again.

Three years later my grandparents died a few months apart. I was at Cal State Santa Barbara, and my mom moved into their house and sold the mobile home. Two years after that, my mom was diagnosed with skin cancer and died three months later. Only William showed up at the funeral, my dad was unable to make it. Two weeks after that, Kaitlyn and I broke up. Two weeks after that, I joined the Army. Seven months ago, after three years in the Army, I was discharged and moved into my grandparent's little house, where, after a quick drive home and the thoughts of my life up to this point flashing before my eyes, Zero and I pulled into the driveway, with our delivery of survival gear.

CHAPTER SEVEN

11/11/2024

Have you ever been hungover, with a travel mug of coffee in your hand as you prepare yourself for the daily grind, gone out to your car, turned the key, and was greeted with a loud blast of music, and immediately you are awake and aware? That's what it was like when I opened the door and entered my home.

"What took you guys so long?"

"What'd you bring?"

"What's going on out there?"

"Where's my blanket?" said Jane, the six-year-old.

As we walked in, everyone turned to us and began talking at once. Not only was it loud, but it was also bright. Just because the electricity was on, did not mean we needed to have all the lights turned on. At least, I will not have to worry about the electric bill.

I had to raise my hand to stop all the questioning. "Give us a sec. I will try and answer your questions later, but first, we need to unload the truck." As I spoke, I noticed some new arrivals. Jenna stood in the kitchen talking to Kaitlyn. Which, at first, took me a few seconds to process. Also present were Drew, Ethan, and someone, a young man, I had never seen before, having an animated conversation.

While we unloaded the truck, I learned that the stranger was, in fact, Jenna's boyfriend. He looked like Shia Lebouf with a Fu Manchu beard, short, with retro glasses and the coordination of a newborn deer. He almost dropped two of the water jugs.

The water jugs were placed in the tiny dining room area, creating a small walkway to the kitchen. All the canned goods were scattered in boxes throughout the living room and kitchen, along with the camping gear. With, now, ten people in the house, it was beginning to feel crowded.

Once everything was inside, I went to the front of the room and raised my hand. Everyone immediately turned to me and went silent, even the children seemed to view me as someone important, as they stood clinging on to their parent's legs, eyes wide with curious trepidation.

"Look, I know everyone has questions, and I gotta be honest. I doubt I have the answers. But, the first thing we need to establish right now is this..." I paused, trying to locate the right way to say what I thought I needed to say. "If you can. If you have family, that you can go to. I would say. Go now." I realized the absurdity of what I was saying, as I was saying it. If they had a family to go to, they probably would have. No one responded. No one even blinked. "Ok. If you are going to stay here. We need to set up some... rules. Not rules. But guidelines. Already the Santa Ana winds have stopped and shortly the ocean breeze will kick in. When that happens, and it will probably be tomorrow morning at the latest. We need to be inside. As secure as possible. Will it be a hundred percent secure? No."

"Secure from what?" a voice I didn't recognize asked.

"Aaron, is it?" I asked. He nodded. "We need to be inside and secure from the radiation. Each hour that passes the better it gets. So, after a week or so, we should be okay. But, I'm not an expert."

"Why don't we just get out of dodge now?" Ethan asked, and I wondered if we should tell him we broke into his apartment.

"It's too late. The freeways and roads out of town will be backed up for miles and miles," Drew replied. "We tried, but it was already backed up this morning."

"Right," I continued. "And you think it's bad in traffic on a regular Monday evening. It's gonna be far worse and dangerous when people fear their life is on the line." I paused for a response. None came. "So, we need to hole up here and wait." Again, I waited for more questions. None came. So, I asked a question myself. "How long? I would say two to three weeks. Then we can see about getting out of town. While the radiation won't kill us immediately like it would if we were closer to the blast site. It probably isn't safe to stay here permanently." I again paused. Nothing. They seemed to be agreeing or at least understanding what I was saying. "I am not saying someone couldn't stay here longer or that it isn't safe here. We are far enough away that as long as we stay inside, we should be good. But, my plan is after three weeks. Kaitlyn and I will leave and head to Utah."

Conversations erupted like someone turned on ten different radios, tuned to ten different channels simultaneously.

Finally, Kaitlyn broke the chaos of speculation from the back. From my vantage point, standing on the linoleum in the entryway, I could see the top of her head. "You can all come," she yelled. Everyone stopped and turned toward her. "My parents own a piece of land and a huge cabin in the mountains. In an emergency or disaster, we were all supposed to meet there. I think this counts. But, more importantly, they were expert survivalist. Mostly for fun and, I guess, boredom. But, they wouldn't mind all of you being there." Again, everyone began to talk at once.

"Hold on. Hold on," I said with my hands in the air trying to grab everyone's attention. "What we do three weeks from now won't matter, unless we can get together now and secure this house tonight. We don't want to be outside tomorrow." That shut everyone up.

"What about news? The TV?" Alicia, Drew's wife, asked. "We tried it earlier, but all we got was static."

I explained that the only TV I received was from IPTV (Internet Provided Television) and we were too far from the broadcast towers to get anything over the air.

"The electricity may not last. It's on now. But, who knows, how long that will be," I said, after another question. "So, we gotta look at ourselves as cut off from everyone else. We have enough water to last a couple weeks. If we are smart with rationing. I have a gas stove, that means the burners will work to cook food. We have plenty of canned goods. That doesn't even include my emergency food-"

"Where are we all gonna sleep?" Jenna asked, cutting me off before I could boast about my emergency food supply. Everyone immediately started throwing out suggestions and volunteering sleep scenarios.

I, again, raised my hand and everyone turned to me.

"I have a plan for that, and we need to hurry up and get to working on it." I looked at my phone 9:30 p.m. 3%. Damn. I need to charge my phone.

Zero was to sleep in the office, Kaitlyn in the guest bedroom and the Welles family in the Master bedroom. Sleeping bags for Zero and the kids. I was to sleep on the red couch, which wasn't as sticky as it was a day ago.

"What about us?" Jenna asked.

"You, Ethan and Aaron are all sleeping next door." My original plan was to have the Welles family next door, and I could sleep in my bed, but that went out the window the minute I saw our new arrivals.

"Next door where?" Aaron asked.

I pointed. "They left last night. The house is empty." We would break in, provide them with the other water dispenser and a few jugs. Open a space in the fence, between the houses. Two homes for the price of one. While I thought, it was a promising idea, the others weren't so sure.

I went through the rest of my plan, as directly and as precisely as I could. We needed to board up the windows in the house. I had plenty of empty, cardboard boxes in the garage that we would use to seal the windows. I grabbed the guns from underneath the sink in the bathroom, which almost caused Alicia, to have a heart attack.

"Those were underneath the sink?" she asked. I shrugged and moved them to the tall filing cabinet in the office. The shotgun and AR on top. The handgun, in the top drawer.

We began to execute the plan just after ten in the evening, by sealing all the windows in my house, including the large slider in the master bedroom. The kids became the masters of the cardboard, and they seemed to enjoy carrying the cardboard around and handing it out as needed.

Once that was finished, Drew, Jenna, Ethan and I went next door with our expert burglar, Zero. He tried the front window. No luck. They installed new windows, a few months back, and the locking mechanism was tougher to get around than the one at Ethan's apartment. In the backyard, we began taking down a few of the vertical fence pickets to make a path from my house to the one next door. Once we got through the fence, you had to duck to avoid the horizontal post that the picket had been nailed into, and we tried the back door. Locked. Next up the kitchen window above the kitchen sink. No luck there either. Zero suggested breaking the window in the kitchen door, but I said, "That kind of kills the purpose of securing the house from radiation." We tried all the bedroom windows. Nope, new windows installed. Finally, the master bedroom slider. While all the windows looked brand new, with a modern locking mechanism, the slider looked like mine, old and original. Probably forty years old.

"Spent all that money to replace the windows, but didn't want to splurge on a new slider," Zero said.

"The slider probably would've cost almost as much as all the other windows combined," Drew said.

Zero pushed on the slider door and started moving the large pane of glass back and forth with slow, deliberate movements. After thirty seconds, he turned to us and smiled. Sure enough, while he kept pressure with his right hand on the glass, he grabbed the outdoor handle with his left and pulled. We were in.

The master bedroom we entered was slightly larger than my own. Even though the house was smaller with two bedrooms, the bedrooms themselves were more generous. We exited the master bedroom into the main hallway. On the left, was the entrance to the main family room and kitchen. On the right, the other bedroom and at the end of the hall, the only bathroom. The interior had plain white walls and was decorated sporadically with framed family photos of Mr. Enrique, his wife, and two daughters. It smelled musty and old, even though it had only been a day since the family deserted the home. We looked in the second bedroom and found their daughters' room, with two small beds. Everything seemed to be in decent shape. The living room had a few more religious pictures on the wall, a smaller TV, and no red couch, but other than that, it was exactly like my home.

Jenna didn't look placated. I noticed the look on her face as we went into the kitchen.

"What?" I asked her.

"I don't know. It's kind of weird to be sleeping and living in some stranger's house." This was a valid response and, truthfully, something I didn't even think of.

"We can grab sheets and blankets from my house, or even wash the bedsheets that are there now. As long as we do it tonight." She still didn't seem to be satisfied, and for a moment, I considered there may be another reason she didn't want to sleep in this strange home, which had nothing to do with the house itself, but more to do with her housemates.

As it was getting late, I went back over to my home, through our new pathway between the houses, out the kitchen door in Mr. Enrique's home, through the fence opening, and into my kitchen door. Eight feet between the two doors. Inside my home, I gathered everyone to grab what was left of the cardboard boxes and a tarp from my garage.

While everyone was working, securing the secondary home with cardboard, the kids again helped by carrying the empty boxes to and fro, I was gathering supplies in the kitchen. Mr. Enrique wisely took most of the canned goods. But, I found some crackers and some fruit in the fridge. I placed on the kitchen counter the portion of survival products for Jenna, Aaron, and Ethan. Twenty cans of a variety of soups. Ten varieties of canned vegetables. Ten canned fruits. A flashlight.

As I was going through the kitchen, I noticed that Jenna seemed to be randomly inspecting different items in the home. Opening drawers. Testing the couch. Looking at the pictures on the wall. As if she were a prospective buyer of the home at an open house. I turned to her as she opened the dishwasher and was absent-mindedly removing leftover clean dishes and putting them in the correct cabinets, which she identified by opening each and every one.

"You okay?" I asked.

"No," she said.

"Everything's going to be okay. As long as we stay indoors for the next three to five days." I was beginning to sound like a broken record.

"I am not worried about that."

"Then what?" At this, she nearly burst into tears.

"I can't." She turned away from me quickly and walked into the living room leaving the open dishwasher. I shrugged it off. Maybe she couldn't process what happened? I don't know. But, I wasn't going to push it. I went back to rationing out the canned food we scrounged. Every now and then I would cast a look at Jenna and see her wandering or half-heartedly helping out, here and there.

"Her parents live in El Segundo," Ethan said while I was in the middle of my count of canned goods.

"What?"

"Her parents, that's why she is upset. After what you said about the Santa Ana winds blowing the fallout over the ocean, she has been pale as a ghost." El Segundo was a few miles west of Los Angeles right on the coast. Right in the path of the fallout. I looked again at her and saw she was quietly talking to Aaron, over in the corner of the living room, while he was trying to duct tape some cardboard to the window sill. He seemed to be listening, but not intently enough, because Jenna slapped him on the arm and he dropped what he was doing. Aaron, instead of reacting angrily, as I anticipated, turned toward her and put his arms around her tenderly and she began to cry.

At that moment, Zero burst into the room with a box. "Look what I found." He didn't seem to notice the unsaid, moment of silence.

"Cartoons!" Immediately Natalie and Jane dropped the cardboard in their hands and ran over to Zero.

CHAPTER EIGHT

11/11/2024

1:12 a.m. Tuesday morning. All the cardboard had been exhausted, and we had to use my one and only blue tarp to cover the glass slider in Enrique's master bedroom. Now, I suppose, it was the house of Jenna, Ethan, and Aaron. I tried to come up with a clever acronym, using their names, but it never came to me. The two homes were secure. Well, as safe as could reasonably be expected to secure a home using cardboard. We put new sheets on the beds. They even borrowed some of my Blu-Ray's (hand me downs) so they could watch some movies if the electricity stayed on.

At midnight, Aaron and Jenna decided to drive to her apartment as she needed some clothes and a few personal items, which I protested, but they were adamant. I wouldn't say I was worried, but I did begin to wonder if they would return at all.

Alicia and the kids went to bed just after midnight, Kaitlyn shortly after that. Which left the four of us seated on my living room floor in a circle. Drew, Ethan, Zero, and myself. The light from the TV lit the room, which kept recycling the DVD menu Janet and Natalie had finished watching an hour earlier, *Happiness Is a Warm Blanket, Charlie Brown*. Not one of the better Charlie Brown films, but they seemed to enjoy it. The four of us were finishing off the last of the keg from my party, which now felt like it took place weeks ago.

I couldn't remember the last time the four of us were together like this, just sitting around talking. Maybe after our high school graduation, eight years ago. It's hard to stay in touch with those you care about, after high school. It's an awkward time, and we had to figure out what each of us wanted to do with our lives. I doubt any of us could even answer that question now. We just drifted further from each other's life. I know this is not a new development. Lots of people with friendships in their youth barely spoke after high school. But, we did manage to keep in touch. It wasn't the same. But, we each tried and that must mean something.

Zero tried the hardest. I don't think he had many other friends in school, besides us. We often wondered who he hung out with in junior high before we met him, but we could never get a clear answer. He was the one who always knew when we were all in town and tried to get us together. At Drew's twenty-first birthday party, he begged me to come to the party, while I was in my junior year at Cal State Santa Barbara. I did manage to make it, but not without Zero promising things he could never deliver.

Drew got married a year after high school. So, he felt the furthest away, yet the most grown up. He had a respectable job, at his father's accounting firm. Which pissed his mother off to no end. "I raised you by myself, and gave you everything, now you are gonna go work for that asshole?" I don't think Drew felt he had a choice. As soon as Alicia was pregnant, he knew he had to get his ass in gear. And that he did. Now, he makes more money a year than my parents probably brought home in the first ten years of my life. While Alicia didn't seem to care for the three of us at first, she eventually allowed him his time with the boys. But, only on special occasions. She would have none of this, I am going out drinking on a Wednesday with the guys. For the first couple years, we gave him a hard time about it when we saw him. But, we also saw how well he was doing. And Drew would get drunk beyond any of us, and that was always fun.

Ethan, meanwhile, reminded me of my brother. He just went where the wind pushed him. A job here. A job there. Hanging out with Zero after work. Or with the people he worked with. If you wanted to find Ethan, just head to the Roadhouse. He was a regular mainstay for years. Always present when we would get together, but I got the feeling it was others who did the planning. Ethan would just arrive and do the drinking.

As for myself? If Zero tried the hardest to keep our merry band together, I was probably the one who did the least. I am the one who left. I went to University for three and a half years. Then into the Army. Even when I was home, I would give my best excuse to not see them. Why? I couldn't answer that. But, sitting here now listening to the past, I felt a great shame and wondered why I forgot or wanted to forget my three best friends.

People may say that 'remember when?', is the lowest form of communication. I would have to respectfully disagree. At least on this night. As we discussed our past and the crazy things we did, I felt something I had not felt in a long time.

Remember when we blew up that smoke bomb in the sewers beneath Haven?

Remember when we stole that crate of beer from Ralphs?

Remember when we went to see that punk band at the Glass House with your brother?

Remember those chicks at Disneyland, who were so high, one of them passed out in line for Pirates of The Caribbean?

For over an hour, it was one 'remember when?' after another. We were into our fifth or sixth beer, trying to keep our voices down, but at one point Alicia came out and just stared at us. We stopped and went very still, making annoying shushing noises. Then, all at the same time, we burst out laughing. She just shook her head and went back into the bedroom, which made us laugh even harder.

This night of remembrance, despite the circumstances, was fun and full of nostalgia. But, I was dreading the inevitable questions about my experience in the Army. It was a simple case of human curiosity that I did not want to extol. But, it wasn't the experience overseas that they asked about, it was a question far more personal.

"So, what happened between you and Kaitlyn?" Ethan asked. "I mean, when you came home for Christmas in twenty-twenty, you two seemed pretty happy. I think she even liked Zero."

"It's true," Zero said. Smiling triumphantly.

"So, what happened?" Ethan continued.

I can see why this was a curiosity, amongst them. The last time they saw me for any extended period was that Christmas. I took a long drink and looked down, trying to formulate the right words. I looked up and felt their eyes staring at me.

"I don't know where to begin," I said. "It was a decision we made at the end of our Junior year. We didn't want our relationship to get in the way of our goals in life." Somewhat truthful.

"What the fuck does that mean?" Drew asked.

"It means, we knew we both really liked each other and it was at the stage in the relationship where we either jumped in feet first, or we take a step back and see..." I paused. "I think we were both scared of each other. We wanted to finish our school, get our degrees, get careers and then if it was still meant to be, it would... It sounded very mature. Rational and practical... At the time. We would remain friends. At least that was the plan." Nobody made a sound. So, I kept going. "But. But, as you all know, a few weeks after that conversation, my mom passed away. And while it was a shock to me, it was more of a shock to learn she had kept her cancer hidden from me. Didn't want to distract me from my studies." I paused again and shook my head. "That was my mom. So, that brought Kaitlyn back to me, in an intimate way. Yet, it was not the same. Since our talk and decision to separate seemed to put a strange distance between us. And I was not in a good state of mind and began to resent her for allowing me to suggest we concentrate on our school and careers than our relationship. I think she felt the same and, although she would never leave me in the condition I was in, there were only a few weeks left of school, and soon she would have to head home. At one point, she even suggested that she should come back to California at the beginning of summer... At the end of April, after the funeral, I made a decision."

I paused one last time.

"What's that?" Zero asked.

"To join the Army and get away."

They looked at each other and then at me.

"That makes no sense," Drew said.

"It did at the time. Like I said, I don't think I was in a very good place."

"But..." Drew was about to continue when the front door opened. Jenna and Aaron were back. Saved by the bell.

Aaron and Jenna, thanks to my advisement, looked like they just returned from a ski trip, bundled from head to toe, which they immediately began stripping off as soon as they entered the house.

"Looks like you guys have been having a pow-wow," Aaron said.

They told us their trip was okay. A few more cars than normal driving around at one in the morning. They avoided most of the intersections with grocery or convenience stores, and when they didn't, it was as crazy as would be expected. At gas stations and shopping centers: tons of cars, a lot of running around but they didn't stick around to see much more than that. But, they did mention a few worrying things.

"I think we heard a few gunshots," Jenna said, seated on the couch. Ethan gave her and Aaron a beer as they recounted their trip. "I'm not a hundred percent sure. But, we could clearly hear loud pops not too far away."

"See any police?" I asked.

"No," she said. "Wait. Yes. On Day Creek. I think I saw a few up by the 210 freeway."

This interested me. "We're they blocking the on-ramp?"

"Not sure. I could barely tell. We were kind of far away when we turned to come here."

"Why would they block the on-ramp?" Aaron asked.

"Freeway's jammed," I said.

No one said anything as we were in our own thoughts for a few seconds.

Jenna broke the silence. "Oh. I almost forgot." She reached into a trash bag, that was mainly filled with clothes and feminine care products. After foraging for a moment, she brought out a pair of Batman Walkie-Talkies. Brand new, still in the box.

"I bought these for my nephews, for Christmas. But, since I don't know when I will see them again. They live in Oregon." She hesitated. "So, I thought we could use them, since the phones are down, while we are in separate houses. I just thought we weren't supposed to leave for a few days. We couldn't talk. So..." She handed them to me. They were black and yellow, with the Batman logo on the back.

"Perfect," I said.

CHAPTER NINE

11/12/2024 - 11/14/2024

I awoke the next morning to the sounds of children laughing, talking and arguing while trying to remain, unsuccessfully, quiet. Sounds from the kitchen. Pots being removed from cabinets. The refrigerator opening. A coffee maker dripping. A movie was being played at an audible level consistent with the ineffective whispering of the children. On the couch, I laid flat on my back, one arm covering my eyes, the other across my chest, doing my best to ignore these noises. I felt somewhat hungover and dry-mouthed. Where did we smoke at? It must've been in Zero's room, my office. I, after a lengthy internal debate, gave up any pretenses of sleep and sat up.

Alicia and Kaitlyn were making breakfast. They appeared to be getting along fantastic. Kaitlyn was wearing a long shirt and shorts, that made her short legs look even shorter, yet at the same time positively adorable. Kaitlyn saw my appreciative gaze and asked if I wanted some coffee. I nodded a positive. Alicia was at the stove and gave me a sarcastic smile, her red hair reflecting the overhead kitchen light, as she continued cooking bacon and eggs.

"Have fun last night?" Alicia asked while Kaitlyn brought me a cup of coffee. I just nodded, and Alicia made a noise that sounded like "haff." A half-laugh, half-sigh.

I sat at my counter height dining table, on one of the stools. Most of the lights were on, even though it was mid-morning at the earliest. With the cardboard blocking all the windows, there was precious outside light entering the home, which I immediately thought was a positive. Inside, it could've been midnight for all we knew, like in a hotel room with thick blackout curtains.

Sitting down and sipping my coffee, I finally noticed the cartoon Jane and Natalie were watching; *Watership Down*. Now that I was awake, the volume was turned up to a reasonable morning level. They must've pulled the Blu-Ray out of my collection, as I doubted it was in the box of cartoons Zero found next door. They probably thought it was just a regular Disneyesque cartoon. My first instinct was to say something about the film to Alicia, as I wasn't sure it was appropriate for a five and six-year-old. But, they seemed to be engrossed in its story and were laughing hysterically at the bird, with the strange Eastern European accident. So, I let it go.

"What's he doing?" Natalie said, in between laughter.

"Huh?" I asked. But, the girls ignored me. I didn't realize it was a rhetorical question and I noticed that both kids eyed me with suspicion. When they turned ever so slightly at my "Huh?" their eyes spied me quickly, and then looked to each other and, finally, back to the cartoon. It seemed they weren't sure what to make of me. I had said not one word to them besides "here" while handing them a blank paper and crayons yesterday, when they arrived. It was Alicia who volunteered them for cardboard duty.

With coffee in hand, I sat next to them on the floor. They didn't move when I sat down, with my back resting on the red couch, but I did sense them flinch a tad. Jane sat cross-legged three feet in front of the TV, a doll completely naked with golden hair, held in the crook of her right arm. I hoped it wasn't one of those artificial life dolls that you had to feed and then it would poop the "food" all over the place. Next to Jane, furthest from me, was Natalie. She laid on her stomach, elbows out in front, chin in her hands.

"You ever seen this before?" I asked.

"No," Natalie said, not immediately. But, with her hands underneath her chin, it came out as a slow, "Noooo."

"It's one my favorite cartoons," I replied.

Jane turned to me and asked, "You like cartoons?"

"Of course," I said.

"Me too," Jane replied. That seemed to seal my entry into the kid's club.

The three of us sat and watched *Watership Down*. As we watched, I couldn't help but notice the parallels between the plight of the rabbits on screen and that of our own. We had created our own warren of outcasts. Unfortunately, we did not have a Fiver amongst the group who had a premonition of the 'attack' and advised us to leave. I was looking for connections when there were none. The rabbits in *Watership Down* were on a fantasy adventure. We were stuck in a stuffy house, watching cartoons.

"Breakfast. Come on over," Alicia said. The kids sat there ignoring her, entranced by the images on my OLED TV. "Natalie! Jane! Breakfast!" This time with a stern, motherly tone. Jane and Natalie both jumped up.

"Oh," Jane said. "Can you pause it?" To me.

"Sure." I found the remote and hit pause, and we all ate an excellent breakfast.

Soon Drew and Zero were seated at the dining table eating their breakfast as well. Everyone appeared upbeat, considering the circumstances. It felt like a vacation or summer camp, rather than a voluntary prison to keep us safe from radiation exposure.

Zero, Drew and I, ended up on the couch watching the end of *Watership Down* with the kids, as it came to the climax.

"Eww," Jane said as the rabbits were fighting each other and blood flew everywhere.

"Holy shit," Zero exclaimed and turned to look at Alicia to verify if she heard his swear. She hadn't. "What kind of cartoon is this?"

Drew said nothing, as he still was in the thralls of a hangover.

"It was made in the seventies. I used to watch it with my mom. It was one of her favorite books," I said.

"You watched this with your mom?" Zero asked.

"Yeah,"

"How old were you?"

"Probably the same age as Natalie."

"She wouldn't let you have a phone, but let you watch this?"

I said no more, as we were shushed by the two girls.

The rest of the day consisted of more cartoons. A board game, The Game of Life, which Alicia won. Some peanut butter and jelly sandwiches for lunch. Another movie, *The Goonies,* which the kids had never seen. Then chicken noodle soup with crackers for dinner.

At 6 p.m. the Batman walkie-talkie spoke, and everyone jumped as we forgot it was there.

"Hello?" Jenna's voice said. Then a click and static. Then quiet.

I picked up the receiver which was on top of the entertainment stand, next to the TV.

"Hello," I said.

"Blake?"

"Yep. How's it going over there?"

"Pretty good... Bored."

"Yeah. We've just been watching movies."

"Same here."

"When you are done speaking, say 'over.' That way I know when it's my turn. Over."

"Sure. No problem... Oh. Over."

There was a long pause, and when I turned around, thinking of what to say, I noticed everyone was staring at me.

"You wanna talk to anyone else? Over," I asked.

"Sure... over," Jenna said. I looked over at the group and held out the walkie as if to say "anyone?". Eventually, after an agonizingly long pause, Alicia got up and grabbed the walkie and went into the kitchen to converse with Jenna.

I left the room, and as I did, I heard Zero mutter to Drew, "That was awkward." In Zero's room (my office) I smoked one of my remaining cigarettes.

The next day was more of the same, except for one noticeable exception. The house had become, almost unbearably warm. It was a problem, I had considered, but was hoping the weather would cooperate. Unfortunately, in Southern California, you could get days in November where the temperatures approached summer levels of heat. The thermostat in my living room read eighty-three degrees, at 11 a.m. The first instinct was to turn on the air conditioner, which Zero suggested, but that would defeat the purpose of sealing the house in the first place. With no movement of air inside the home and seven people in a one thousand square foot area, it was beginning to smell like a locker room.

If the first day of our confinement felt like a vacation or holiday, the second felt like a day at the DMV. The kids were irritable, the newness of the 'adventure' was beginning to wear off, and they emphatically rejected any suggestions to alleviate their boredom. They just wanted to go home. At one point, both were protesting in my master bedroom and wouldn't leave. They, eventually, fell asleep on their sleeping bags. Thankfully, that bedroom was on the north side of the home and was the coolest room in the house. An hour after they had fallen asleep Drew and Alicia joined them for a nap.

At 3 p.m., eighty-four degrees, Kaitlyn, Zero and I were back on the red couch, watching one of the newer movies from my obsolete, Blu-Ray collection, *Star Wars: Episode 9 The Last Jedi*, released seven years ago, which I thought was okay, but Zero loved. We had a verbose conversation about the merits of the "newer" *Star Wars* films, but I won't bore you with the minutiae. I guess, now, it really doesn't matter.

Zero was wearing shorts, which completed his outfit and I suggested he should probably put on a shirt, just in case small doses of excess radiation were entering the home. He shrugged and said, "Fuck it. I would rather die of radiation than be miserable." At that moment, I almost agreed with him.

At 6 p.m., we ate dinner. Eighty-five degrees. More peanut butter and jelly sandwiches. No one wanted soup. We used up all the eggs and bacon that morning. Alicia asked if that was okay and I said "sure" because I wasn't confident the power would stay on much longer, and we might as well eat what was in the fridge while we could.

Shortly after dinner, Jenna called again and, this time, Alicia answered. Over at the second house, things were just as bad. They had burned through the movies they borrowed from me and were just as hot and bored as we were.

Our generation never really had to experience boredom. Everything was right at our fingertips; movies, books, television, games. We could experience any distraction we wished at any time we desired. Everything was designed to provide us, through sophisticated computer algorithms, an ever-growing match of things we could enjoy. Advertisements based on watch history, browsing history, and purchase history. Calculated news, that lined up to an individual's political and social beliefs. We never had to experience anything that may clash with what we already believed or desired to see. Modern life had become a box that people were enclosed in, whether by choice or not. It took a conscious effort to fight and break out of this self-imposed container, to free yourself from your own long settled beliefs. With the advent of virtual reality and artificial intelligence, human beings really had no reason to do anything, except remain upset about everything, from the comfort of our own home. People walked around wearing glasses or goggles that allowed them to see reality, not as it is, but as they wanted to see it. Truth mattered less than how an individual felt. News from around the world brought to our doorstep, without any way to process the information. If it upset you, you would just put on your VR glasses and disappear into another world.

One of the best things that came out of my time in the military was the simple unplugging from this Huxleyan world for a few years.

Day three started a little better. Most barely slept, as it only cooled down to seventy-nine degrees in the home. But, everyone seemed to put on a brave face. I think we all knew it was not likely to get any easier; so let's make the best of it. Natalie and Jane were in a good mood. As if the previous day was a nightmare that never happened. They watched a DVD, *Spongebob Squarepants*, from Enrique's daughter's collection, all morning.

Zero was right there with them and was treated as one of them. He had acquired full membership in the kid's club, with little effort and laughed without cynicism at the same moments as the children.

Kaitlyn, Alicia and I, made an inventory of the fridge. There wasn't much left. There wasn't much food, to begin with. I did have some tortillas and cheese, so we had quesadillas for breakfast. Beyond that, nothing left, except for a few bottles of water and a variety of condiments. We had peanut butter and jelly sandwiches for lunch, again.

Which was alright because at 12:48 p.m. the power went out.

Everything went dark.

The young girls screamed.

They were right in the middle of season three, episode ten of *Spongebob*.

The amount of light in the home was about what you would get from a quarter moon at midnight. The main source of light came from the peephole in the front door. Eventually, our eyes adjusted and we could see gray shapes, with minimal contrast. I grabbed a flashlight and some old scented candles from the top cupboard in the kitchen and lit them and placed one on the dining table and the other on the entertainment stand. Eventually, we had enough light to see everyone without much effort, and the scent helped with the locker room odor.

Alicia was trying to console Jane and Natalie, who looked like they were about to have a nervous breakdown. They had made it this far, but this was the straw that broke the camel's back. They would not be consoled.

"Are we going to die?" Natalie asked, between sobs, arms wrapped around her mother.

"No. Of course not," Alicia said, holding her daughter close to her chest. Drew had Jane in his arms.

"Hello... over," The walkie spoke, followed by a burst of static. It wasn't Jenna.

I grabbed the Batman walkie from the entertainment stand. "We're here... over," I said.

"What's going to happen to us?" Jane asked her dad.

"We're going to be fine," Alicia replied before Drew said a word. It looked like he didn't know what to say.

"Just checking that the power was out over there... over," Aaron, whose voice I now recognized, asked.

"Yep. Everything's out. Do you guys have candles or flashlights? Over," I asked.

"Yeah. We have the flashlight you gave us and found some candles in the bathroom... over," Aaron said.

I didn't respond. Neither did he. Everyone sat in quiet, except for the kids crying. Everyone, waiting for the next shoe to drop. Imagining the worse. I could just imagine the thoughts of the others. What was going on outside? Was the world truly ending?

I went into the office, stepping over Zero's clothes and sleeping bag, which were thrown across the room haphazardly, and found what I was looking for on the top bookshelf. I smoked one of my last cigarettes (two remained) and sat on the cheap, non-ergonomic, office chair and enjoyed the silence for a few minutes before returning to the living room.

Kaitlyn was alone at the dining table staring off into some unknown thought. Zero was in the kitchen, looking in the refrigerator, maybe searching for something to cheer the children up or something for himself. Drew, Alicia, Natalie, and Jane were as I left them. Parents holding their children close on my red couch. I approached cautiously.

"Natalie. Jane. Do you like stories?" I asked. Doing my best to be consoling and calm.

Natalie turned her head from her mother's shoulder and caught a glimpse at what I was holding in my hand and asked, "What kind of story?" I gave the book to her, and she grabbed it with her small hands that buckled under the weight and began investigating the cover with her eyes.

"It's a book my mother used to read to me when I was your age," I said. Jane was now curious as well, looking at the book Natalie had in her hands. The book was thick, with a green dust cover that had actual dust on it, which Jane, reaching across her father began slowly wiping away. In the center was a picture of a red dragon. At the top was the title in bright yellow letters.

"The hoe-bit," Natalie said.

"*The Hobbit*," Alicia said.

"What's a hobbit?" Jane asked.

"You want me to read it to you, and we can find out?" Alicia asked. They both nodded. Jane and Natalie both unhinged from their parents and sat on each side of their mother, as she opened the book.

"This has pictures?" Jane asked.

"It looks like it," Alicia said. They both leaned over the book looking at a picture of a wizard, in a funny blue hat, walking on a path in Hobbiton. Alicia looked at me and mouthed "Thank you." I just nodded and sat down at the dining table next to Kaitlyn, and she put her hand on mine and squeezed.

Later that night, after dinner, the candles providing the dancing light throughout the room, everyone sat in a circle either on the couch or on the floor. All the adults took turns reading by flashlight, providing our unique voices to the story and as the heroes in Tolkien's story were escaping the clutches of the goblins and Bilbo was playing games with a strange creature named Gollum, the doorbell rang, followed by a loud knock at the door.

CHAPTER TEN

11/14/2024

When the doorbell rang, it was as if someone hit the pause button on the movie of our life. Nobody moved. Even the children went still. The outside world had come knocking.

I was the first to react and went to the office and grabbed my Smith & Wesson 9mm, made sure the safety was on and put it in the band of my pants behind my back.

The doorbell rang again. Followed by another knock. This time more insistent, followed by a loud, muffled voice, "This is the San Bernardino County Sheriff's Department. Please open up."

At the door, I tried to peer through the peephole. Two figures, but nothing distinguishing. It was too dark.

"I would rather not open the door," I yelled through the door. "I sealed it with duct tape." I heard some indistinguishable mumbling.

"That's good. We're going around to all the neighborhoods and informing anyone who's still around, that there is a mandatory evacuation order for this area."

"Mandatory?" I said through the door.

"Yes," the voice responded.

"How big is the area?"

"What?"

"How large is the evacuation area?"

More muffled, incoherent voices behind the door. "The whole Inland Empire," the voice answered.

I paused to grasp the magnitude of this development. If I remembered correctly, the Inland Empire had almost five million people in its geographical area. How was this even possible? Where would everyone go?

"There are evacuation centers set up in the high desert along I-15, just after you reach the summit of the Cajon pass. East along I-10, just past Banning. South along I-15 as you pass Temecula. And many others." Answering my unasked question.

"Who's in charge of these, evacuation centers?"

More mumbling, followed by, "I believe it's a joint effort between the Army, FEMA, and The Red Cross, along with other volunteers. I have all the information right here." I looked through the peephole and saw a dark shadow holding up a black rectangle to the peephole. Obviously, a piece of paper.

"How long?" I said.

"What's that?"

"How long until we have to evacuate?"

"Three days."

"What happens then?"

Another bout of muffled mumbling behind the door. Then the voice said, "The National Guard will be doing sweeps of the area making sure everyone is out."

"Why?"

"What?"

"Why a mandatory evacuation? We were far enough away from the... blast."

"I can't answer that."

"Can't or won't?"

"I personally, do not know. It was given to us as excessive radiation fallout. Whatever that means. I am no expert. We were given our orders, and here I am." I could tell the voice was getting a little flustered with my questions. He probably thought I was some kind of doomsday prepper, who had long been waiting for this day.

"Right. Just leave the paper on the doorstep, and I will grab it later."

"Alright then." Through the peephole the dark figure on the right bent down. "Have a good day," he said and turned toward the house next door.

I turned away from the door and went quickly, ignoring everyone's questioning gaze, and grabbed the Batman walkie, depressed the button and said, "Don't answer the door. As soon as they are gone, put on a thick coat, gloves and come over here. We have a lot to discuss. Over."

Twenty minutes later, I was standing in the hallway opening, that lead to the bedrooms. To my right were Jenna and Aaron, seated at the dining room table facing me. Also at the dining table, on the opposite side, were Ethan and Zero, with their backs to me. On my left, Kaitlyn, Drew and Alicia, on my red couch. On my rug in front of the TV were the kids, flipping through *The Hobbit*, looking for the pictures. The whole area was illuminated by flickering candles, that provided enough light, but also added to the 'end of days' discussion we were having.

"I think we should go and go now before it gets too crowded," Aaron said.

"To the evacuation center? It will already be packed. I mean how are they even going to accommodate everyone?" Alicia responded.

"Well, it's better than waiting here till the Army forces us out," Aaron replied.

"Maybe the roads are clear, and we can just head to Utah now," Zero said.

"I'm not going to Utah," Aaron said.

"That's fine, but what Zero said is not dependent on going to Utah, if the roads are clear we can head anywhere we want," Alicia said.

"Yeah. We can go anywhere," Jenna said to Aaron.

"So, do we head out tonight?" Aaron asked, ignoring her.

"I would guess so," Ethan said.

I finally spoke up. "I wouldn't do that."

"Why not?" Aaron asked, not politely. "We've been bunkered down for three days like you suggested and now you want us to stay for at least three more, when we can get out of here now."

"I wouldn't go anywhere… yet," I reiterated. Everyone stared at me, waiting for an explanation. Instead, I walked to the front door, ripped off all the duct tape around the door frame, unlocked the door and opened it. After three days in our cave, the evening air felt amazing and I smiled as the lovely, gentle, cool, breeze swept across my face. It had been four days since the bomb exploded and interrupted our lives. I reached down to my doormat which said "Welcome," it was about as generic a doormat as one could have. Underneath the mat, sticking out halfway, lay the piece of paper that the sheriff had left. I grabbed the paper and closed the door. I didn't bother with the duct tape. I think we ran out anyway.

Back inside, I read out loud the contents of the order: "'Release date November thirteenth, twenty twenty-four. Time, ten a.m. By order of the United States government and the state of California, the following areas are under a mandatory evacuation due to the fallout and radiation, caused by the cowardice attacks,'" Attacks? As in multiple. "'On this nation, occurring on November tenth, twenty twenty-four.' There is a list of cities here. All in the Inland Empire. A city with a letter correlating to our evacuation zone. Rancho Cucamonga is supposed to evacuate to Zone C. At the bottom it says; 'this is a mandatory evacuation. Residents should leave the area immediately. Be sure to take any medications, pets, family valuables, etc. with you, close all windows, and leave all doors closed. All residents need to be evacuated from the area by November seventeenth.' And that's it." I turned over the paper and looked at the map, and my biggest fears were confirmed.

"So, that settles it. We go tonight," Aaron said. No one argued.

Alicia asked to see the paper, and I handed it to her. "It shows that we need to go to the zone at the top of the Cajon pass, right past the summit on the west side of the fifteen. Zone C," Alicia said.

"What's there that could be an evacuation center?" Ethan asked, and I smiled, not out of amusement.

"It's not a center. It's a camp," I said.

"A camp? Like Camp Cucamonga?" Zero asked.

"No. Definitely not like that. It's a refugee camp." I heard some audible gasps.

"You can't know that," Jenna said.

"Oh yes, I can. I spent over a year in one," I said, and they all looked at me as if I told them that I was secretly Santa Claus.

My time in a refugee camp began in the summer of 2021. Just three months after my enlistment in the Army. A few weeks out of basic training, our unit was assigned to southern Syria. This was not a safe area. In fact, over the prior ten years, Syria was about as bad as any place on Earth. But, thanks to a variety of deals struck in 2020, mainly between Russia and the United States, the area had slowly settled down from horrible to bad. One of the components of the deal was for Russia and the US to set up temporary housing for the displaced Syrian population. Neither side called them refugee camps. This was supposed to be a joint effort between all parties, including the United Nations. The Red Cross and other emergency organizations were expected to be in charge of the 'temporary' camps and work with the respective countries providing the supplies and infrastructure. That had lasted about a week before each side heard the other used military troops to keep the peace inside the camps. That's where I came in.

I arrived in late July at Mezze Air Base, just outside of Damascus, by helicopter, after spending the previous week in Israel. The one thing you feel when you are in the middle east is the history. Compared to the United States, Syria and Israel were ancient, and you could see and feel it everywhere. You could also feel and see the massive destruction that the decades of fighting had left across the landscape. I was probably as wide-eyed as any infantryman, on their first assignment.

Right off the helicopter, we were loaded into a transfer truck. As I stepped inside the truck, which had wood benches for seating, I was already sweating as the temperature was well over one hundred degrees and I had arrived with all my equipment, which weighed at least ninety pounds. We headed west from the air base and into the middle of nowhere. After a half hour, we could see the rising mountain range approaching and at the base of the hills, rising out of the brown and gray landscape, a large chain-link fence, twelve feet high. This was supposed to be the temporary housing? I thought. Only one word came to my mind; Prison. And we were to be the custodians.

The camp was divided into twenty-five sections. Each section had around one thousand people. The camp was set up like a spoked wheel. The center hub was where the military and red cross were to live. Spreading out from there in a grid were the tents. Each tent held five people. Each section had two hundred tents. In the center of each section was the mess hall for the individual sections. It was all very straight and precise. Obviously, military design.

My job was simple, between ten in the evening and eight the next morning, I was to patrol Section C of the camp. Joe and I spent our nights wandering around discussing our past. He was from Boise, Idaho and came from a family of soldiers. I was not, which surprised him. Even though I had seen him in basic training, we never spoke until our late-night walks. Everyone he met, he told me, came from a military family.

"Why join the military, if you weren't trying to please some relative," he said with a smile on his face.

"I thought it was my duty to the country," I told him. A lie.

Joe just smiled and said, "Well, you're a better man than I am. I joined because that's all I've known. My dad joined right after 9/11, a few months later I was born, and I didn't see him until I was four."

We talked like this, most of the nights. Some frivolous, sometimes serious discussion between two strangers. Most of the nights were quiet. At least in our section. We heard horror stories from elsewhere in the camp about the things they've seen and stories they've heard. But, for Joe and I, it was easy-going. I was beginning to think I had lucked out with my first assignment with this unit. But, two months later, I would start to think otherwise.

It's hard to pinpoint where the animosity began. Was it the soldiers taking advantage of the people they were supposed to protect? Or was it the occupants slowly realizing their luck at being assigned to a U.S.camp, was a fraud and that they had actually been taken to a U.S. military prison? Or was it the fact that the supplies that were supposed to arrive on a regular basis, were now coming, alarmingly, at random? Whatever it was. Whatever the reason, there was no turning back from the inevitable.

There was fighting. People killing each other over food. The school, at the center of camp, was closed after a homemade bomb was detonated in the main classroom (tent). Luckily, this happened when no one was inside. Not to mention the question of how someone could smuggle an explosive into the camp. But, the message was clear. The people wanted out. Now, when we would patrol, people would mutter under their breaths or swear at us in our faces.

A massive brawl broke out, at the mess hall in Section C as I was in bed. I ran, half-asleep, to contain the situation along with twenty other soldiers. Twenty soldiers against, at least, a thousand people. Luckily the 'prisoners' were disarmed, and ninety percent just wanted to be left alone. But, the other ten percent were determined to cause chaos.

That's when the rumors began. Stories of U.S. soldiers hauling people off in the middle of the night, to never be seen again. I can confirm they were not rumors. We were targeting potential undesirable individuals. Where they were taken, I do not know?

One night, Joe and I had to grab a man, while his wife was kicking me and his two children were crying. We took him to the main headquarters and never saw him again. He kept asking the same question over and over again, as we dragged him through the dirt streets, "What did I do?" in broken English.

During the first three months; Breakfast, lunch, and dinner were served daily. The last three months; only lunch, and a small meal at dinner, if available. Not only was it miserable for the inhabitants, but also for the soldiers. We were not trained as prison guards, we were trained as soldiers to kill enemy combatants. By, the end of my time there, and it shames me now, I did view them as the enemy. It was the only way I could survive.

I sighed and looked at all my friends sitting or standing in front of me and continued, "The reason I tell all of you this and believe me when I say, that is the last thing I want to do. Is to try to make you understand. We do not want to be anywhere near these camps."

"But, surely it can't be that bad here, right?" Jenna said, "I mean this is America."

"I actually, think it will be worse here," I said.

"Why's that?" Aaron asked.

"The Syrian refugees and whoever else were there, wanted to be there at first. Most Americans, we included, will not react well to being confined to a prison camp. This is America. Don't Tread on Me. Liberty or Death. Our ideals and freedoms, clash significantly with a military controlled refugee camp."

"What are you saying?" Aaron asked.

"He is saying that people in this country would rather die, then be locked in a cage," Ethan answered.

The next hour was an exercise in futile debate. On one side was Enrique's temporary residents; Ethan, Jenna, and Aaron wanted to leave as soon as possible. On the opposite side; Drew and Alicia, along with Zero. Even though Zero would bounce back and forth if someone made a good point. Drew and Alicia wanted to stay until we were forced out. As for Kaitlyn and I, we abstained for the time being.

"Look, we are safe here for now. Why leave?" Alicia said. "What's the rush?"

"We need to go as soon as possible, so we don't get left behind," Aaron said, the most fervent proponent for leaving tonight.

"Left behind?" Drew asked.

"Right now the government is acting. Organizing. FEMA has set up these, so called, camps. What if they decide to move? Or set up people in temporary housing? I don't believe for one second these evacuation areas are as bad as Blake makes them out to be. We need to be there when they decide where we need to go."

"That's great and all, but once we are there, we are in their hands, at their discretion. Our freedom will not be our own," I said.

"Freedom?" Aaron asked. "What freedom?" He took a step toward me. "You call locking ourselves in these homes, hoping the radiation isn't that bad. Sitting on our asses, until you decide when we can leave. What's the difference?"

"You can go at any time, no one is forcing you to be here."

"You would like that wouldn't you?" Now he stepped right into my personal space. I could smell his breath, which was poignant with the clam chowder he must've had for dinner. I didn't say anything. Just kept eye contact. His fist clenched. Zero and Ethan approached on either side of us as if they could see what was coming.

"I know you were trying to fuck my girl, at your party," he said.

Jenna grabbed Aaron by the arm, "Aaron!" she said. He pulled away with a brisk movement, that left Jenna grasping air.

"Your girl? You don't own her," I said.

"It's never gonna happen," Aaron said. "You can act all nice and friendly. Have us all over here at your piece of shit home. But, I know your type. You never wanted us here. Any of us. Ethan told me you had to be forced into having your party. You probably would've been happier if we never showed up here."

It came like a beam of inspiration. Or desperation. I was not even aware it was happening. My right fist flew from my side in a flash, connecting right where the jaw curves up to the ear on Aaron's arrogant face. There was a loud pop heard. He staggered backward instantly, while also raising his right hand to swing at me, as he grabbed his jaw with his left. But, before he could swing, Zero grabbed his right arm and pulled him away from me. Ethan stepped in front of me and held me from going after Aaron any further. I don't think I would've. Zero, eventually, wrestled Aaron down to the ground.

"Fucking cheap shot," Aaron said. I think. I saw red, so my memory may not be accurate. The moment that seemed to enact in slow motion was over in two seconds.

Aaron got up, holding his jaw. Jenna was trying to help him up, but he just shoved her away. "I'm leaving, right now. Gonna grab my stuff and getting the fuck out of this lunatics house. You all should as well."

I saw a look in Jenna's eye, as she locked eyes with me, that screamed disappointment. Alicia was taking the kids away and into the master bedroom. Zero had a grin on his face. Drew was standing behind me. Ethan was looking at Aaron and then back at me.

"Well?" Aaron asked.

"Sorry, dude, I ain't going anywhere without Blakey here," Zero said. Aaron ignored him.

"If my family wants to stay. I stay," Drew said from behind me.

Aaron looked at Ethan, who he seemed to have a close friendship with. "Ethan?" he asked, with hope.

"Nope. Staying here," Ethan said. "I think Blake is right. If we do anything, we shouldn't do it half-cocked, just cause we're scared."

At the word, scared, Aaron flinched. He was scared, as we all were, and it seemed he believed that going to the evacuation area was the solution to his fear. Most likely, fear of the unknown. The government was the known, and he could relax once he was someplace that told him what he needed to do. Someone in authority. Not someone whom he believed tried to fuck his girlfriend.

"Fine," Aaron said. "Let's get our stuff and get out of here." He walked to the kitchen and was a few feet from the kitchen door when he noticed someone wasn't following him. He turned around. "You coming?"

Jenna had tears in her eyes and wasn't looking at him. She was shaking her head. Finally, she said, "No. We should stay here."

"Whatever." He turned to leave, then spun around and addressed me. "Good luck with her, you're gonna need it." He exited stage kitchen door right. A few minutes later, he drove off into the night. We all watched him leave from the window next to the front door, where I removed the cardboard.

CHAPTER ELEVEN

11/15/2024

I awoke with my arms wrapped around Kaitlyn. I smelled her hair before I opened my eyes, a hint of coconut, and for a brief moment, before the memories came back to me, wondered what I was doing in bed with a stranger. I rested with my arms around her and took in the comfort of her warm body against mine, while I replayed the events of last night in my mind.

After Aaron had departed, the household began making plans. All of us that is, except for Jenna, who sat on the couch and said nothing. She had made her decision, and whatever we came up with was her penance.

"I don't care what you say about Aaron, but he was right about the fact we need to get out of here," Ethan said. He still wanted to leave, but not on a whim, he was pushing for a plan, but offered none of his own.

"How and where? All of the freeways that lead out of town, pass right by an evacuation center," Drew said. "Refugee camp. Or whatever you want to call them. That is not a coincidence. They want everyone to go to those places."

"Why is that?" Alicia asked. "Why can't we just drive by and tell them were going to family in Utah?"

"Maybe we could," Kaitlyn said as she read over the evacuation notice. "There is nothing in here that says we have to go there. It just says, here are the evacuation areas. If we just drove by, or if they stopped us, just tell them we have a place to go." Her voice rose a pitch as she spoke.

"I wish that was the case," I said. "But, I don't think that will work." I put a hand out for the notice. Kaitlyn gave it to me. I flipped it over to the backside with the, hastily drawn, map of Southern California. "They placed them all over to funnel everyone into the camps. There is no question of that. The question is why?" I paused, waiting for a response. I was hoping someone would come up with an answer that made sense. A hopeful answer. Not the one I had in my head. Any reason, other than the one I was thinking.

"Maybe those were the only areas big enough and close to major freeways that could handle that amount of people," Zero said, peering over my shoulder. He had been quiet until now. Instead of seeing Zero, we were starting to view the man, Jason, emerge in bits and pieces.

"Could be," I said. "It could be that simple."

"Right. Maybe we are overreacting for nothing," Ethan said. "I know you went through some shit, but maybe you are spooked for no reason."

"Maybe," I said.

"Come on Blake," Alicia said, in her mom tone. "Stop pussy footing around. What do you think? You obviously have an idea."

I did, but I was hoping I was wrong. "I think we need to stay as far away from these camps as possible. You know that. That is my suggestion. As for the why they would force everyone into the camps. I think it has to do with resources."

"Resources?" Ethan asked. His brow furrowed as if trying to work out a philosophical question.

"Think about it. Not twenty-four hours after the bomb went off ten million people tried to get out of town. At least. From Los Angeles to San Bernardino to Orange County. Tens of millions of people. Panicked. Heading north along I-5 towards San Francisco. I-15 to Vegas. I-10 to Phoenix. South to San Diego. Can you imagine the chaos that brings to a city? What the fifteen looked like through the high desert? My guess is not an hour after the bomb went off, the camps were being planned and set up. While we were all sitting here remembering the past, drinking. The national guard, the Army and FEMA were setting up these camps all over the place to alleviate the influx of people to the various cities."

Ethan rose from his seat on the couch and walked past me, and grabbed a drink of water from the water dispenser. We had five full jugs still left. He took a drink, swallowed and then said, "That's alot of guessing."

"I am not saying I am one hundred percent right. And if there is another possibility I would be glad to hear it. This is just a hunch."

"Okay. So say it is true. Then what?" Alicia asked. "We can't stay here forever."

"No. We can't. Aaron was one hundred percent correct about wanting to leave, and that was always the plan. This just moves up the timeline and the way we get out of town. I was hoping we would stay here, at the longest a month or so, and by the time we decide to leave, the freeways would be clear. It wasn't until I saw the evacuation notice that I understood the naiveté of that original plan. I didn't think of the backlash that would rise in other cities over the incoming... refugees."

"Then what's the answer?" Drew asked.

"We leave. But, we have to find a back way out of town. We can't take the freeways, obviously. That is the only way we can hope of getting out here, without ending up in one of those camps."

"Which way?" That was the question. It was Alicia who asked, but it was in all our minds.

As I laid in bed with Kaitlyn, the following morning, I was still trying to uncover the answer. Only one road out of town was mentioned, and that was the one I was thinking of; through Big Bear, over the mountains, and into the high desert. I believed that road would be blocked. If it was the first option we considered, then it would be the first one the military considered as well.

I climbed carefully out of bed, not wanting to wake Kaitlyn. A clock on the wall in the guest bedroom displayed 6:55 a.m. Only five hours of sleep. I tiptoed out of the room. In the living room, Jenna was asleep on the red couch, and Ethan was in the last sleeping bag on the floor. Neither one of them wanted to go back to the separate house. So, we gathered all the supplies from next door and brought them over. Light leaked into the home through the thin, vertical, window beside the front door.

The coffee pot began to gurgle as I poured the boiling water from the stove into the coffee filter and it began to drip into the pot, hoping not to wake the rest of the house. As the glass coffee pot began to fill, my mind went back to the problem at hand. There had to be a back way out of town. But, we needed maps. None of us had used a map since we were kids. Our directions were all given to us by our phones. GPS was how we found our destination. Our phones were dead or soon would be. Drew said he had GPS in his car, but that only gave them directions to a target. No way to create your own back roads trip.

If we entered, into the GPS system: Duck Creek, Utah, it would tell us to get on the 15 freeway and head north. It may offer an alternate route, but it would still be by major highway. We needed an old school foldout map of the area. Like the ones my grandfather used to own. Then it hit me like an uppercut from Juan Marco; my storage unit.

My storage unit contained boxes upon boxes of stuff from my parents and grandparents. Things I couldn't get rid of, due to sentimental value or laziness. Maybe inside those boxes, a map? It was a long shot, but one we needed to take if we were going to get out of here safely. If I left early enough, I could get to my unit, find the maps and return by noon. Then we could attempt to head out tonight.

I snuck out the front door like a thief in the night. Only in this case, like a thief in the morning. I left a note on the kitchen counter. It read, "Went to look for some maps. Be back soon." The sun had just peaked above the homes to my left. The air smelt intoxicating after my confinement. I was wearing a black sweatshirt and beanie. I wasn't too concerned with radiation. It wasn't that I didn't care anymore, it was the realization, if we survived the immediate aftermath, then five days later, we should be okay. There was a nice chill in the air, as the ocean breeze we were so afraid of, had now brought in a cold front. Clouds accumulated to the west, and I hoped it would not rain. That would introduce another radiation issue.

For now, I put those thoughts aside. I was tired of worrying about radiation, about keeping myself safe and about keeping everyone else safe. It wasn't supposed to be like this. I expected to be sleeping in my hallway. Alone. Going through my food supply, which would last me a month. Drinking boiled water. Just alone with my thoughts. Maybe I could find that old typewriter of my grandparents and write that book since I would finally be devoid of distractions. Instead, I was full of distractions and worry.

I started my car, saw I had half a tank of gas and pulled out slowly, maneuvering around the Welles family SUV, which was parked in my driveway cockeyed behind Zero's truck and I drove off.

I made my way to Day Creek Boulevard and stopped at the first light. The traffic light was out. I looked both ways and saw nothing. No cars. I turned left (south) and still saw nothing. Either everyone had evacuated or were late sleepers. This city of almost two hundred thousand people was now a ghost town. A few blocks south of my home, I drove past the pride of Rancho Cucamonga; a major outdoor mall. I saw broken windows and unused merchandise drifting through the streets like tumbleweeds. Clothes kicked up into the air, thanks to the stiff breeze. But, I saw not a single soul.

When I arrived at Storage Units R Us, a new problem arose. A thick iron gate divided the storage units from the public parking lot. I parked in one of the four parking spaces. I would have to hop the wall. It's too early in the morning for this, I thought to myself, as I used a decorative rock right next to the brick wall that surrounded the compound and heaved myself up and over, and I landed on my feet with a thud.

I visited this storage unit once since I returned home. I had to decide to keep it or sell off all the junk. I decided to keep it and pay a hundred bucks a month. But, I moved all the stuff to a smaller unit. It gave me something to do and allowed me a chance to filter out the unwanted items. Now, I was glad that I moved it to the smaller unit because the previous unit was in the interior of the building, which was now locked behind a solid, thick, door. The unit I stood in front of, on this lovely morning, was a direct access unit from the outside.

I put my key in the lock, unlocked the lock and pulled up the metal roll-up door. It rattled all the way to the top, making a god-awful creaking, grinding sound, that I was sure would wake up everyone in a hundred-mile radius.

The smell that spilled out of the opening was pure memory. The musty smell of old papers. Of grandparents, who lived far longer than I probably would and real books with their wonderful paper. The smell was overwhelmingly nostalgic. I felt my body warm, as images danced in my head.

After the initial shock of nostalgia, enhanced, I guessed, by my four-day imprisonment, and possibly nicotine withdrawal, I began to examine the strewn white and blue boxes. I found old newspapers, my mom's schoolwork (she was like me, a "B" student), real estate documents, old tax returns and no maps.

After forty-five minutes, I began to think this was a fool's errand. Besides, the nostalgia, I thought I wasted a beautiful morning. I was sitting on the cold concrete floor and about to give up when I heard a noise behind me, coming from the unit's open door.

"Don't you move!" a voice said. An old, raspy voice. I raised my hands slowly, stood up and turned around. Technically, ignoring his command. "I told you not to move!" In his hands was a shotgun. He raised it higher for dramatic effect as he yelled. He was a tall man, probably in his seventies, with silver-white hair that started at the top of his head and flowed long past his ears. I recognized him at once. He was the owner of the storage facility. His eyes were darting to and fro, searching the unit. Presumably, to verify I was the only one inside.

"Sorry. I hope I didn't scare you. But, this is my unit," I said. My hands now out in front of me, palms up in the universal signal for "calm down." The old man squinted his eyes as if trying to recognize the owner of the unit.

"Scare me? I am the one with the shotgun." He didn't know I had my 9mm handgun concealed behind my back.

"No. I meant showing up here. Gate locked and all. But, this is my unit, and I was looking for something before I head out of town."

"Show me," he said.

"Show you what?"

"Show me proof that this is your unit?" I ambled toward the light. He backed away keeping the barrel of the shotgun pointed in my general direction. I reached up and grabbed the lock hanging from the rail, then unlocked and locked the lock in front of him. His brow furrowed. He looked at the lock then at me. "What's your name?"

"Blake Anderson." He didn't seem to recognize the name. The shotgun still pointed at me. "This unit used to belong to my grandparents and my mother. Probably under Joel MacIntyre." At that, I saw it. An eyebrow raised and a gleam in his eye. He knew my grandfather. Of course, he did. They would've been about the same age. He and my grandfather probably talked each other's ears off when he delivered the monthly payment by hand.

"Joel MacIntyre?" he asked.

"My grandfather."

"Well shit son, you did give me a fright." He lowered the shotgun. "I thought the damn looters finally decided to take my business."

"There were looters?"

"Hell yes. You didn't hear them? All hours of the night. Police sirens. Gun shots. The Target over there." He pointed to the west. "Was a damn war zone." He noticed my quizzical look. "You didn't hear any of it, did you?"

"No. I've been bunkered in my home for the past four days."

"Smart man."

"When did it stop? The town is dead now."

"I guess." He paused, put his hand up and cradled his chin. "Maybe it was last night. I heard nothing except the damn National Guard."

"The National Guard?"

"Yeah, I guess they finally restored some order."

"Enforcing the evacuation order."

"What evacuation order?" he said, and it was my turn to explain. After I was done. "Damn, I ain't going to no," He raised his left hand, the one not holding the shotgun and made the universal quote sign with two, twisted, fingers. "Damn evacuation centers."

"That's why I'm here. I came to see if my grandfather left any maps in here."

"Maps?"

"You know the old folded kind, that had all the roads on it. Maybe one for the western states. For now, I will just take anything that will help me get out of town."

He smiled and shook his head. "I know what type of maps you mean son. But, no one has those maps anymore. Hell, even I used the GPS in my car to get anywhere."

"Yeah. I know. I thought I would try. No luck, so far."

"Where are you going?" he asked.

"Eventually. Utah. For now, just trying to avoid getting sent to the evacuation center."

"The wife and I aren't going anywhere. We are staying in the units themselves, right in the center. Got plenty of food. And for fun, we open the units to see if there is anything of use. Any board games, books, to help pass the time."

"You going to stay there long?"

"As long as we need to." He eyed me suspiciously. "Then when everything calms down, we may try and go see our sons in Bakersfield." Sounded a lot like my original plan. At this, we went quiet. I looked back into the unit. "I can help you look for a little while, but I wouldn't stay out here much longer," he said. I couldn't tell if he wanted to get rid of me or genuinely wanted to help. Either way, I understood. I wouldn't want someone younger and stronger than me, close to my bunker, with plenty of food and my wife.

"That sounds good. I have this row to the right to get through yet. Then I will head out, map or no map." He nodded, and we spent the next hour enjoying our time in my storage unit.

The final result; no map. Nothing of use was found that morning. I shook his hand and shut the metal shutters to my storage. He waited for me to lock the latch. I didn't and said, "I don't think I will be coming back here. So, what's the point." He just nodded.

I was halfway to my car. Thinking about what to do next when I heard, the old man yell, "Power lines and fire roads!"

I turned around. "What?"

"Follow the power lines! There are always roads around power lines, and there are roads through the mountains for fire trucks."

"Thanks!" I said. Power lines and fire roads? How do we even find them to begin with? Oh well. At least it was a start.

As I drove out of the parking lot, I made a rash decision. I had to know if my assumptions were correct. Was the government filtering everyone to the camps? Were the freeways blocked so you could only go one way? Was I overreacting and making an unpleasant situation worse? Could we just hop on the freeway north, pass right by the camps and on to our destination?

I turned right onto Milliken Road and headed north toward the

210 freeway. A block from the storage unit a police car went flying by, sirens blaring, heading south. It was the first car I had seen all morning. I turned right on a side street to avoid the intersection of Baseline and Milliken, the intersection Zero and I avoided on the first night out to gather supplies and I ended up on a side street through a residential neighborhood. Eventually, I passed by my old high school and pulled into a city park, next to a shopping center that appeared deserted. Concrete barricades blocked all the entrances to the shopping center. Just north and behind the shopping center was the freeway. I left the car in the parking lot for Kenyon Park. It was a park that was hidden from the main road, and I parked in a spot no one could see unless they drove into the lot itself.

I made it across Kenyon Way and headed north along the sidewalk on a street that ran into a Mormon church. I kept my head on a swivel. The weather was still cooperating. No rain yet, and a temperature in the fifties. I turned right into the Mormon churches parking lot. I didn't head straight because the freeway was dead ahead. I came around the backside of the white church, with its steeple pointing to the sky and saw the freeway. It was separated from the neighborhood, by a single chain-link fence. As the freeway ran through Rancho Cucamonga, it was mostly isolated from the communities by either being below ground or behind a brick wall. But, right here, next to this church, it was a chain-link fence, which would allow me to see for miles in each direction.

I ran across the road from the church to the fence and hid behind a small tree, one of many that lined the road to disguise the freeway. I peered out onto the road. I was ten feet from a National Guard vehicle, parked at the top of the on-ramp and next to it was a sheriff's car. As I watched a small, blue, Toyota crawled up the on-ramp, the vehicles split and made way for the car to merge onto the freeway. As the car passed, the two government vehicles closed ranks.

Across the freeway, on the westbound side, there was nothing except another sheriff's car at the top of the off-ramp. So, no one could go the wrong way and get on the freeway heading west. It was as I feared. Once you were on the freeway, there was no getting off, presumably until you reached the camps.

Along the concrete median separating the west and eastbound lanes, were lines of cars. All empty. Cars that must've died and left behind. Hundreds of them lined up heading east. So many, that the fast lane was now a junkyard of cars. *How long had the backup been for cars to be abandoned? Ran out of gas? Or just shut down?*

I shook my head and turned away from the freeway and leaned against the tree. Was I still making assumptions? Was the entirety of the freeway blocked as I have seen? I didn't want to believe it. But, it made the most sense from an evacuation point of view. Get everyone on the freeway and control the population until they arrived at the destination. The 'Evacuation Centers.'

I turned back to look at the freeway, straight into the eyes of a National Guardsman. He was walking along the shoulder when he spotted me. We both wore shock on our faces, as I am sure he thought the last thing he'd see is a young man alone standing at the fence, dressed in a black beanie and sweatshirt. I nodded and gave a little wave. He nodded back. Better to act like everything is normal than to show the panic I felt inside. My heart was racing. I turned slowly away and walked across the street back toward the church. I don't know why I was so scared and paranoid, he wasn't going to chase me down. I was just one man. But, I didn't want to take the chance, and I ran back to the car, cursing my smoking habit.

I drove home, passing by the high school, by the freeway, again, near Day Creek Blvd., and saw the same setup. Police cars blocking the on-ramp for the westbound lanes and the eastbound off-ramp. At the top of the eastbound on-ramp was another National Guard vehicle. I just assumed there were more cars on the freeway blocking the on and off-ramps. I, finally returned home, just before noon, with no clearer direction of what to do before I left. But, at least I knew my instincts were correct. We did not want to get on the freeway.

CHAPTER TWELVE

11/15/2024

When I pulled into my driveway, I had a moment of selfishness. I put the automatic gear shift in park, but left the car idling. I wanted to take off, right then and there. Take off for gods knows where. Maybe try to find my brother in Oregon. It had been nice being on my own. Exploring. Not having every decision scrutinized by a committee. Inside was responsibility. Worrying about others. Leading a group of people dependent on me. A week ago, I wanted nothing more than to be left alone. I doubt anybody would've shown up here after the bomb if it wasn't for that damn party. I deliberated with myself, sitting in silence, but, of course, shut off the engine, sighed, and went inside.

It was just after noon. Everyone was eating lunch. Peanut butter sandwiches as we finished the last loaf of bread in the pantry. They did not look surprised to see me.

"How's the outside world?" Zero asked.

"Fine," I said.

"Any luck with the maps?" Ethan asked.

"Nope."

In the living room along the wall with the TV stand, carefully placed around my left home theater speaker, were ten suitcases. The dining room had eight boxes of canned food, and all the Welles family camping gear. Sleeping bags rolled up. The five, unused, water jugs were lined up around my right home theater speaker. They were ready to leave.

"Find anything?" Ethan asked.

I sat down on the red couch next to the kids who were trying not to get peanut butter all over the place. Trying, but failing. I observed them one by one. The kids. Drew, Jenna, Ethan, and Alicia were at the dining room table. Kaitlyn standing behind the others in the kitchen by herself. She appeared to be the architect of lunch and was making me a sandwich as I sat down.

"What's wrong?" Alicia asked.

"I don't know how we are going to get out of here," I said.

"Why? What happened?" Alicia said.

"The freeways are a definite, no go. Unless we want to be taken straight to the evacuation centers."

"You saw it for yourself?" Ethan asked.

"The freeways? Yes," I said. "The off-ramps and on-ramps are all blocked by either barricades, the national guard or police."

"What's that mean?" Zero asked.

"It means once we're on the freeway, we are not getting off until they let us," Drew answered for me.

"Thanks," I said to Kaitlyn as she handed me a sandwich. She sat down beside me, there was enough room for her to squeeze in between the girls and me. I nodded and said, "Drew's right. Once were on the freeway." I took a bite of the sandwich, "We're not getting off."

We sat in silence. No Maps. No Freeway. Nowhere to go. Then

I remembered what the old man said. "Any of you know anything about roads along power lines and fire roads or any back roads through the mountains?" They turned toward me, mid-bite, like I was mad. "I didn't think so."

"I know what you mean," Drew said. "But, I don't know where we could even find them. Sometimes when we go camping, you run across a lot of those types of back roads." He paused and took a bite of his sandwich. "But, who knows where they would lead."

"I came to the same conclusion."

We ate the rest of our lunch in silence. Kaitlyn was leaning against my shoulder. I sat staring straight ahead, searching my mind for an answer that never came.

It was Alicia who broke the situation down to its bare components. "We have two options then," Alicia said, while she took the empty lunch plates from the children. Natalie had been using her finger to clean off the excess peanut butter and gave her mom a dirty look when she turned her back toward the kitchen. "We can stay here and hope whoever comes to enforce the evacuation, doesn't bother with us. Or, if they do come, we could hide somewhere, in the attic maybe."

"Like Anne Frank," Zero said.

"Yes," Alicia said, rolling her eyes. "The other option is to try and get out of here and the only route we know of, that won't get us on a freeway is either through Big Bear or Lake Arrowhead or take a chance on some back road where we have no idea where it may lead."

"That about sums it up," Ethan said.

"So, we should vote, either we leave and try to get out of here tonight? Or we stay here and play it out?"

Everyone looked around at each other. Zero shrugged. Drew beamed at Alicia with pride. Ethan and Jenna, still seated at the dining table, were whispering to each other. I looked at Kaitlyn, and her eyes told me how I needed to vote.

"I vote we head out tonight," I said.

"Me too," Zero said.

"Jenna and I are down," Ethan said. Jenna said not a word.

Alicia looked to Drew. "Whatever you want babe. You know I can't make a decision," he said.

"We go then," Alicia said. Then she turned to me. "What other supplies do we need?"

I looked at her, with sincere admiration. As I was complaining about being in charge, internally. Alicia had stepped up and got things moving again. "We need to go around and find gasoline. Find some way to take it with us. We should go in Zero's truck and your SUV. Which gets what miles per gallon?"

"About thirty six on the highway, less than that, maybe twenty five, on the streets," she replied.

"Right so we will need at least a half tank of extra gas to get to Utah, and I would rather not have to stop at a gas station." I paused thinking. "Zero, what gas mileage does your truck get?"

"Thirty two. Thirty three. On the freeway. Twenty-four on average. I think. The dashboard will tell me," he said.

"Okay, we need to siphon the gas from the rest of our cars and fill up the truck and SUV. Then we head out tonight as soon as it gets dark."

An hour later I found myself with a garden hose in my mouth, blowing air into my cars gas tank. A second tube curved out of the tank into a one-gallon gas can I used for the lawn mower. Thankfully, Zero showed me the correct way to do this. I tried to accomplish this task, as I saw it performed in the movies. Sucking on the hose till the gas came out. Zero said I could kill myself doing it that way, or at least, it would make me sick. The way I was doing it now, was less toxic. It was slow going, one gallon at a time, but by three in the afternoon, we had the truck and the SUV filled. The math in my head said the SUV and truck could both go about four hundred miles, on a full tank of gas. But, that was if we were on the freeway going seventy. That wasn't going to happen. So, we figured we would need an extra ten gallons of gas, to make the trip. Three, empty, three-gallon water jugs plus the one-gallon gas can, equals ten.

"You sure that's gonna work?" Ethan asked as were taking out one of the empty water jugs.

"No," I said. "But, I don't think we have any other choice. I think if we were planning on storing gas in them, for a long time, that would be a bad idea. But, they should be okay, as long as we don't take weeks to get there."

"You know it's gonna take weeks, now that you said that," he said and gave a half-smile.

"Yeah, I always seem to do that. We should stop every hour and top off the tanks. Just to be safe."

"Sounds like a plan."

"What plan?" Zero asked as he came outside with another empty water jug.

"Oh you know, just a plan to make sure we don't blow up your truck with all this gas in the back," Ethan said.

Zero stood straight up. His eyes darted from the truck to the empty jugs. "Could that happen?"

Ethan and I laughed. "Not if we do this correctly?" I said.

"Assholes," Zero said.

We found an abandoned, or rather we hoped it was an abandoned car, a block from my house and siphoned that gas. We filled another one and a half jugs of gas with that car. We loaded it onto Zero's dolly and wrapped it with my blue tarp and heaved it into the truck.

At that moment, it started to rain.

"We need to get inside now!" The ferocity with which I yelled, made Zero and Ethan jump and we ran into the open garage for cover.

"What's going on?" Zero asked, once safely inside the garage.

"Radiation," I said. Zero looked around as if to say "where?"

"The rain. It could be carrying a high dose of radiation."

"Could be?" Ethan asked.

"Could be." I shrugged. "Better safe than sorry, right?"

"Look what I found!" Zero said as he was looking at one of my shelving units along the wall of the garage. In between a pair of empty coffee cans, he pulled out a pack of Camels. "Smokes!"

"Sweet," Ethan said.

I went to the walkie-talkie that was on the washer, at the back of the garage, and radioed the host inside. "We are stuck in the garage since it's raining... We will head inside when it stops. Over." Since my garage was detached from the house, we were stuck inside the damp, dusty garage until the rain deceased.

"Okay. You guys have enough gas?... over," Alicia responded.

"Almost. Another trip around the block to find one more car should do it... over."

"Great. We are all getting pretty anxious in here. The girls have almost finished *The Hobbit*. I told them we were about to go on our own adventure like Bilbo. But, that seemed to scare them more than it meant to," she said and laughed. "Over."

"Yeah, I doubt we will run into any goblins," I said. "We need to change clothes since it rained a bit on us. So, we'll see you inside shortly. Over."

I put the walkie on top of the dryer. At the front of the garage Zero and Ethan sat on green foldout chairs smoking, watching the rain come down outside the open garage door, like two Hobbits.

CHAPTER THIRTEEN

11/15/2024

At 5:14 p.m., our journey finally began. The Welles family, along with Kaitlyn, were to lead in the SUV. Zero, Ethan, Jenna and I followed in Zero's truck. Drew led because he knew where he was going. By his estimation, we could take Baseline Street, all the way to the road that went through Lake Arrowhead or even further east to the one that passed through Big Bear. I wasn't thrilled about taking that route the entire way, but it was the only non-freeway road we knew of, that could get us to our destination. If we saw any official vehicles, we would pull over or down a side street. I had my AR (Windham Weaponry Carbon Fiber SRC AR-15, Semi-Automatic) with me in the front seat and my handgun (Smith & Wesson M&P9 Pro Series) behind my back. If we ran into any major trouble, Zero would pull in front of the SUV. If we needed to, we could drop down to a side road for a bit, but Baseline was the road we were to stay on. My real concern were intersections with freeways. We had to pass at least one, and I was worried about the number of official vehicles around those locations.

We exited the north side of the suburban development onto a side road to avoid the intersection with the 15 freeway and headed east with the sun already set behind us.

I grabbed the walkie-talkie and depressed the yellow button, with the Batman symbol. "Keep at this speed. And before we get on Baseline take a long look before we turn. Over."

"Gotcha... over," Alicia said. If we were within a car length or so, the walkie worked fine. Any further and we ran into static issues.

We passed under Interstate 15 on Victoria Street and materialized into an area that was undeveloped, that reminded us that we did live in an over developed desert. With the vehicle lights off and the sun set, it was dark and ominous, as we passed under the freeway into another world. Next, we arrived at a dead end and a right turn on Cherry Place.

At Baseline Street, there was a gas station and a small shopping center on the left. A crowd of cars, scattered around the parking lot, and at the gas pumps. People moseyed around aimlessly. One man was pulling on the gas pump, over and over, like it was a lawn mower. Finally, he considered the nozzle, confused at its inability to perform its one function, then slammed the pump back into place. One important thing to remember when the power is out; most gas stations no longer function.

"I think we're good to turn," Alicia said. "Over."

"Okay, let's go for it. Over," I said.

Slowly, Drew pulled into the intersection with overhead traffic signals as dead as the rest of the city and turned left. Zero followed close behind. We stayed in the slow lane, traveling thirty-five miles per hour. We were no longer in Rancho Cucamonga and now were in the city of Fontana. If Rancho had seemed dead, Fontana was on its last legs. Every now and then a car would come up behind us and pass by.

As another vehicle passed us on the left, heading the same direction it honked and flashed its lights on and off. How nice, I thought, he was trying to warn us our lights were off.

As we continued East, the suburban sprawl of prosperity, slowly gave way to the suburban sprawl of poverty. While Rancho Cucamonga would be considered a wealthy city, despite its certain areas, like a mobile home park, Fontana and Rialto were far more typical of the Inland Empire. A vast suburban sprawl of mixed races and average to below average incomes. A concrete jungle with gang violence and some neighborhoods you would not want to visit at any time of day, let alone at night after a mandatory evacuation.

"Blake." I heard Alica say over the walkie. I had been peering out the side window as the neighborhoods passed. I looked ahead and saw a host of police lights.

"I see it, turn left here," I said. We had been on the road twenty minutes. We turned left at an intersection with another non-operating traffic signal. "Keep going and try to find a way around. Over."

"Will do. Over," Alicia replied.

We headed north on an unknown street. Reading the street signs was difficult in the evening light. We stopped at another intersection which led into a residential area. Drew kept us headed north. We passed an elementary school that was deserted. Went through a stop sign. Then ran into a dead end. I saw the sign as we passed that read: Not a through street.

"We are gonna turn back on the last street... over," Alicia said. We turned around, and as we did, I noticed the big brick wall at the end of the cul-de-sac. The 210 freeway.

We headed east and continued to weave ever so slowly in the direction we wanted to travel.

It was Zero who saw the lights first. "Blake," he said. I looked up and saw flashing red and blue lights about a quarter mile ahead, along with white headlights. Five police vehicles and many large vehicles that I could not make out. Drew pulled over, and Zero followed.

"What do you see? Over," I asked into the walkie.

"Not sure. It looks like a shopping center on the left and tons of police cars. Some, maybe Army vehicles and about ten school buses," Alicia said, slowly. "What's with the school buses?" I wasn't sure if she was addressing me or not. "We are going back the way we came. Over"

"Okay? Over," I said.

"This is getting to be ridiculous," Zero said. Ethan and Jenna sat in silence. We were headed back the way we came. Drew turned south on a side street, and we followed close, crawling through the streets of a residential neighborhood. Small, single story, two or three bedroom homes, built in the late sixties. Most had bars on the windows.

Abruptly, Drew pulled over next to a large tree with branches that hung over the street, in front of a single-story home with two dark front windows between a red front door. In the darkness, our eyes had adjusted, and besides the few moments where we ran into other cars, or one of us used our brakes, the world had acquired the look of a low-contrast black and white movie.

"We are not sure which way to go. Over," Alicia said.

"I think if we just head east we can find a way through. Over."

"Blake," Zero said, but it was the way he said it that got my attention. An alert. A seriousness that made the hair on my arms stand up. "You see them?"

Thirty yards in front of us, I could see four or five human-shaped shadows approaching the SUV.

"Alicia, you see the group in front of you?" I said and forgot to say over.

"Yes," she replied.

"Do not move or say anything, I will be there in a second. Any sign of trouble and you tell Drew to take off."

"What do you mean?"

"Just go! Hit the gas, everyone get down and go. Over."

The men were now within ten yards of Drew's SUV. They wore beanies and dark clothes. But, it wasn't the clothes that bothered me, it was the way they were flanking us and the spacing between them. One stopped dead in the center of the road in front of the SUV. One had already passed the SUV, walking down the middle of the road and headed toward the truck. The other two approached Alicia's window.

"Take this," I said as I handed the AR to Ethan. "If you see any trouble, you roll down the window and make some noise so they can see the gun."

"Okay," Ethan said with trepidation.

"Don't I get a gun?" Zero asked.

"You just come and get me," I said.

"And me?" Jenna asked, from the seat behind Zero.

"Just stay down," I said as I exited the truck. By now, the taller of the two men arrived at Alicia's window. I walked swiftly, ignoring the guy who was examining the back of the truck, five feet from where I exited the vehicle.

"You guys need some help?" I heard the tall man ask Alicia in the window.

"N-no, were okay," she replied through the window. As I approached, the taller man was tapped on the shoulder by the other man and pointed toward me. The taller man backed away from the SUV and turned to me.

"Hey. How's it going?" I said as I approached and maneuvered myself between Alicia and the taller man. I put on a smile, but inside, my heartbeat was pounding a hundred beats per second and my adrenaline was spiking, giving me a sensation I had not felt since Afghanistan. A feeling I had missed.

"We're alright. But you guys look like you need some help." The tall man said, with a thick Spanish accent. I kept my eyes focused on him. But, in my peripheral, I could see the man standing in front of Drew's SUV and the other guy peeping in on Zero's truck.

"We're just a bit lost," I said.

"Where you trying to get to?"

"Out of here," I said with extra flummox. "Don't want to go to one of those evacuation places."

"The FEMA camps? Yeah, fuck those places man. That's smart," he said and smiled. "So, where you headed then?"

The man at Zero's truck had walked around the truck bed and now was on the passenger side, just behind Ethan's seat. Eyes still on the tarp-covered gasoline.

"We were trying to get out through Big Bear or Lake Arrowhead, but kept running into the damn police and National Guard."

"Yeah, they already started the evacuation east of here."

"Is that right? I have a map. Can you show us a way around?"

"I might."

The man at Zero's truck lifted the tarp covering our supplies and gasoline. I took a step forward, my left hand up in the universal sign for "Give me a sec" and I reached for my map behind my back.

I did not pull out a map.

As quick as I could, I pulled my gun, took a step forward and placed the muzzle against the tall man's forehead. He was over six feet, I was just below, so I had my gun at an angle on his forehead, that if I pulled the trigger, the bullet would explode out the top of his head. I heard the tires squeal as Drew took off behind me. The man in front of the SUV dove out of the way. I saw him out of my peripheral land on the grass by the sidewalk, roll, and back on his feet in an instant. The man at the tarp had pulled out a gun of his own and was pointing it toward me. The man in front of me, the taller man, had his arms raised at his side. Behind him, the other man stood still. To my left, the guy, who was dusting himself off from his dive into the grass, also pulled out a gun.

"There's no need for this man," the tall man said. I usually would not put my weapon that close to another person. Too easy to knock away. But, in this instance, I wanted to intimidate more than execute. I wanted him to feel the nozzle against his forehead.

I slowly began to walk backward, removing the gun from his forehead, never losing eye contact or my aim.

"Maybe. Maybe not. Tell your guys to put their guns down."

The tall man said something in Spanish.

"Hey asshole," I heard Ethan say from my right, and the man by the truck slowly lowered his weapon.

The taller man again spoke Spanish, with a steely voice this time.

My adrenaline was spiking, and I started to feel lightheaded. I could hear Zero's truck, slowly pull up behind me, and I continued to walk backward and into the street. Never taking the gun or my eyes off the man in front of me. As soon as I felt the truck behind me, I reached for the door handle with my left hand and with my right kept the gun forward, my eyes never leaving the target. I opened the door and backed into the seat, pressed the button to roll down the window with my left hand as I sat down. Then, also with the left hand, shut the door and showed the gun out the open window. Drew had opened the window in the cab and the big assault rifle was pointed at the tall man.

"Go," I said. Zero slammed on the accelerator, and the truck sped away with tires screeching. I relaxed in my seat, with a sigh and Ethan brought the rifle back in the vehicle. The breathing was heavy as if we all ran a marathon.

"You are one badass motherfucker," Zero said.

"I was afraid I was gonna accidentally shoot someone," Ethan said.

"Did you turn the safety off?" I asked.

"There's a safety?" Ethan said. Zero laughed so hard the truck swerved erratically. "Why did you give me a gun with the safety on?"

"If you can't figure out whether or not the safety's on, it's probably a good thing it was." I turned and grabbed the rifle back from Ethan. Jenna sat in shock, wide-eyed and staring at the three of us as if we were lunatics. "You okay?" I asked as I put the rifle down at my feet in the front seat.

"No," she said. I nodded and turned back to the road ahead.

"It's a good thing they didn't shoot at us as we left, with all the gasoline in the back," Zero said.

Yes. A good thing.

CHAPTER FOURTEEN

11/15/2024

We caught up to the SUV at another cross road. It appeared they were waiting for us. The red brake lights from the Welles family vehicle lit the interior of the truck, like a dark room for processing photographs.

"You guys okay. Over?" I asked.

"No. My husband almost ran over a man, who pulled out a gun not two feet from my children. No, I'm not okay," Alicia said. Her voice was higher pitched than normal. I waited for her to continue. "Was that necessary?" she finally said. I continued to wait. "Blake?"

"Say over when you finish. Over," I said.

"FUCK OVER!" she yelled, causing the walkie to screech loudly in my ear. I looked over to Zero who just raised an eyebrow.

"Blake," said Drew, on the walkie. "Sorry about that, we are a little shaken up. Over"

"I understand. We are as well," I said. Zero just shrugged his shoulders. "Over."

"You could have given us a warning. Over."

"No time. Over." There was a long pause on the other end. I waited patiently. Zero had his arms crossed over the wheel, with his head laying on his arms. I looked back at Jenna who was staring out the window, chewing on her fingernails. Ethan was looking right at me listening intently.

"So, what now?" Drew asked. "Over."

"It's up to you? If you can get us through this, we can continue. If not..." I left the sentence hang. "Over."

"I think I can. Over."

"Okay then. On we go. Over," I said.

And on we went, passing through numerous residential developments. I could see flashing red and blue lights to the north of us and sometimes to the south. It was slow going. At every intersection, there was an unbearably long pause. But, we continued like molasses flowing down a tree. I no longer had any idea where we were. I knew we had passed through Fontana and possibly, Rialto. We must've been close to the 215 freeway, with our destination just beyond. The only light and color came when Drew hit his brakes, casting an eerie red glow into the night. Drifting from empty street to empty street. Every so often I would see a light from the inside of a home. It seemed some people were still hiding out.

"Here we are. Over," the walkie crackled. It was Alicia again. The road in front of us slowly rose into the air, and there was a red and white glow from both sides of the road below us. It was the 215 freeway. As we glided over the overpass, I could see thousands of cars on the freeway heading south. To our left, white headlights. To our right, red taillights. When we crested down the other side of the overpass, I thanked Drew for finding us a way past the freeway that avoided on and off-ramps.

"Just a few more streets and then we will turn left toward Lake Arrowhead," Alicia said. "Over."

We passed a stop sign that was barely visible and entered another residential neighborhood. Another stop sign. A right turn and a quick left. We continued.

Abruptly Drew slammed on his brakes. The red light blinded us momentarily. Zero almost slammed into the back of the SUV. I reached my hand out to the dashboard and braced for the whiplash.

"It looks like a road block up ahead. Over," Alicia said. I didn't respond. I looked to my left and saw a side street. Drew had seen the same thing and turned the SUV north up the side street... which ran right into San Bernardino High School.

At the end of the street, to our left was the football field and we could see hundreds of people standing around, under temporary lights scattered along the track that ran around the field. To our right, the parking lot and a variety of military vehicles. Multiple helicopters. At least thirty school buses. It was a staging area.

"I think we took a wrong turn," Zero said.

"We need to turn around. Over," I said into the walkie as Drew kept creeping closer to the school.

"We know. Over."

We kept trying to turn East, but it was of no use. The National Guard had blocked off all routes headed east of the school. Drew pulled over on a side street and stopped. Zero pulled in behind him. It was quiet.

"What do you thinks going on?" Ethan finally asked.

"They are probably discussing possible ways we could go," I said. This night had not turned out like any of us thought. It was far worse than I could've imagined.

Finally, the walkie spoke. "I think... we need to turn back," Alicia said. "We can't find a way through, without coming into contact with..." She paused, and I heard her sigh. "We should go back. Over"

"I think so too," I said. "Over." I looked back at my fellow passengers, and while they didn't say so, I could read it on their faces.

"You sure?" Alicia asked. "We may not have another chance. Over."

"True. But, I don't think we want to risk it. Not with the way this night has gone. We can go back to my place and try to hide out there. If we keep going, we will end up at the camps for sure. Over."

"Okay. Over," she said, barely audible.

"We'll think of something," I said. "Over."

"What?" Zero asked as I put down the walkie and Drew made a U-turn in front of us.

"I don't know," I said, and I didn't.

We took the journey back to my house without incident. At eight-thirty in the evening, we pulled into my driveway. A three-and-a-half-hour drive to nowhere. The second time I ventured outside my home since the explosion and both ended up fruitless. Maybe we were meant to stay here.

"So, what now," Alicia asked as she dropped down two suitcases in my living room and I lit the candle next to the TV.

"I don't know," I said. "We have a day, or so before we need to be out of here, we can think of something." I was not sure I believed that, but I was the de facto boss and was trying to give the people what they want.

"Like what?" she asked. The kids sat on the couch, yawning, rubbing their eyes and kept looking around like 'why are we back here?'

"I don't know," I said. "We need to think and figure it out."

I ended up in my garage, alone, after we had unloaded all the water and food. We stored the excess water jugs and canned food in my garage because it created more space in the house. It also would enable us to ration better. Like a smoker putting his pack of cigarettes in the garage because he was trying to cut back. It usually didn't work. But, it was a good attempt. I smoked one of those cigarettes from my pack in the garage. It was stale and smelled dreadful. I sat, relaxed, on one of the folding chairs. The garage door was open, so I could see into the night. It was quiet as it had been most nights. But, now I knew what it sounded like did not make it so.

Sitting in my garage with my stale cigarette it could've been any night. I could be going to work tomorrow morning and would be worried about my reports that were due on Monday. Out on the road, you could feel the chaos of the rest of the world. In my home, it felt safe. It was a mirage. A lie. A well-meaning lie. But, that lie had been exposed, and now I worried for the psyche of my compatriots.

What now? The single question being asked by the group. I could not answer that, and I fear that my experience and knowledge may have belayed a sense of safety. Now, they had seen the truth. The world is in chaos. The power is in the military.

So, what now?

"Can I borrow one?" Jenna said, interrupting my thought.

"Sure," I said and handed her the pack of cigarettes. I only had three left, and I was not looking forward to the lack of nicotine. Jenna grabbed one out of the pack and lit it with a lighter she provided. We sat in silence for a minute.

"Would you have actually shot that guy?" she asked.

"Umm... Not unless I needed to."

"I guess it's a good thing Aaron only ended up with a sore jaw," she said, with a grin.

"I am sorry about that." I took a hit of my cigarette. "I should not have hit him."

"It's alright he had been an ass the whole time. He wanted to just stay in his apartment and said it was dumb to come here and then I made a mistake of telling him about the party."

"Why, we didn't do anything?"

"True, but I kind of threw it in his face when we were arguing, and I guess he assumed the worst." That explained the dynamic change.

"Still, I shouldn't have hit him."

"Whatever. I should have left him a long time ago."

"Do you worry about him?"

"Nah. He is a survivor. I am sure if we end up in one of the camps, he'll be there trying his best to get on my good side and showing me all the rules and how it all works."

"Right," I said.

"Do you think we will?"

"End up in the camps? I hope not. I think we can hold off here for a little while longer."

"We may not have a choice."

"We always have a choice," I said and put out my cigarette.

Back inside, the household began to return to normal, or as normal as when we left three hours ago. The kids were reading *The Hobbit*, again, or at least looking at the pictures. Zero and Drew were playing cards on the dining room table. Kaitlyn and Alicia were talking on the couch. Ethan was in the kitchen making an updated inventory of our food supply that was then placed on the fridge with a magnet. He had separated what was inside and what was in the garage.

As I sat on the couch next to Kaitlyn and Alicia, Jenna went and sat at the dining table with Drew and Zero, everyone stopped to look at me. I knew what they wanted, but I did not have a definitive answer for them. Only the same thought I had previously. Stay here for as long as we could.

I told them this.

"Then what?" Alicia asked.

"Well, we stay here until we can find a road out of here or we go to the camps. Those are the answers right now. The only solutions I can think of. If you have any others, I would be glad to hear them," I said.

"We can try again tomorrow, during the day so we can see where we are going," Drew said.

"We could," I said and nodded. But the way I said it, they knew I did not think that was a promising idea.

We argued like we did a few nights ago, back and forth. To go to the camps. To stay here. To try the roads. The only guaranteed safe place was my home.

"We need to have one person be a lookout, at all times. From here on out, until we decide what we need to do or the decision is made for us," I said.

"Who will that be?" Drew asked.

"For tonight I will. Then tomorrow, early morning..." I waited for a volunteer. Finally, Drew raised his hand. "Good. This is just a lookout. If you see something, don't do anything just let the rest of us know."

"What if the National Guard comes and tries to evacuate us?" Alicia asked. The question we were all thinking.

"I will wake all of you up, and we will try to hide. That's all we can do."

"What if we don't want to hide?" Alicia asked.

"I know you are upset about what happened tonight. I know it was shocking for me to pull out a gun in front of your children. But, the world has changed. We need to all be on the same page. We all need to look out for each other, or we will end up in one of those camps, or we will be split up and alone." The thoughts just came to me as I said them. Alicia didn't say any more.

I brought a folding chair from the garage and set it up inside the front door next to the window that faced the street. With my AR at my side, I sat down with a clear view of the road and as soon as the candles were out, an invisible view. In short order, everyone went to bed. Jenna slept on the red couch and Ethan on the floor in a sleeping bag. I spent the night thinking. Trying to unravel this puzzle. If we sought to hide, I knew if the National Guard were on our doorstep, they would not do a cursory search, it would be thorough and complete. It was an M.C. Escher problem. No matter what path we chose, somehow, we end up going in a circle, and it all ended the same. With all of us at the camps.

I opened the front door as quietly as possible. I could hear Jenna's snoring, and I produced a half-smile at the sound. I stepped out and closed the door. I wanted to smoke one of my remaining cigarettes. I lit the cigarette and inhaled the toxic smoke with a loving sigh. A few birds were chirping in the night. Every now and then I could see on the horizon to the south a red and blue light flashing. Police cruising in the evening. But, no sirens, which I thought was odd. The night was cold. How could this have happened? I thought for the first time since that first night. It was a thought I knew that could not be answered by me, but a thought I had none the same. That first night I had felt confident I could survive this. Even when everyone showed up, and I felt responsible for them, I still felt confident things would work out alright. We would all make it to Utah and live happily ever after. Now?

Now, I felt different. If we were to survive and make it to Utah, we may have to do some things we would not have done in the former world. I understood this, but I was not sure my friends did or would. And that scared me.

I finished my cigarette, with no clearer answer than before. I sniffed the butt out with the heel of my shoe, picked it up and flicked it into the gutter. I quietly opened the door, with Jenna's snoring providing comfort. I sat down at my lookout post and thought one hopeful thought. What if they never came at all? What if no one came to enforce the evacuation? That may be our only hope. I smiled and shook my head. If that happened, we would be the luckiest survivors in the world. I looked out the window and said a small prayer to whoever was in charge of this crappy universe and asked for that miracle. Just leave us alone, I thought.

Alone.

CHAPTER FIFTEEN

11/16/2024

I awoke the next day just after noon, alone in the guest bedroom. The sun shone into the room from the no longer boarded window. I shifted slightly and hesitated to get up. Usually, I could remember my dreams, but after the long night I must've slept like a rock, I couldn't remember anything.

I arose from the bed and did some slight stretches, an old military habit, and walked out of the bedroom into the hall, and as I turned into the family room, I saw all the eyes of my guests turn to me.

Zero was now on the lookout. Ethan and Drew were discussing something when I came in and turned toward me with a smile on their faces. The women of the household were nowhere to be seen.

"What's up?" I asked.

"I think-" Drew said, before being interrupted, as the back door opened and Alicia, Jenna, and Kaitlyn entered the home from the kitchen, with Natalie and Jane at their side.

"Blake. Good your up," Alicia said. "We got something to show you." This was interesting. I wondered what they've been doing while I slept.

"Ok," I said. "But can I get coffee first?" I pointed toward the kitchen.

"Oh, yeah. Of course," she said.

I walked past the women and children and prepared myself some coffee. Standing in front of the stove I felt their eyes on me. I turned my head toward them and smiled. They smiled back. I lit a match and turned one of the gas burners on, to boil some water. As I placed the pot down on top of the lit burner, I looked over again and smiled. They all smiled back. I just shook my head. They were waiting for me. They wanted to show me something, and by their never-ending stare, I guessed they had waited all morning.

I poured the boiling water slowly through the drip coffee maker's carriage that had a coffee filter and a half a cup of ground coffee inside. Eventually, I took a sip of black coffee, as I did, I turned and faced the living room. Where I found fourteen eyes staring back at me. Zero was the lone exception as he was on the lookout.

I walked into the living room and finally said, "Ok. So what do you have for me to see?"

They all looked at each other. Then Alicia stood up and said, "It's not something, in particular, it's…I believe a solution to our problem."

This was intriguing, they all seemed to be behind whatever it was they were selling.

"Okay. What is it?"

"I need you to go outside and pretend to be the national guard," she said, and I gave her a quizzical look. "And when I mean pretend, I mean pretend. I want you to act as if you were the national guard and you were coming here to evacuate us."

"Okay." They were practically pushing me out the door.

"Start down at the end of the street," she said as I took a step outside the front door. She closed the door before I could respond. While it wasn't early in the morning, I had only been up for ten minutes. I shook the cobwebs from my head and tried to make sense of this development. Apparently, they think they found a solution to the problem of evacuation, and instead of just telling me, they wanted to impress me with the act. Okay, I can play along.

In my garage, I opened the main garage door, grabbed a cigarette, one remaining. Lit the smoke and sat down on one of the fold-up chairs. If they really wanted to play this out, I needed to surprise them. So, I waited ten minutes. Finally, I put the cigarette and coffee down, then walked down the sidewalk to the end of the street.

What would the national guard do, when they were evacuating citizens? It would not be a stealth operation. They would pull into the cul-de-sac and go door to door, most likely in pairs. Since it was just me, I walked right down the middle of the road. I turned to look at my front door, just to see if I could identify anyone at the window next to the front door and saw nothing. The reflection from the sun off the vertical window, which Zero was behind, hid him from my perception. I turned toward the house. Crossed the sidewalk, onto my front lawn, then the paved path to the front door. At the door, I knocked.

"This is the National Guard. There is a mandatory evacuation. If anyone is inside, please come out, and we can help you get to the evacuation centers. If you have no mode of transportation, we have buses at the local high school, that can take you to the appropriate... place." I was just making this up, but I thought it was fairly accurate, after what we saw last night.

I knocked again. Nothing. I grabbed the door handle and turned. The door opened into my home, only now I needed to view it as a foreign place with potential undesirables. It was empty. I slowly crept inside, keeping to the left with one eye on the kitchen, the other on the opening to the hallway and back rooms. As I came up parallel to the hallway entrance, I took two long quick steps and side-stepped my way to the hall archway. I walked backward a pace keeping both the kitchen and hallway in my view. Looked right, then left, down the hall. Then slowly crept toward the bathroom at the end of the corridor. Nothing. The guest bedroom. Nothing. The office, nothing except Zeros sleeping bag and clothes. Down to the master bedroom. Again, nothing but sleeping bags, suitcases lying opened and clothes scattered on the bed. I retreated into the living room. Acting cautiously, I entered the kitchen and could smell the coffee, which was still warm and smelled great, and I had an intense desire to grab another mug. But, I kept going. I was generally interested in playing this out.

Out the kitchen's back door and into the yard. I noticed immediately that the pathway we had made in the fence, between the houses, had been repaired. Clever. I looked around the backyard, nothing out of the ordinary, except an empty keg. I strained to hear any whispering or unusual or at least human sounds. Again nothing.

They sneaked over to Enrique's home. So, I went back out of my front door, just as I assumed a National Guardsman would. I probably should've done a cursory check of the attic, but I knew in a realistic scenario, there would not be enough time for us all to get into the attic and be quiet enough to stay there. If they were in the attic now, I would have to shoot down that plan. I was confident they were next door.

I went to my neighbor's yellow front door and knocked. I said the same speech I said at my front door. As I finished, I heard some footsteps coming from the backyard, along with a slight creak of a door opening and closing. I went into Enrique's home, the door was unlocked, and immediately went to the backyard. Outside I saw no one. I looked at the spot where the fence had been taken apart for our pathway and saw what now looked like a door. New hinges had been placed on the fence, along with two new horizontal pieces of wood, which appeared to now allow someone to pull or push the whole two-foot section open and enabling them to close it. Clever, now they were back in my house. I went back out the front door and back to my home.

I walked inside.

"Ta.Da," Zero said. I smiled and looked around at everyone beaming with pride. Natalie and Jane stood next to their mother, hands covering their mouths trying not to laugh.

"So, what do you think?" Alicia asked.

"Very good," I said. I meant it. But, I also understood its faults. What if they didn't go door to door one at a time? What if they hit all the houses at once? I kept those thoughts to myself.

"Do you know what we did?" Drew asked.

"I think so. You went next door as I approached and when I went next door, you came back here," I said. They were kind of disappointed I figured it out. So, I continued, "But, like I said I knew the pathway was there and that was an option. I am just glad you all didn't climb into the attic." They laughed.

"It was Jenna's idea," Alicia said.

"No. It was all of us," Jenna said.

"Did you notice the door?" Zero asked.

"Yes. But, I was looking for it."

"I made it."

"It's a beautiful door."

"Do you think it could work?" Drew asked.

"Yes. I think it might. But, only if they truly believe the houses are empty. I did hear some shuffling and the makeshift door opening and closing. Which would mean they would do a more thorough investigation." Everyone seemed to take this correctly. I wasn't trying to destroy the plan, just saying we needed to be perfect for it to work.

"Okay, so what do we need to do? To make it better," Alicia asked.

"First, we need to make sure if someone enters the home, the house looks abandoned. If I was a soldier, I could tell right away that someone was here recently, based on how the clothes, suitcases, beds, candles, books, dishes were all around."

"What else?" Drew asked.

"Practice. Going quietly from here to next door," I said. "Let's see how you do it now, and we can see if we can make it quicker and quieter."

And practice we did. It was only ten hours before we would have to enact our plan for real.

CHAPTER SIXTEEN

11/16/2024

Zero stood up from his lookout position and snapped his fingers three times. On hearing this, Drew who was sitting on the couch reading to Jane and Natalie stood up and went to the kitchen to let Alicia know the drill was on. Alicia went to the living room, grabbed Natalie and Jane, turned back to the kitchen and out the back door. I had been seated at the dining table, and as soon as I heard Zero's fingers snap, I went into the hallway and checked all the rooms to make sure everything was put in its proper spot. All suitcases were to be hidden away, mostly under beds or in closets. Sleeping bags rolled up and hidden as well. The rooms needed to appear deserted. I found Jenna and Kaitlyn in the office and let them know the drill was in motion. I grabbed my handgun from the top drawer. Kaitlyn oversaw the living room, making sure the candles were put away, all books and movies were in their proper place, and dishes were nowhere to be seen. Jenna was in command of the two bathrooms. All the toothbrushes, towels and other daily hygiene objects were to be stored below sinks and in drawers. Ethan, who had been outside, was in the kitchen as Kaitlyn, Jenna and myself made our way out the back door. Ethan oversaw the kitchen, making sure the coffee, dishes and all other used items were placed in the dishwasher. If the coffee maker was still warm, he was to wipe it down with a cold rag and the coffee dumped outside. Zero, was the last man out, he stood watch and made sure we all were outside before he followed us. Once we were all out of the house, Drew would close the kitchen door and shut the fence door after we passed into Enrique's backyard.

"How'd we do?" Drew asked Zero. The lookout kept the time and executed the random drill.

"One minute and," Zero said as he looked at his watch. It was my watch, an old digital one that I had to teach everyone how to use. "Eight seconds." We had been steady at around a minute all afternoon.

"That's about the same as before," Alicia said.

"Yeah, just a few seconds off," Ethan said.

"I think we're ready to go," I said. "I don't believe that we can improve much on that time."

"Is it good enough?" Ethan asked.

"I don't know," I said. "We may have to move the lookout to catch them coming sooner."

"Where?" Zero asked.

"Down at the end of the block. We need at least a minute to get into position before they approach the door."

"Use the walkies?" Alicia asked.

"Yes. We need to test that first. If that doesn't work, we will just have to make do."

I took one of the Batman walkie's from the house and walked

down to the end of the block. The sun had just begun to set behind me. I depressed the button on the side and said, "Can you hear me?"

"We...hear... some.." was all I heard back. But, I wasn't worried, it would be good enough. The walkies were never designed to work that far away. They were toys for children to play in the house or backyard. But, the fact they heard something would be enough. That's all we needed. It was only thirty yards from the intersection of Seagull and Gully to my front door. Seagull Dr. was the street I lived on. The cul-de-sac had six homes from that intersection, three on each side.

I reported my opinion to the group, and we all agreed that it was enough. I pulled my car down to the very end of the block, so whoever was sitting in the car, could see any vehicle descending Gully Drive.

We spent the rest of the day waiting for the inevitable.

At six in the evening, I took Drew's place in the lookout spot. I told everyone I would be the lookout for the rest of the night, despite their protest. They thought that was too long. I told them I wanted some alone time. Zero made a masturbation joke, and I was 'allowed' to sit in my car all evening.

The truth of the matter was: I wanted to write. I felt I needed to start getting our experiences down before I forgot them or ended up dead. So, under the overhead car light, I began to write our story, which you are currently reading.

It was a chilly night, and I was clothed in my post-bomb standard attire, a black beanie, and black sweatshirt. Kaitlyn said it made me look like a prowler. I just thought black was easier to wear repeatedly since dirt didn't stand out so much. I had a black ball point pen and my notebook. I wrote furiously, the sound of my pen on paper was all I heard. Outside the car, I heard birds chirping, a car strolling over the pavement, far away, as now sound carried much further in this dead town, and from time to time a dog would bark. But, those sounds became white noise. Every few minutes I would stop, raise my head, and listen for anything out of the ordinary.

By 10 p.m. I could see my breath, in the compact Hyundai. I wasn't sure if the writing was any good, but at this point, it mattered little to me. I needed to get this down. If we ended up in the camps, I wanted to leave this behind for some future generation to know where we ended up. Whether they would care, was not a question for me. I needed to document as best I could.

I heard footsteps before I saw the figure approach on the passenger side of the car. My right hand immediately dropped the pen into the cup holder between the front seats, I reached behind my back and tried to see who was approaching using the side mirror. It was nearly pitch black out, and I saw a little shape, just a black mass about five feet tall. The overhead dome light was sending a glow out into the street and as the blob passed the trunk, the glow from inside the car shined a light on Kaitlyn's wonderful face. My hand relaxed, and I hit the unlock button on my door.

"Sorry. I hope I didn't scare you," Kaitlyn said as she sat down in the passenger seat.

"No. Just didn't expect to see anyone."

"I know. I couldn't sleep. Not much to do and everyone else had gone to bed."

"So, you wanted to come hang out with me, in forty-degree weather?" I said. She was wearing the brown and red *Superbad* beanie, that used to belong to my brother, a V-neck fluffy sweater and her red converse.

"Maybe. I'm not used to sleeping by myself."

"Is that why you asked me to join you, the other night?"

"Kind of. Well. And Jenna needed the couch. I knew you would do your self-sacrifice thing and sleep on the carpet with just a blanket. So, I thought what the hell, we can be adults, and sleep together as friends. Friends without benefits," she said and laughed at her own joke. She did that quite a bit, and it used to drive me nuts.

"It is strange," I said.

"It is. I know."

"But comfortable as well," I said as she gave a strange look. "I mean. We cannot see each other for years and yet when I woke up the other morning it seems like just yesterday we were at Cal State together."

"That's not how I felt at your party. I thought our friendship was over for good," she said.

"What did I say? I still don't remember."

She rubbed her hands together and blew on them, creating a wisp of steam from her warm breath. The dome light catching her green eyes as she turned to me. "You asked to talk to me, and we went to the room we now sleep in, and you proceeded to rail into me about showing up to your party and bringing my husband. Thankfully, for you, I knew you were drunk and wasn't going to take it too personally." She paused and looked down. The corner of her mouth twitched. Which I knew was a tell, for when she was holding something back. That damn twitch always lets me know when she was going to really let me know something I didn't want to hear. "But the worst and the moment when I knew or at least thought I knew I would never see you again, was when you began to blame me for our break-up. Saying I should've done more. Saying I abandoned you," her voice broke, "after your mother died. That was when I started to yell back, and eventually, you started crying, and I started crying, and I grabbed Jeff, and we left."

I was horrified. I reached out to her and put my hand on her shoulder, and she began to cry.

"You don't actually believe I abandoned you, do you?" she said.

"No. Of course not," I said. "I know it was mutual."

She stopped crying, shrugged my hand off her shoulder and looked at me as if I was the biggest blockhead in the world. "Are you fucking kidding me? Mutual? You." Her index finger pointed at me. "It was you who left me. All I ever wanted was to be with you. I offered to come with you back to this damn town and be with you. You wouldn't have it. After your mom died, you shut down. I tried everything. I even visited you only a week after you left school when I didn't have any money. Finals coming up. I came to this fucking place, even though you told me not to and what is the first thing we did. You said, 'let's go for a walk.' I was so in love with you, I didn't see the damn signs. I thought in my ignorance, this will be nice and then you spring on me, you are going into the Army and we should be friends. The Army? Friends? It made no sense. None. I couldn't even come up with a response, as you know. So, I said, 'okay,' and I went back to school."

"We are friends now, right?" I asked.

"I suppose. Now, that the world has ended," she said and laughed as she wiped away a tear with her sleeve. "But, that's why I brought Jeff and even showed up to your party in the first place. I wanted to be your friend. I missed you."

"I missed you as well. I am sorry. Sorry for everything. The party. For being a distant, total asshole at the end. I am beyond glad we are now friends. Even if the situation is fucked up."

"Really fucked up."

"Really fucked up. I know you miss Jeff and your daughter. I promised to get you to them and I will."

"I know. I just wish you got to know him. You barely spoke a word to him at the party."

"I barely spoke to anyone at the party."

"You seemed to hit it off with Jenna."

"Yeah, but we were both so drunk we could've been talking about anything, and we would've found each other fascinating."

"Well here's the deal then. We make it to Utah, I want you to stay with us at least long enough to get to know him and my daughter. You promise me that, and I will not hold anything you have said or done against you." She smiled one of her wry, curved, smiles.

"I promise."

"Good. Now talk to me about Jenna."

"What?" I said.

"Do you like her?" she asked. But I didn't hear her because I heard another sound that made the hair on my arms stand up. I leaned out the window and listened. It sounded like a heavy truck. Multiple heavy trucks. I saw headlights down at the end of the road.

"What is it?" Kaitlyn asked.

"They're here," I said, and her eyes widened. "Go. Get everyone up. I will be in, in a minute." She didn't move, her eyes just kept focused on the headlights at the end of the road. "Kaitlyn. Go. Wake everyone up. No lights. I will be there in a sec." She slowly turned away from the scene unfolding down at the end of the road and exited the car.

As she left, I turned off the dome light, grabbed my notebook and exited the vehicle. I crept onto the front yard of the house on the corner of my street and Gully drive that lead to the main road where I could now see multiple headlights. I stood behind a tree watching.

How stupid we were, we had plenty of time to hide. All those exercises for nothing. As I watched, a military transport truck stopped at the end of the road and made a U-turn. The vehicle now blocked the exit of anyone wanting to head east. Another vehicle slowly pulled down the road toward me, and I bolted before the headlights found me.

 I ran as quietly as possible.

CHAPTER SEVENTEEN

11/16/2024

We stood in silence in the darkened room. Waiting for me to give the signal. Inside, you could barely perceive the sound of idling engines far-off in the distance. Kaitlyn was at my side, fidgeting in place, her shoes squeaking ever so noticeably thanks to the silence in the room. Jenna was behind me, her breathing heavy and intermittent as if she was conscious of the sound it made and kept trying to suppress it. Zero was the only one seated, alone on the red couch, eyes staring out the front window. The rest were already in the kitchen. Jane in Drew's arms, Natalie in Alicia's. Ethan at the back door, ready to open once the signal was given.

"As soon as we see headlights. We go," I said with no response from the group. They understood. I already repeated the same objective three times. When I first entered, they were already heading out the back door. I told them to wait. It would be a while before they arrived. We went through the house and made it look as abandoned as possible. Hid all the suitcases. Made the beds, but not too well. Hid the sleeping bags and camping equipment in the attic. The AR and shotgun stored and locked in my gun safe. It took three minutes. Twenty minutes later we were still waiting.

"Come on," Zero said in a whisper. He stood up and walked over to me. He was going to say something when we heard voices. I stood still staring toward the sound. The noises came in the direction of one of the bedrooms.

"Did you leave the back window open?" I whispered.

"No," Zero said, on my left.

"Maybe," Kaitlyn said, on my right.

I walked into the hallway and listened. Yes, the voices were coming from down the hall and the guest bedroom. The door was closed, but I could still hear them. They had to have been in a neighbor's yard on Gully Drive, their backyards ran along my yard on the east side.

I turned toward Kaitlyn, Jenna, and Zero and put my index finger up to my lips. I waved for them to follow me, as I headed toward the kitchen.

"They will be here any second," I said as quietly as possible. Everyone nodded, and Ethan grabbed the doorknob.

Thirty seconds.

Ninety seconds.

One hundred and twenty seconds.

An eternity.

Headlights on the street, as a truck turned down Seagull drive. I signaled, but there was no need. Ethan had already opened the door. Out went Drew with Jane, then Alicia with Natalie, followed by Jenna and Kaitlyn. Zero and I brought up the rear. Ethan had already opened the door in the fence. Once outside the need to go quietly was unnecessary as the trucks sounded louder than a rocket taking off after sitting in quiet for a half hour.

We took our positions in Enrique's back yard. Seated with our backs along the back of the house, under the kitchen window. I sat closest to the fence. In the distance, I could hear faint voices. I looked over at my companions. Each one staring into an undetermined space. Their breath could be seen, yet not heard, in the cold darkness. Alicia was patting Jane on the back, and I could see her whimpering into her mother's shoulder.

A loud knock came from my home.

"National Guard!" The digital voice sounded like it was coming from inside a trashcan.

It was not as nice as my practice announcement.

Another knock. Then the doorbell rang. Some indistinct, digitally altered, voices. Then a loud clank. That was my doorknob knocked out and hitting the linoleum in my entryway. If we can get through this, we would need to fix that.

I could see little, between the picket fence slots, but every now and then I could see a light coming from my home.

Then another knock. This time from the front of Enrique's house. The house we were hiding behind. Shit. Everyone turned to me. I held up my hand, indicating to wait.

"National Guard! Open Up!"

The doorbell rang. Another clank, this time louder, as another door knob and lock was sent to the linoleum.

My patio door opened not five feet from where I was sitting. Through the fence, I saw a soldier in my backyard. He was whistling a digitally modified tune. I couldn't make out the song. His footsteps on the concrete of the patio were loud and expressive.

"Nobody here?" a soldier with a muffled, electronic voice said from my patio doorway to the soldier outside.

"Nope. Just like the rest of the houses. Did you clear the bedrooms?"

"Did I clear the bedrooms? Of course, after what happened to the one-eighty-fifth in Corona. Fuck if I am gonna let that happen."

I needed them to get inside before it was too late. We needed to get back over to my house before the soldiers inside Enrique's house checked the back yard.

"You know they've got a water dispenser in here?"

"Yeah. I saw that. There is a keg out here. You want some?"

"From the keg? Sure, why not?"

"I meant the water."

I heard the doorknob on the patio door, on the other side of the wall from me, rustle and then turn. We were caught. No victory for Blake and his gang of misfits. The soldier inside Enrique's home would be out here in two seconds. The soldiers in my backyard were taking their sweet ass time getting back inside. If we ran through the fence, we would probably be shot, and I couldn't blame them. Any quick movements would be met with force. My head lowered. I looked at everyone and shook my head. Each one of them, huddled in winter coats, breathing heavily, nodded and lowered their heads. I stood up with my hands raised. And turned to face the kitchen door as a soldier exited from Enrique's home.

He was about five-foot-nine, wearing the usual modern military fatigues and a black, protective gas mask that made him look like Darth Vader. The patch on his shoulder had the California bear on top of a yellow insignia with red and green stripes. I kept my hands raised. He appeared in shock for a second and took a breath before he raised his rifle and aimed it at me.

"Keep your hands up!" she yelled through the mask. It was not a man, but a woman.

I was blinded by the small light attached to the rifle as she raised it, but I did as I was told, fighting back the instinct to cover my eyes and said, "There are nine of us back here with two children." She motioned for me to take a step back. The rest of my companions were in the process of standing as she rounded the corner.

"Everyone stand up and keep your hands in the air," she said.

Another soldier joined us in the backyard. "Holy shit!" he said, apparently not expecting us.

"Yeah. Call this in. So we can search them."

"Right," the male soldier said, wearing the same outfit.

Alicia took a step forward. "I can't put my hands up." She nodded to Jane still in her arms.

"Put her down," the woman soldier said. Alicia's eyes narrowed, and she gave the woman a once over, but eventually got Jane to stand on her own.

"Mommy!" Jane cried.

Alicia reached down to put pat her back. "It's okay."

"Put your hands up!"

Two more soldiers arrived. One was about six-foot-four and towered over all of us. He immediately gave off the impression of being in charge. That and the sergeant patch on his uniform.

"Well, what do we have here?" he said in a distinct booming voice that made him not only look like Darth Vader but sound like him as well. "You all know you were supposed to evacuate, right?" We didn't respond. By now our arms were getting tired. "Private Smith?"

"Yes, Sarge," The soldier who called in the order responded.

"Search the men. Private Kennedy?"

"Yes, Sarge," said the woman soldier.

"The women." The Sergeant then turned to us. "My name is

Sergeant Jones. Don't worry. This is just routine. Then we can get you out of here and to safety."

Private Smith said to me, "Turn around." I looked at him and smiled. I turned around with my hands in the air.

"Gun!" Private Smith yelled and smacked me in the back of the head with his rifle. The force of the blow drove me to my knees. A strong forearm slammed into the back of my neck, pushing my body and face down into the concrete. Someone grabbed my gun. Another someone sat on my back, knocking the air out of me.

"I forgot," I tried to say, but it came out mumbled. I honestly did forget I had my gun in the band of my pants. With my arms in the air, the sweatshirt lifted and exposed the black gun for all to see.

The pain in the back of my head was throbbing, and I felt a warm, wet flow of blood traveling down both sides of my neck. My face felt like it had been dragged across a carpeted floor. I turned my head to look as best I could at my friends, who all wore expressions of shock and fear.

"Let him up!" Kaitlyn said. They ignored her.

"Anybody else have a gun?" Sergeant Jones said. Everyone shook their heads vigorously. I felt a weight remove from my legs. Then Smith, on my upper back with his forearm still on my neck, began searching me. To my left, I saw Private Kennedy searching Kaitlyn. Once she was done, she moved her to another soldier and left my view. This continued for a few minutes until all of them had been frisked and disappeared from my sight.

Finally, Private Smith got up from his perch atop me and had me stand up and face him. He searched the front of me.

"Sorry about that," I said. "I completely forgot about the gun."

Private Smith grunted under the mask. "At least you were smart enough to leave the safety on."

He turned from me and motioned with his rifle for me to move. We went into the house. The home was empty, but the front door was open.

"Where'd they go?" Private Smith said to himself.

"Probably next door," I said. He turned his head my direction and then gave me a nudge with his rifle to keep moving.

Outside I saw two large military trucks parked on the street. One facing the cul-de-sac parked right in front of Enrique's home. The other across the street facing the other direction. Not the heavy-duty weaponized ones, but the transport trucks.

We came to my front door and found Sergeant Jones drinking a glass of water. "They say this is your home?" he said as we approached. I nodded an affirmative. "They also told me you are the one in charge and it was your idea to not go to the evacuation area." I nodded again. "Cat got your tongue?"

"No."

"Good." He reached out to me with a gloved hand and grabbed me by my face, turning my head left, then right. "Get Specialist Graves up here to take a look at this and tell him to bring a medical kit," he said to Private Smith.

"Thanks," I said. The pain was throbbing, and my legs were starting to feel like noodles.

"We are here to help."

"Where are the others?" I asked.

"Packing. Gathering clothes and anything else they need. Two bags, no more. Each."

I made a move to go pack as well when he grabbed me by my shoulder. "You've got a pretty good set up here," he said. "Plenty of water." I flinched. Did they find the supplies in the garage and attic? "Yes, we found the stash. The sweet, short, brunette, slipped about the sleeping bags being up in the attic. The water, and the gasoline you have in the garage we will take. The canned food we will leave, we don't need it. Maybe some poor schmuck years from now, will find it and make use of it." He said all this with his hand still on my shoulder. I just nodded, and he continued. "Why did you want to stay here? You knew the area was being evacuated. You seem like a smart guy. You know about radiation, right?"

"Of course," I said. I felt my adrenaline beginning to rise, and the head wound slowly disappearing.

"So, why not go to the evacuation area? There's food. Beds. Water. So, what was the plan? Stay here till you ran out of food?"

"The original plan was to hang out here until the roads were clear and make for family in Utah."

"Oh. I see. Did it ever occur to you that you could just go to the camp until this calms down and then head to Utah? At least be in a place of safety, not hiding out in here without power?"

I jerked away from him when he said safety. "Safety? Please. A military controlled camp?"

"It's not just the Army. There's FEMA and The Red Cross."

"Who has the power?"

He just looked at me. Or at least I thought he just looked at me, maybe studying me, but behind the mask, it was hard to tell.

"Whoever it is, it's safer than being on your own right now?"

"Why are you asking me this?"

"Just trying to understand why we keep running into people that don't evacuate. To be honest, most of them were nut jobs. But, you seemed to be in control, so I thought I would ask."

I didn't know whether I should thank him or not. I think that was a compliment.

"Can I go pack now?" I turned to leave, and again he grabbed me by my shoulder.

"One more thing. The gun safe?"

"What about it?"

"I need you to open it."

"Why?"

"I just do."

"What if I say no?"

"Then we will find another way to open it. But, I don't think you want us to do that."

I nodded. Private Smith entered the house with Specialist Graves, who looked just like the rest of them, besides the sergeant. Specialist Graves nodded for me to come to him. I did, and he turned me around and looked at my head wound. "This is gonna need some staples," he said, sounding like the rest of them as well.

I was maneuvered to my red couch and told to lay face down. Specialist Graves began rubbing an ointment on the wound, that he said would numb the area. He had a small flashlight in the crook of his arm, shined on the back of my head.

Sergeant Jones said, "The gun safe? What's the code?"

"Zero. Three. Two. Four. Seven. Nine," I said. They had me in a precarious position.

"Your mom's birthday or something?"

"My dad's," I said, and the sergeant just nodded and left us.

They gave me three staples for the wound in the back of the head. Even with the numbing solution, it still hurt like someone using a stapler on your skull. Specialist Grave put a bandage over it and then he gave me some painkillers.

"Nice couch," he said. As he got up.

"Thanks. It was my mothers," I said, standing up and rubbing the back of my head.

"Have someone take those out in two weeks." Then he turned, grabbed the medical kit and left.

Over the next half hour, we packed up our clothes and bathroom supplies and loaded up Zero's truck and Drew's SUV. Everyone kept asking me if I was alright. To the point, it became annoying.

"I'm fine. Don't worry about me," I told Kaitlyn as she was trying to get a look at my head wound. "Seriously, I'm fine. Make sure you gather everything you need. Concentrate on underclothes and put on one heavy-duty jacket." I told everyone the same thing, "as many pairs of underwear and undergarments, toiletries, as possible."

Eventually, we were ready to go. I packed a backpack and a rolling suitcase. The same driving situation as the other night. I had made sure we had everything we would need in a prison camp before we were to leave.

Oh, and the National Guard stole my guns.

CHAPTER EIGHTEEN

11/16/2024 - 11/17/2024

I felt a cold surface against my cheek. A vibration rattled throughout my body. A low murmuring sound was coming from some far-off place. Two people talking, although they seemed miles away. And a relentless throbbing in the back of my skull.

My eyes opened. I was in Zero's truck, Jenna was in the cab with me, and it took a few seconds to remember what had happened. The pain killers the National Guard supplied must've knocked me out. Out the window I had been leaning against, I saw a red sedan in the next lane over. Two children were asleep in car seats, in the back, a female sleeping in the front. I turned to Jenna and saw she was staring off into the void out the other window.

"How long do you think this is gonna take, we've been sitting here for an hour?" Jenna asked Ethan, who was seated in the front passenger seat.

"What time is it?" I asked. My mouth felt dry, and I was not sure I said it loud enough for the other passengers to hear me.

"Blakey, you're awake?" Zero asked.

"I think so."

"How you feeling?" Jenna asked.

I turned my head her direction, and it felt like my skull was full of sand. "A little groggy." She nodded and put her hand on mine and squeezed. "Where are we?" I asked.

"At the top of the Cajon Pass. We've been sitting here for over an hour," Ethan said.

I looked around more clearly this time. In front of us were red taillights. Behind us white headlights. I saw Drew's SUV clearly behind us, but could not make out any passengers with the headlights blinding my view. We were at the top of the Cajon Pass, on our right was the famous Summit Inn. Rebuilt a few years back, after a forest fire wiped it out. Now, it was black and closed for good.

The red tail lights were heading off to the right just past the Inn. I could see lights from an Army truck shining down the empty road at us, like the waiting eyes of a monster hiding under the overpass. The left two lanes were full of stalled cars, and a barricade was placed at an angle to force us off the freeway at this exit. The interstate past that point was inky black. This was where we were to get off.

Ethan turned to me. "It was just like you said, all the exits ramps were blocked by police cars or Army vehicles. We only had one way to go."

I nodded. "How long has it been like this?" I motioned my head to the traffic getting off the freeway.

"We've been sitting here an hour. But, up until we got here, it was smooth sailing."

"Finally," Zero said. I looked up and saw a few red brake lights flicker off and move at the top of the exit. "Looks like we are moving."

The cars in front of us began to slowly merge and move onto Exit 138. It was automatic. No wondering which way to go. The Army had every way, but one, blocked off. As we passed by the Summit Inn and a gas station, the road curved to the right. At a stop sign, we turned left but did not stop. Just a slow crawl to our destination.

I looked behind to make sure Drew and the rest were behind us. They were. The last thing I wanted was for us to get split up and never to find each other wherever we ended up.

I removed my heavy gray jacket but left my trusty black sweatshirt on. Everyone was wearing heavy wintry weather clothes before we left and looking around the truck now, I saw everyone had stripped off the jackets except me.

"Any idea where we're going?" Ethan asked Zero.

"None. I've never been around here before," Zero said.

After the stop sign, we slowly made our way to the overpass and crossed over Interstate 15. I looked to my right and saw, to my surprise, way off in the distance a haze of light on the dark horizon.

"Look, the power must be on out there," Jenna said, pointing to the north.

No automobiles littered the freeway to the north, beyond the off-ramp for Exit 138. There was the horizon with its faint glow that we could not see beyond as the road rose to its summit before heading into the High Desert.

We continued our slow crawl through the desert. Passed an RV camp, with no RV's and a few commercial buildings on the left as we turned north running parallel with the freeway. We turned back west at one point and headed into a small valley that housed a few ranch-style homes, barely visible in the dark. No one was home.

"Where the hell are they taking us?" Ethan asked to no one.

On the evacuation map, it showed the camp right off the freeway. Twenty minutes after exiting the freeway, on little desert roads, we still had not reached the destination.

At a couple of points, I thought maybe we could make a run for it. Ridiculous fantasies of heroic escapes flashed in my mind like a movie projector projecting images one frame at a time. I never presented these fantasies out loud as a real alternative to our fate. That and the fact at every quarter mile or so, I saw a military vehicle blocking all other roads or just sitting on the shoulder watching all the cars drift pass.

As we began to wonder if this was all some cruel joke, we saw a light in the distance. Immediately, everyone in the car was at attention. The truck slowly cruised to the top of a small ridge, and the camp was below us.

"Holy Shit!" Zero said.

Across the desert valley as far as the eye could see was the evacuation camp. A sprawling city, miles in length. It appeared to have no end. Two chain-link fences surrounded the camp. Every hundred yards, portable high powered lights provided light. The tents looked like thousands of black Legos organized neatly on a dirt playground.

"How many people are here?" Jenna asked.

"I have no idea," I said.

Zero guided the truck slowly down the gravel road to the entrance. At the entrance, heavily armed vehicles and military personnel on each side, the outswing gate was open to allow the new arrivals to enter. As we passed through the gate, a soldier pointed us to turn right. Not that we needed to be told, we were following the vehicles in front of us.

As we traveled further down the road between two chain-link fences, there was enough room for two cars abreast, Zero said, "It's like parking at fucking Disneyland."

"Except cheaper," Drew said, and Zero gave a hesitant laugh.

After five minutes, traveling on the dirt road, we reached the northeast edge of the camp, and then we saw another Army personnel pointing us to turn left, and we exited through a gate in the outer fence. Now we were outside the camp again and only had the outer fence on our left as we entered the desert parking lot. A vast and endless row of vehicles.

We kept trudging along passing rows upon rows of cars that lead without end into the dark desert. By now, it was after midnight, and I could feel the drugs wearing off. My head began to throb where I had three staples in my skull. I thought about taking another pill, but I wanted to be aware of what was to come. On my left, out my window, I could see little of the camp, except for the outermost tents. They appeared to be standard issue military tents, but it was hard to identify since the camp was in darkness, except for the lights, every hundred yards. I made sure to count the lights as we passed.

After, what seemed like another mile, we were told by a waving soldier, to turn right, between a row of cars and found our parking spot. Which was just desert, but the vegetation and landscape had been removed.

"Twenty-four," I said as we parked.

"What?" Zero asked, and Ethan turned to look at me.

"Twenty-four lights since the entrance to our parking spot."

"Okay?" Zero asked.

"Just in case we need to find your truck. Now, we have a starting point."

Jenna was gathering up her coat and preparing to exit the vehicle. I put on my thick coat as well. The SUV had pulled into the spot next to us, and I could already see Kaitlyn and Alicia helping the kids, who were rubbing their eyes and yawning, exit the vehicle. Drew had already opened the back hatch.

I stepped out of the truck and was hit with a frigid blast of air. If I thought it was cold in Rancho, it was freezing in the desert. I pulled the beanie down lower over my head and went to the back of the truck and began to unload the suitcases and backpacks.

Once we were all set, we started the long walk back to the front entrance. There was no question which way to go as there was a stream of people all heading the same direction. We walked along the edge of the outer fence. No one said a word. After about ten minutes we came across another soldier motioning all the pedestrians to enter through a gate in the outer fence and onto the road that wrapped around the whole complex. We could now see clearly into the camp as we walked along the outside of the inner chain-link barrier. It was deathly quiet, except for our footsteps and the electricity pumping through the large lights.

In front of me was Alicia carrying Jane. Alicia and Drew would pass her back and forth once each got tired. At one point, Kaitlyn offered to volunteer, but Jane started screaming, so back to Alicia she went. Natalie walked, holding hands with either Kaitlyn or whoever was not holding Jane. She was wearing a thick pink coat with a hood, that had a white puffy ball on top, that bounced as she walked.

Behind me was Jenna, Zero, and Ethan. Zero was wearing a sweatshirt, that had a picture of a unicorn holding a football that said, "Fantasy Football." He didn't play fantasy football, he thought it was funny. Ethan was talking quietly. He had no beanie on, just a red hoodie. I could hear bits and pieces of their conversation as we walked. Thankfully, we had backpacks and suitcases that could roll. Otherwise, carrying all our clothes this far would've been painful. It still was tiring trying to get the bags to roll on the desert dirt, but at least, we weren't carrying a forty-pound suitcase.

"Who are the soldiers in blue?" I overheard Zero say behind me. I turned and looked into the camp. Two people wearing blue jackets and black khakis walked the perimeter.

I turned around and said, "FEMA."

"What are they doing?" Zero asked.

"Looks like they are patrolling. Having FEMA personnel patrol the inside of the camp, makes people feel safer than having the Army do it."

"Are they armed?"

"I can't tell, but as far as I know, they shouldn't be."

We kept walking until we hit the northeast portion of the camp. By now, my toes felt frozen, and I could tell everyone else was feeling the same way. We were ushered into the camp at the gate in the inner fence, by another soldier. We had caught or been passed by quite a few other people taking this long trek. A line of misery had begun to form.

Inside the camp, we passed straight rows of tents, stretching beyond view. Between each row was a small path, just large enough for a vehicle to pass. At the end of each row was a sign posted into the ground about four feet high. On each of the signs; a letter and a number. As I looked, I saw one that read: B4.

Eventually, we came to the end of a line of people. At the front of the column was a tent, much larger than the sleeping tents that made up much of the camp.

"Now it is like Disneyland," Zero said behind me. It had been a thirty-minute walk from the truck to the front of the camp and the intake tent. I felt tired and cold. I kept trying to make sense of what I was seeing. The other soon to be tenants, in line with us, appeared as surprised and unhappy as we were. Children crying, hushed whispers laced with bitter resentment. Some spoke with quiet awe. Aaron was right about one thing. This was completely different than the camp I was stationed at three years ago. This was at another level. The size was almost incomprehensible. How did this function? I tried to concentrate, but all I wanted to do at this point in the night was get to the tent and go to sleep.

It was another half hour before we finally entered the intake tent. Just after one in the morning. In the center of the tent were two foldout tables, each with two soldiers conducting the intake, with a laptop in front of them. Standing behind them at the back, FEMA volunteers were gathering the new arrivals and guiding them out into the camp.

Drew, who was at the front of our group motioned me forward. "You wanna talk to them first?"

"I don't think it matters," I said. "As long as we all stay together." I could see a pleading in his eyes to take control. Jane was whining in his arms. "But, sure, I'll go first."

As the group in front of me parted, I walked up to the desk, and my companions followed. The young man at the laptop had to be barely eighteen, bright blue eyes and eyebrows thicker than the head on my hair.

"How many in your group?" he asked, without looking up.

"Umm, nine."

"Each tent can hold only five people. Three cots. Two doubles."

"That's fine as long as we can be next to each other."

"No problem," he said, "And your name is?"

"Blake Anderson."

"Is this your family?"

"No. Friends."

"Fine. What's your occupation?"

"My what?"

"Occupation. What did you do to earn a living?"

"Oh, umm. Business Analyst." That technically wasn't true. But, it was close enough.

"Your address?"

"Eleven-twelve Seagull Drive. Rancho Cucamonga. California. Nine-One-Seven-Three-Nine."

"Thank you," he said while his fingers flew over the keyboard.

"Are you connected to a network?" I asked. I was curious.

"Just to the central hub here," he said, finally looking up.

"Not connected to the outside world?"

"No," he said, and I nodded. "Your housing is in section, CD. Tents thirty-six and thirty-seven. In the center of each section is the mess hall. It's not really a mess hall, basically just a bunch tables where we serve the food and water. That's also where you'll find a few porta-potties and the shower stalls. Breakfast is served between seven and ten. Lunch eleven and two. Dinner four to seven." He reached under the table and handed me a printed ID card. It had my name, tent number thirty-six, height, weight (I didn't provide), an unflattering picture (taken without my knowledge) and previous address. "Curfew is at ten. All persons must be in their tents by ten. Please keep that on you at all times. Present it at the mess hall as you get food between the times printed on the back. Only one serving per meal."

"Do you know when we can get out of here? We have family in Utah we'd like to get to, at some point," I said, even though I knew it was a longshot that this guy could know such a thing. But, I thought I would ask.

He looked up at me, studied me for a second and said, "I really have no idea. But, I can put that in the system here, so the big bosses know you have someplace you can go."

"Thanks."

He nodded and typed the information into the laptop. Or at least appeared to, he could have been pretending for all I knew.

"Next," he said, and I stood off to the side and waited as my companions went through the same questions and the same unflattering pictures. Drew had to hold the children up and point them at an unknown source for their snapshots.

Once we were all processed, we headed to the back of the tent and the exit. There we were greeted by a FEMA volunteer. "Hello, my name is Jill, and I can show you to your tents," Jill said. She looked to be about seventeen and as bubbly as a cheerleader. Blonde hair and a permanent smile on her face. This night had officially entered the surreal.

Zero looked at Jill and said, "Why hello Jill it's a pleasure to meet you."

"Hi, and your name is?"

"Jason, but all my friends call me Zero."

"Zero? That's a strange name."

"It sure is."

"What section are you in?"

"Oh, we are in the lovely section called," Zero pulled out his ID card, from his front pocket. "Section CD."

"Well, that's a long walk from here, we better get going."

"That sounds great."

Jill ignored him and opened the flap and led us into to the camp. Alicia gave Zero a dirty look as she walked by, while I couldn't help but smile.

After another long walk, pulling along two suitcases, as Drew and Alicia both had to carry the kids, which meant every ten minutes or so, we had to stop and let them catch their breath. The paths between the tents were composed entirely of desert dirt, but every now and then you would stumble on a rock, that had yet to be cleared. It was hard to see anything as we walked, besides Jill's little flashlight lighting the way. Once we were in the heart of the camp, I couldn't tell which way was which. Like being in a casino. But, she knew where she was taking us.

We reached the center, where hundreds of trailers were lined up running north to south down the middle of the encampment. At the trailers, we made a right turn and made our way toward the parking lot. Another left turn, until, finally after another thirty-minute walk Jill shined her flashlight on a sign at the front of a row of tents that read: CD3.

"Your tents are right up ahead," she said, leading us to our new homes. At the sixth tent on the right, she shined a light on a plywood sign attached to the tent at the peak, where the tent poles met, that read: CD36. Finally. "Here you go," Jill said and left with a quick turn and a smile.

No one said a word. We all looked around. But, no one went inside.

"I can't believe we are here," Alicia, finally spoke, holding Jane in her arms, in front of tent thirty-seven.

"How are we going to sleep?" Jenna asked. "Four in one, Five in the other?"

"We'll take this one for now," Drew said. I thought that was obvious.

"Who cares, let's just do this," Zero said, and I agreed. Jenna, Zero, Kaitlyn, Ethan and I entered tent thirty-six, after saying goodnight to Drew and family. A battery powered lantern sat on a small table in the middle of the room. Zero turned on the lamp, fumbling with its switch in the dark, eventually casting a pale, blue light into the room. The tent was ten by ten with three cots. The cot at the back was the single. The other two at the right and left of the tent were the doubles. We threw the suitcases in the back corners.

"Me and you?" Kaitlyn asked me with a smile. I nodded, and we took the cot to the right. Jenna paired up with Ethan. Zero had already plopped down on the single bed in the back and under the covers of the thick, green, blanket. I pulled back the blanket and saw a standard cot, that was as uncomfortable as it looked. At least there were two thin pillows.

I got in first, pulling off my shoes and jacket, but leaving my beanie and sweatshirt on. Kaitlyn took off her shoes only, and we fell into our usual position, which wasn't very comfortable on the cot, but comforting none the same.

"What do you think?" Kaitlyn whispered.

"I really don't know. I guess we will find out in the morning."

She said nothing further. I felt a sting in the back of my head, and some more throbbing. I forgot to take another painkiller. I moved to get up, but then I heard a slight snore from the warm body against mine, so I decided to stay in position. It didn't matter ten minutes later, as I fell to sleep.

CHAPTER NINETEEN

11/17/2024

Standing in line the next morning I looked down at my I.D. card, and it had printed on the back the times we were to eat. Breakfast between 9:00 a.m. and 9:15 a.m. We waited just off to the side of the mess hall between two ropes guiding us to the serving tables. Excluding Zero, he was still fast asleep and only made a grunt when we tried to wake him while waving us away. To our left, two porta-potties, which also had a lineup.

The weather remained no better in the morning than it was the previous night. Kaitlyn, standing in front of me, kept shivering and blowing warm air into her hands. Jenna, behind me, kept shuffling her feet to keep the blood flowing. Everywhere I looked, people were bundled up. One elderly couple in front of us wore, what appeared to be FEMA issued jackets, but without the insignia. I imagine that in haste to evacuate when it was seventy-eight degrees, they ended up here without any warm clothes.

To our right, was the dining area. Ten, white, folding tables, in five rows of two. Or two rows of five, depending on perspective. Some families were still seated. They must have been part of the 8:45 a.m. group.

The dining area was shaped like a horseshoe in the center of our section. The serving area curved outward in front of two trailers where the food was prepared. Two porta-potties on each side and even two shower areas, which also had a line. I looked again down at my I.D. card, and it said I could shower on Thursdays and Sundays. At least it didn't tell me when I could take a shit.

We finally reached the serving tables, at 9:10 a.m. A man scanned the front of our I.D. card, which had a barcode on it, to verify it was our time and our first and only serving. I grabbed a paper plate and a plastic fork and was served by a lady from the Red Cross, from aluminum trays containing scrambled eggs and toast, which was buttered or not. Your choice. At least we had some choice. At the far table, were the drinks. Orange juice, milk, and water, in generic, small, plastic bottles. But, I went to the end, where they had coffee. Thank God. I filled a Styrofoam cup full of black coffee. It smelled wonderful.

We found an empty table to sit at, near the back and we ate breakfast swiftly. There wasn't much to it.

"I wasn't expecting a complimentary hotel breakfast. But, that was still disappointing," Drew said.

The kids were eating just fine and seemed to be oblivious to the camp surroundings. Jane dropped some eggs on the floor, and Natalie began laughing.

"She dropped her eggs," Natalie said in between giggles. Jane turned and punched her sister on the arm. "Hey!"

"Stop that. Jane. Here have some of mine," Alicia said while spooning out some eggs onto her daughter's plate.

"You want the rest of mine?" Drew said.

"No. Not that hungry."

"Me neither," he said and then stuffed a fork full of eggs into his mouth.

The food wasn't good. But, I expected nothing else. I remember the quality of food at the camp in Syria and this was much better. Not good. Better.

"So, what do we think?" Ethan asked.

I leaned forward resting my elbows on the table and said, "I will say this. When I told you that story about the refugee camp, I was stationed at." I paused and looked around, "Well, this place is the Ritz compared to that camp."

"Really?" Jenna asked.

"Yes. But, I don't think it changes much of what I said and the reason I didn't want to come here. Look around. What do you see?"

They all did as I asked. Jenna was staring at the showers, Kaitlyn back at the food. The others working their heads around in a one-hundred-and-eighty-degree motion.

"Not much," Ethan said.

"I see the Red Cross and FEMA," Jenna said.

"That's all good right?" Kaitlyn asked

"Yes. For now. But, there are probably a hundred thousand scared, cold and tired people in a what?" I looked to my left. Then back to the right. "Three-mile area. That's crazy."

I must've had a look of awe on my face because Alicia said, "It is pretty remarkable. How they built this whole area in... a week?" It had been seven days since I saw the mushroom cloud in that moonlit sky.

"It really is, and it's far more organized than I anticipated," Drew said to his wife.

"Yes. And for now, we just need to go with the program," I said.

"Are there any other options?" Ethan asked.

"No. Definitely not. But, it doesn't mean we should be content. I think we should try to find people to talk to, if we can, to get any info on the situation here. Cause the longer we are here, and the less we are told, I think the worse it will get."

"You're always so positive," Ethan said.

"I am just trying to look out for our best interest." I couldn't help being pessimistic after all I've seen and experienced, I am sure they would have been the same.

A few hours later I announced to everyone that I wanted to take a walk around the perimeter of the whole encampment and I asked if anyone wanted to join me. Jane and Natalie had my Hobbit book, which I stowed away in my suitcase and were, again, having Alicia read it to them. I also brought my *Lord Of The Rings* hardcover, just in case they wanted to know more. They pulled a cot outside to soak in the sun, that had finally broken through the clouds just after breakfast. Most of us were either sitting around in the dirt listening or in the tent napping. Or still asleep like Zero. Jenna had returned from using the porta-potty twenty minutes earlier.

"It was disgusting, as expected. Thank god, we brought our own toilet paper. One guy even offered me one hundred dollars for it as I was leaving," she said with a bemused smile. But, this caught my attention.

"You probably shouldn't go alone again. We should go everywhere in pairs, and try to keep the toilet paper hidden," I said. Jenna's smile evaporated. I hated being that guy. The Doomsayer. But, damn, if my friends didn't need a little education on prison etiquette.

Now I was stuck, I couldn't walk the perimeter alone because I insisted we needed to go everywhere in pairs. When I announced my intentions, I wasn't expecting everyone's hands to raise but thought I would get at least one interested party. Instead, I got silence.

"One of you?" I said. "We may miss lunch, but aren't any of you curious about the rest of the camp?" Alicia's hand rose, with one hand still on *The Hobbit*.

"No," Jane cried.

"You have to read to us," Natalie said.

"You two can read on your own. You're just being lazy having me read it to you," she said as she stood up and placed the book in Natalie's hands. "And if you don't understand a word, just ask your dad."

"You sure about this, you may miss lunch?" Drew asked. Our lunch was scheduled between 1:00 p.m. and 1:15 p.m.

"After breakfast this morning, I am sure I won't mind," she said and then kissed Drew on the cheek.

Alicia and I walked in silence toward the fence to the north of us. We journeyed past two more rows of section CD. Then all of section CC. The sections appeared to be lettered in a snake fashion. We walked along the main path which ran through linked sections north to south, connecting the mess halls. As we reached the fence we could see the cars, in their dirt parking lot, spread out evenly and orderly throughout the desert. We turned west, the opposite direction from the main entrance, walking along a car-width dirt road that ran just inside the fence, like a warning track in the outfield of a baseball stadium. Every now and then we had to move off the road as a truck passed.

We hit the western fence and headed south. This area of the camp did not seem to be as populated as the others. Probably, the last few sections left for occupation. To the west, we could see the desert and its vegetation that was rudely destroyed in creating our new campground. A brown and green landscape, littered with small plants, tumbleweeds, shrubs, and rocks.

Alicia said little up to this point. But, I would catch her looking right and left, just observing the different areas as we passed, her red hair sparkling in the sun.

"I count twenty rows of tents in each section," she said.

"Yeah, that's what I got. Twenty rows of ten tents each. Two hundred tents. Five people in each one. One thousand people per section."

"That's sounds right. And these would be the last sections and…" She looked to her left at a row of tents. "Section C.V. was the highest lettered section… so that means what… a hundred sections?"

I nodded an affirmative. "Over a hundred thousand people could be housed here."

"Crazy," she said. "I know that's what you said the number could be, but to have it confirmed, is something else."

We kept walking. The sun shined bright, warm. And I began to sweat, wearing all black as I was.

"You guys think I'm a bitch, don't you?" she said as she inclined her head to look at me.

I stopped and said, "We never thought that."

"Don't lie. I was at first when Drew and I met. I can admit it. I was jealous of you guys, and I wanted him all to myself."

"I always thought you seemed right for him."

"Thanks.

"The few times I met you, it seemed like you were keeping an eye out for him."

She laughed. "Yeah. Well, when your husband, never invites you out with him and his friends. And then when he does. You end up just drinking by yourself. It can get awkward."

"I can imagine."

"You know I wanted to go to your party. But, we couldn't find a sitter."

"Drew didn't mention that. He just said you were home with the kids."

"See. That's what I mean. I wonder if I always come across like the wife who won't let her husband do anything," she said, and I must admit that's how I felt when I did see Drew. "But, and I am gonna let you in on a little secret. Drew was the one who did not want to go out anymore. He knows he can't hold his liquor." She laughed. "Once I caught him texting with Zero, blaming me for not going out with him, to some bar. I almost knocked the phone out of his hand, I was so pissed. But, then he told me that he couldn't tell his oldest friends he didn't want to hang out. So, I became his excuse."

"I was surprised to see him at my party."

"You're crazy. He wasn't gonna miss it for the world. He had been so excited to see you. I know you talked or texted a few times since you returned, but he wanted to see you. And I did too. I am glad he went. Because if he didn't, I don't know where we would be right now."

"What do you mean?"

"If he didn't go to your party, I am not sure we would've gone to your house after we tried the freeways to get out of town. You were on our minds. Without the party..."

"You probably would've ended up right here," I said, and she laughed.

"Probably... I've always liked you, Blake. Your one of the few friends of his that I actually admired."

"Thanks."

"Now, Zero on the other hand," she said and laughed.

We continued our small talk and I, after all these years, finally got to know Alicia.

"I am afraid, everyone is looking at me like the Worry Wart. Always on everyone's case. But, with Jane and Natalie, I kind of default to that state of mind," she said, changing the subject.

"Well, I am the Doomsayer."

"The Doomsayer and the Worry Wart. Sounds like a good team to me."

"Yes, it does."

"Maybe we can keep these idiots alive, for a little while longer," she said, followed by another laugh.

By now we had reached the southern border and headed back east. Section CM was empty, except for a few tents right next to the dining area, where we saw a man sitting on a cot playing with his infant son.

The chain-link fence was constructed the same throughout the camp. Every one hundred yards a light. Every five hundred yards a small gate that lead to the road that wrapped around the entirety of the camp. At the camp in Syria, there was barbed wire at the top of a twelve-foot fence. Here, it was an eight-foot fence with no barbed wire.

"Do you think you could climb the fence?" I asked Alicia

"Why? We making a run for it?" Alicia said.

"Just curious."

"Yeah. I don't see it being a problem."

"That's what I thought. So. Why have a fence at all?"

"To keep everything organized and contained. So we have to have our neat I.D. cards."

"Yeah. I guess so."

To our left, we saw two FEMA volunteers, walking toward us. We may have been staring at the fence for too long. I grabbed Alicia by the arm, and we began walking again. As they approached, they stopped us.

"You two out for a walk?" A young male, with blonde hair and a Southern California tan, asked us. His companion wearing the same FEMA uniform was a young African-American girl and a foot taller than all of us.

"Yes, just checking out the camp," Alicia said.

"Good. Just be careful walking on the road. Stay to the inside. A lot of vehicles use the outer road to transport supplies."

We made a move to continue walking, and I said, "Thanks and we will."

"Have a nice day," The young man said.

As we continued to head East, the more crowded the camp became. More and more desperate looking people were also walking along the path. An old man with a cane and a small dog nodded to us as we passed. The rest just walked by with eyes down, headed to who knows where.

We finally reached the center lane where the line up of trailers ran north to south and saw hundreds of the FEMA volunteers.

"That must be the housing for all the FEMA people," Alicia said. I nodded in agreement.

In section AX, we saw our first act of violence. Two young men were arguing when one of the men sucker-punched the other. They both flew into the desert dirt wrestling. Their friends and significant others tried to pull them apart. Alicia and I stopped to watch the melee.

Not fifteen seconds after the fight began, we saw FEMA volunteers descend on the area, in golf carts. They ordered one of the men to stop, as he was on top pummeling the smaller man on the ground. As he rose to throw another punch, one of the female FEMA officers shot him, with what looked like a taser gun. A type I had never seen before. It appeared to emit the electricity in a precise wave and knocked the guy flat. At first, I thought it may be some sort of sonic gun, but when the man hit the ground, he began convulsing.

"Whoa," Alicia said next to me. A crowd began to gather around as two of the FEMA officers grabbed the man on the ground and rolled him over, zip-tying his hands together. Two other FEMA personnel turned the man over that took the beating and zip-tied him as well.

"Hey. He didn't do nothing," said a woman who broke apart from the crowd, pointing at the beaten man. She then pointed to the aggressor. "That guy. He was trying to steal from our tent. My husband just tried to stop him," the wife continued, right in the face of a FEMA officer who put a hand up for her to back away. "Please. He didn't do anything."

More FEMA officers showed up. One began to administer first aid to the beaten man, but they did not undo his binds. The woman tried to get to her husband but was pushed back.

"Don't push me," she said. "Let my husband go!"

"Ma'am. Please back up. We will sort this out." I could see the eyes of the FEMA volunteers, widen at the sight of the growing throng. A group began shouting for them to let the woman's husband go.

From behind us, we heard a truck approach, Alicia and I turned around and saw a military vehicle approaching. We moved aside to let it pass. As it pulled up six Army soldiers jumped out the back, with their rifles ready. The crowd instantly backed up.

Two soldiers approached the two men on the ground and grabbed them each by their elbows and stood them up. The FEMA officer administering first aid said something to the soldier, but the soldier appeared to ignore him. The soldiers began walking the two men away, toward the truck.

"Where are you taking him?" the wife asked. She tried to follow but was blocked by a soldier. He didn't say anything, just stood in front of the woman motionless. "Let me go." No response. She tried to push past him, but the soldier grabbed her by the elbow and, with a curt shove, flung her into the dirt. The rifle was then pointed at her. She began to cry in the dirt. Others came to her aid, trying to get her back to her feet, but she just sat there, tears streaming down her face, hands digging into the dirt. Then the soldier turned and climbed into the back of the truck with the other soldiers and the two prisoners. The FEMA volunteers were already in their golf carts, speeding away. Finally, the Army truck started up and headed north.

The whole incident took five minutes.

"Where do you think they took them?" Alicia asked.

"I don't know," I said.

We continued on our way. But the appeal of the hike had left our steps. The incident was on my mind. How did they respond so quickly? Surveillance cameras? I looked around and saw nothing that would indicate a camera. So, I asked Alicia, "Do you see any cameras anywhere?"

"No," she said, looking to and fro. "Why?"

"FEMA responded almost immediately. They had to have seen." We both looked around again. We saw tents. Signs indicating tent numbers or sections, nothing on the fences.

"I don't see any, but that don't mean much. Cameras today are so small they could be anywhere and everywhere," Alicia said.

"Yeah. I think they are everywhere."

We stood still for a second. I wondered if Big Brother was watching us now. Wondering what this young, brown-haired man and red-haired woman were doing wandering along their fence line.

"We should head back," Alicia said, probably battling her own bout of paranoia.

"Yeah. I don't think there is any more to learn about the camp. The fence is the same the whole perimeter."

CHAPTER TWENTY

11/19/2024

Two nights later, there was no sleeping for anyone in the camp. The Santa Ana winds had returned with a vengeance and were blowing desert sand and dirt high into the air. Finding cracks and crevices to push their cold and dust filled breath into every tent.

I found myself snuggling up to Kaitlyn underneath the thick cotton, Army green, blanket, to keep warm. No longer in our comfortable positions after an awkward encounter the previous morning, when my friend below my waist stiffened in the morning and woke her with a poke in the back. Now, we were back to back. It was enough to feel her warmth radiating from her body and into mine.

I heard someone stirring, and then the lamp in the center of the tent flicked on, casting a pale blue light around the tent. My eyes picked up the change in light as a glow behind my closed eyelids was visible.

"Fuck me."

My eyes flickered open at the voice. I saw Zero standing straight in the blue light, and all around him was a fog of dirt. Dust particles flying in the air as the winds battered and shook the whole tent. The sound was akin to a group of annoying teenagers dancing around the tent hitting the canvas exterior with their fist all at once.

The lantern in the center of the tent was a circular device that was permanently attached to the center table. It also doubled as a heater, and the warmth felt wonderful as the winds depressurized the tent with frigid air.

I slowly swung my legs over the edge of the cot and sat assessing the situation. Zero was moving suitcases to the northeast corner of the tent. A smart move. I arose and grabbed my bag and drug it over to the corner with the others.

Soon, my eyes adjusted, coherent thought returned, and I saw how bad the dirt infiltration had become. My mouth could taste it, and my eyes began to sting. The culprit was the tents one flaw. While the tent was one heavy-duty cloth wrapped around sturdy tent poles, where it connected with the ground was not sturdy. There was no floor, except the desert dirt. A cheap twenty-dollar tent would've had a plastic floor. Not these tents. The wind was flowing beneath the tent with flapping pieces of cloth creating the loud music.

Zero was attempting to stop this infiltration by placing the suitcases along the bottom edges. It wasn't easy, as the cloth had to be pulled straight down and stretched to its limit before a suitcase could be placed on top of its bottom edge. We spent ten minutes with different configurations until we had the bags piled high, creating a small wall at the northeast edge of the tent. We spoke not a word. Just grunts and pointing.

I attempted to go back to bed, and after playing around with the light, we figured out a way to leave the heater on and dim the light to its lowest setting. The warmth felt good. I asked Kaitlyn if she wanted to switch positions so she could be on the side facing the heater. She just shook her head and hid beneath the blanket. Only the top of her brown hair was visible.

It was no use attempting to sleep. While we had stymied most of the dirt from entering the tent, the noise was unbearable. When a large gust arrived, the tent shook, and I feared the whole contraption would come tumbling down on top of us. Every instance of sleep was awoken instantly by a gust of that foul wind.

By morning I was exhausted. Five minutes of sleep here and five minutes of sleep there. The winds had been relentless and seemed to have picked up their pace by the dawn. I looked at my watch seated on the edge of the cot. It was 6:42 a.m. I stretched a bit and saw Jenna staring at me. She and Ethan were sleeping back to back. The blanket was pulled up to the curve of her bottom lip, and the exposed parts of her face had a thin layer of dirt. When she pulled the blanket down, you could clearly observe a line just below her nose. I gave a quick smile, and she smiled back but did not get up. Was my face also covered in dirt? I touched my forehead with my forefinger and looked at the residue on the tip of my finger. Everyone was coated in the desert sand.

I grabbed my jacket and stepped outside the tent. The decibel difference was like walking out of a loud club. Inside the tent the sound was constant. Outside, the noise was all around but less intense. The sun was just peaking over the eastern skyline behind the small hill that led into the valley of our imprisonment.

To my left, twenty tents down, I saw several FEMA personnel and many residents attempting to put a tent back together. A golf cart drove toward me from that direction with two more FEMA officers in tow. A strong gust of wind almost tipped the little cart over, but the driver kept his cool and kept it steady. I stepped aside as the vehicle passed.

I pulled my beanie down lower on my head. All around the camp similar scenes were unfolding. Tents collapsed, people trying to get the tent upright, and poles back into the ground. Some were with FEMA help, others on their own. I stopped and helped a family whose tent had collapsed on the north side. I didn't say much, just helped. They thanked me, and I went on my way.

When I reached the edge of the camp and saw the fence, I found another emergency scenario unfolding. Half the large lights that surrounded the camp had been toppled by the wind. Soldiers swarmed the area like ants around a fallen candy bar. Many trying to put the lights back up, others just appeared to be checking the fence, for any insecurities. One soldier caught me watching and nodded. I nodded back and turned around.

By lunchtime, the winds had died down. The camp began to operate as normal. Since we had skipped breakfast, our little band was eager to eat. Huddled together we now, officially, looked like refugees. Dirt was caked all over our faces. Jenna had that dirt line framing her face. The children looked like they had played in the dirt all morning, dirt streaks streaming down their face from where they must've been crying. Even Zero seemed to have a permanent frown on his face. Looking around, the rest of the residents appeared to have the same look. Even the red cross volunteers looked miserable. Good thing our scheduled shower day was tomorrow.

"I'm going to sleep in Alicia's tent with her family from now on," Said Kaitlyn, as we waited in line, standing behind me. It wasn't surprising, but the timing was.

I turned around and smiled. "I understand." I did. It was one thing to sleep in the same bed in extraordinary circumstances. It was quite another to begin to develop a routine. I felt the change over the past few days. Comfort. Love. It was the practical and rational thing to do. Yet, I felt a sting down in the deepest depths of my tired heart. I missed her, and I forgot how much I had loved her, until these days together.

"You sure?" she asked.

"Yeah. I'm fine."

"Okay," she said.

We had reached the front of the line. Ham sandwiches, a bag of chips and bottled water. Nothing more, nothing less. We ate in silence, on a dust covered table and chairs, at the back of the mess hall. Every now and then a gust would arrive, not as destructive as that morning, but enough that it had all of us reaching for our paper plates to make sure they didn't fly across the table and into the desert.

"We've got to get out of here," Zero said breaking the silence. I had not thought about what it must've been like for a free bird like Zero to be stuck in this monotonous camp routine. I spent years in a routine. It was a way of life in the military. Zero had no such discipline. He came and went as he desired. If he didn't like a job, he left. If he wanted to go to Vegas, he went. He was also alone. I had Kaitlyn or at least I did. Jenna and Ethan had a long friendship and now seemed closer than ever. Zero had all of us, yet none of us.

"Easier said than done," Alicia said.

"What about demanding they let us go? We've got some place to go. We told them so when we got here. Why keep us, if we don't want to be here," Zero said.

"We could ask them?" Kaitlyn said and hesitated before continuing. "But, who do we ask? I don't think the FEMA people would know or care. I have only seen a few soldiers."

Ethan interrupted, "It's as if they are all in charge, yet none of them are."

Another blast of wind interrupted our conversation, and it was our time to move on anyways, we had to make room for the one-thirty lunch crowd, so we went back to our tent and piled everyone inside.

"Who do we go to then?" Alicia said. "The Army, FEMA, Red Cross?"

"All of them," Zero said. "I don't give a shit. Take a shot at all of them and see if we can get out of here."

I had remained silent. I knew, intimately, that it was futile. The camp was designed with multiple divisions so not one of them could be held accountable or could know all the answers. If we asked FEMA, they would pass us on to the Army. The Army back to FEMA. And the Red Cross would direct us to either one.

"Let's set up a plan then," Drew said, seated on one of the cots, next to Alicia. The kids, while providing no ideas themselves, were preoccupied in the corner playing tic tac toe. A game they must've just picked up, since kids born in the twenty-tens did not play games with a stick and dirt, yet there they were. I was standing by the entrance. Jenna and Kaitlyn on the cot to my left. Drew and Ethan to my right. If someone walked in, they would've thought I was giving some sort of sermon. Yet, I was the one silent.

"We all try and talk to someone from each branch," Alicia said. "Army, FEMA, and Red Cross. Try and find out who the bosses are and we can go from there. We should be able to find out who is in charge for each branch and then we can talk to them about getting out of here. Or at least if they have a plan for us."

"Good," Zero said.

"Okay. How do we want to attack this?" Alicia said, looking at each of us. Unfortunately, I had already checked out. I would go along with whatever their plan was. I knew it wouldn't work. But, for the first time since we arrived, I heard something in their voices, that I did not want to take away. Hope.

After much deliberation, assignments were handed out. Since I was in the Army, it was my job to try and find out information about the distribution of power here at the camp from someone in the Army. I argued for a bit, saying that because I was in the Army, I should not be the one looking for information from the Army. This did not make sense to the rest of them.

"Do you think there is a chance?" Kaitlyn asked me, a few hours later, alone in the tent together.

"It might," I said.

"That's what I thought," she said, reading between the lines. It was a familiar feeling. We could always talk to each other without saying what we meant, and yet we would always understand the truth behind the lies.

"I'm sorry. It's just, I think we have to accept that we are not getting out of here unless we force our way out."

Kaitlyn raised an eyebrow and nodded. I began to walk away when she grabbed me around my waist and pulled me into a crushing hug.

"I'm glad I am here with you."

"Me too. But, that's selfish. You should be with your family."

"I miss my baby girl."

"I know."

"Damn Jeff and his stupid work trip, that I just had to tag along with." She pulled away, her arms still around my waist, and stared into my eyes. I could feel the stirring in my heart again. She was always so beautiful with those full green eyes. "Yeah. I think it's better that we don't sleep in the same bed anymore." She pulled away, averting her eyes.

Echoing across the camp came a voice, a loud male voice and in surround sound. "Zone C residents. This is your weekly update." The voice seemed to be coming from everywhere, yet nowhere in particular. "I know it's been a tough week or for that matter a tough month. But, we do have some good news. Next week on Thursday. It will be Thanksgiving. And in honor of this uniquely American holiday, we will be serving a special turkey dinner. And gathering at 5 p.m. in all your individual sections for a celebration. To repeat, a special Thanksgiving dinner will be prepared at 5 p.m., on Thursday the twenty-eighth, for all residents in each section." Kaitlyn and I looked at each other with the same expression, one raised eyebrow and crinkled brows that expressed a cynicism that almost made me laugh out loud. "In other good news, and one that I am sure every one of you will appreciate. Each tent will be provided with a television. That's right, each tent will be getting a TV which will broadcast news, movies and TV shows broadcast directly to you. Only one channel, but better than nothing, right? That is all for this week. Thanks, and have a good day!"

The execution of the announcement reminded me of high school, during homeroom, when the annoying PA system would announce school news, that no one cared to hear. But, the damn voice was always so excited to announce the band would be selling candy bars for a fundraiser.

Kaitlyn and I looked at each other, wondering what strange planet we landed on. A television? Why? No news on what is going on in the outside world? Who attacked us? Did we counter attack? Are there any plans to move us to a more permanent location? To let us go on our merry way? Any actual news? Instead? Thanksgiving dinner and a fucking TV for our tents.

"What the hell is going on?" Kaitlyn asked.

"Keep the local systems in line," I said.

"What?"

"It's from *Star Wars*. Except instead of using fear to keep us in line, they will use distractions." I forgot Kaitlyn was not as ingrained in the world of *Star Wars* as I was. "My guess is they felt the depression going through camp this morning and wanted to give everyone a lift."

"Smart," she said.

Yes, it was, I thought. Zero entered the tent in a huff, and smacked his hand on my shoulder and said, "This doesn't change a thing, right?"

"Not that I could see," I said.

"Good. I'll be damned if they buy me off with a fucking TV."

CHAPTER TWENTY-ONE

11/21/2024

Two days later, I found myself alone, attempting to follow through on Zero's plan. But, finding anyone in the Army to speak with was becoming a mission unto itself. They just did not show themselves in the camp. I spent the morning walking the perimeter and saw not one fatigue-clad individual.

I set off by myself, despite my insistence we go everywhere in pairs, thanks to the uneven number of adults and wanting to be alone. The last six months of my life I spent by myself, except when I was at work, which I may as well had been. Being cramped in the tents, with, now, three other people was exhausting. A man needs his space.

As I approached section A (northeast corner of camp), I saw a woman talking to herself or to the exterior fence. She wore a filthy jacket that was tucked into her dirty jeans on her right hip. She turned toward me as I approached. Her face was still covered in dirt from Tuesday's wind storm. Her eyes darted around me, up and down, as if giving me an x-ray. Then she turned her whole body swiftly in my direction. It was a jerky turn as if her arms and torso understood the command before the rest of her body.

"Have you seen my husband?" she asked as she approached. I thought about the question for a second and almost laughed at the absurdity of it.

"Not that I'm aware of. What does he look like?" Maybe I had.

"Oh, you know," she said and cocked her head sideways, looking at me with only her left eye. "Are you military?"

"No."

"You look military?"

"Do I?"

"Hmm," she said. Growing up in the Inland Empire and in a mobile home park, one tends to recognize a person under the influence of drugs. Or, as on this occasion, one on the influence of withdrawal. She could not stand still. One leg kept moving up and down. She would switch eyes to give me a look. Right eye. A pause. A head turn. Left eye. One arm always grabbing the other arm, again in an alternating pattern. "I know they took him."

"Who took him?" I asked.

She waved her arms in the air wildly pointing all directions at once. "They! They!"

"The Army?"

"I'm not telling you. You." She took a step forward. "You. Can't get me to talk. No way."

"Maybe I can help."

She smiled at me a crooked smile, with missing teeth. "You can't help. No one can help." Her head swung low, shaking back and forth. "Nope. No help."

"Why not?"

She swung her head up, so quickly that I thought the momentum would throw her head over heels on her back, and whispered, "Cause we're already dead." OK. This was getting bizarre. "Like on that show from when I was a kid. Umm. Ummm. Umm."

"*The X-Files?*" I said, trying to help.

"No. No. No. The one with the island."

I knew which show she meant. "*Lost?*"

She nearly jumped ten feet in the air and pointed, excitedly at me with crooked fingers. "Yes. Like *Lost*. All dead."

"That's not what happened on *Lost*. The plane crash didn't kill them. They were on the island. They all survived. The ending is only confusing if you don't realize that time doesn't matter in the afterlife."

She looked at me as if I spoiled her lunch. "What?"

"The ending only showed what happened after all of the survivors died at different times. Since, you know, we all die at some point. Sooner or later," I said, while also wondering why am I discussing the end of a fifteen-year-old show in the middle of a refugee camp.

"Huh?" I lost her. She turned away from me and continued muttering to herself as she headed toward the interior of the camp, every now and then turning her head toward me, maybe afraid I would follow her. I watched her go with what must've been a goofy grin on my face.

One fragment of her rambling stuck in my mind as I continued with my expedition. Where did her husband disappear to? Typically, I would've chalked it up to a drug-addled mind, but I had seen a man dragged off against his will and I began to wonder if that situation was unfolding throughout the camp. Did her, no doubt, drug-fueled husband get dragged off to some unknown destination as well? If I had not seen what I saw, when I was the one dragging off unsuspecting men in the middle of the night, I probably would've ignored it. But, I couldn't. It was there in my mind like a small splinter stuck on the bottom of my foot.

I arrived at my destination just before noon. The main intake tent for the camp. The one place I knew I would find Army personnel. At the opening of the tent facing the camp, I saw two FEMA persons, both were chatting with each other as I approached. They stopped talking as I approached.

"Can I help you?" the young blonde-haired man to the left of the opening said.

"I hope so," I replied. "I am looking for the man in charge." I laughed at myself internally after I said it. It was a ridiculous thing to ask. But, I was in a sarcastic mood, and it was worth it to see the blank expression on their faces as if I asked them to send me to the moon.

"I'm sorry what is this concerning?" the lovely brunette to my right asked.

"I have some questions that need answering about our tent?"

"We can help with that," the male said. "What is it you need?"

"Was it the wind?" the female said.

"No. Not the wind. And no offense, but I don't think you two are the ones in charge."

"No. Maybe not. But we are authorized to help in any way we can," the female brunette said. "What do you need with your tent?"

"I was hoping to discuss this with someone inside the tent your standing in front of."

This seemed to throw them for a loop. Both looked at each other waiting for the other to take charge. "I am sorry that is not possible. This tent is for authorized personnel only," the male said.

"Well, can't you go inside and ask if someone would come out here and speak with me? Someone in charge? A boss maybe?" They both, again, looked at each other. They probably thought I was on drugs.

"The only people inside are part of the Army," the female said.

"Perfect. That is exactly who I want to speak to."

They were beginning to become annoyed with me. Tension began to creep into their facial expressions, and the tone of their answers became firmer.

"That is not gonna happen. They are only here for protection. Not for matters concerning your tent," The male said.

"I think they are the people I want to speak to. You see, the problem with my tent is I want to leave it."

"You want to move to another tent?" the naïve brunette asked.

"No. I want to leave the tent and all the tents in this fucking place. I want out of this camp." The expression on their faces made this so much more fun than I anticipated. Their brows furrowed. Their eyes peered down to the ground. Both trying to find the correct answer from their training. "Come on. I can't be the first one to ask?"

Before they could respond, a soldier burst out of the tent, looked at me and then to the young FEMA workers to each side of him. "What is going on?" He was about six feet, with what I guessed a permanent grimace on his young, yet mature, face.

"This man wants to talk to someone in the Army," the brunette said.

"About what?"

I stepped up to him and said, "I was wondering if you guys had any plans for moving us out of this camp."

He gave me a once over, then turned to the now cowering FEMA volunteers. "Move him along."

"Aww. You don't know either," I said. "Can you at least let me talk to someone who does know what's going on? A Major? Lieutenant? I don't expect a private such as yourself to know the answers to such important questions."

He had his back to me and was about to enter the tent, when he stopped and turned back to the brunette, "Get him out of here." He then entered the tent in a pronounced movement, equivalent to slamming a door. The Army tent cloth gave no satisfaction.

The FEMA personnel now had their hands on their hips, wrapped around the taser gun I saw used a few days ago. "Sir, your gonna have to leave now," the male said, losing all the niceties previously in his voice.

I raised my hands and backed away. "No need to get angry. I found all the answers I needed." I bowed a mock bow while raising my left hand in the air in a flamboyant gesture. "Thanks for your help." I turned and left.

That went about as well as I expected.

CHAPTER TWENTY-TWO

11/22/2024 - 11/28/2024

For the next week, a routine was set. After breakfast, two groups went about in a grid-like fashion, trying to gather as much information from anyone that we could find. The other group stayed behind with the children. After lunch, the alternate team would head out. We did our best to not approach the same area twice.

What have we learned after a week on the job? Jack about squat. Oh, we learned what we already presumed. The FEMA volunteers oversaw the camp where it concerned organization, security, and procedures. The Red Cross and other non-profit organizations monitored the food, water and other supplies, such as clothing, blankets and the wonderful TV's we all were to receive. The Army remained on the outside of the camp. Except at the intake tent or in emergency situations, like high winds knocking over lights. Or a disturbance inside the camp that needed a more powerful hand. Such as a brawl that erupted in section D, that everyone was talking about, yet no one had seen.

As for my part? I spent the afternoons walking the camp. I never went back to the intake tent. I passed the tent often but never attempted to discuss our request with anyone. I knew it was pointless. After dinner, we would all gather around inside one of our temporary homes, or outside, depending on the weather and discuss our daily inquiries.

On the Wednesday night before the scheduled Thanksgiving feast, we, again, were all outside, in the space between the two tents and were discussing that day's investigations. (When we first had these loud and sometimes boisterous discussions, I worried that Big Brother was not only watching, but listening. If they were listening, I am not sure they cared, because nothing came of it and after the second night I thought nothing more of it.)

The night was chilly, but refreshing, and lit by a nearly full moon. Jenna and Ethan said they talked to a lovely Red Cross lady in section BB, who empathized with their plight, but could only offer a "Well, if they have your request in the system, I am sure they will grant it soon."

Drew and Alicia talked to multiple FEMA workers in section D, but all they got was, "Well, we can't give you a timeframe, but I am sure there will be a movement towards a more permanent location forthcoming." I am positive that was an interpretation of what was said since I can't imagine one of the young FEMA volunteers using the word "forthcoming."

Zero and Kaitlyn, an odd pairing for the day, that made me smile, reported that Zero tried, unsuccessfully, to hit on a young FEMA volunteer. Kaitlyn said, "I had to drag him away and apologize."

"Hey, I was trying to get an in, with the enemy. You know, sleeping with the enemy, is the best way to get information," Zero said. All the guys laughed, the women not so much. So, another day and night came and went, without any additional information gathered.

"We can't keep going like this," Drew said. "We are gonna get in trouble."

"Trouble?" Zero asked, "We're just asking questions."

"Look around. This is not the place to ask questions. We may ask the wrong question to the wrong person and find ourselves disappeared." I told the group about my encounter with the disturbed woman by the fence, and how she was looking for her husband. We also heard rumors from some of the other families in our section, specifically those we shared our eating times with about other people who had family members disappear.

"Those are just rumors," Jenna said. "We don't know if that is even true. Maybe they took that woman's husband for health reasons. Nursed him and now he is back with his crazy wife."

"Okay, maybe they are not stealing people in the middle of the night like Blake said what happened at the camp in Syria," Drew said. "But, if we keep harassing people, it's gonna get some attention, and attention is not what we need. It could eventually lead to people asking questions to the wrong person, and that may lead back to us."

Drew may have stumbled over the meaning, but I knew where he was coming from. The last thing we needed to do was draw attention to ourselves.

"So, we just sit here and do fucking nothing?" Zero said. "Sit on our asses. Wait for our shiny new TV's and for them to tell us how everything is great and sooner or later we may or may not be able to go."

"No. That's not what I mean. But, I do think we should pull back on our question asking," Drew said.

At this Zero turned to storm away. "Hold on Zero," I said. "I think Drew is right. We do need to stop harassing people who have about as much information as we do."

Zero turned to me and said, "Then what do we do?"

"We keep our ears open. But, the questioning is getting us nowhere."

"I can't live like this," Zero said, with a pleading note in his voice.

"I know. That doesn't mean we stop trying to find a way out. But, we may have to change our tactic."

"What do you suggest?" Drew asked. Jenna, Kaitlyn, and Alicia were quiet, seated on one of the cots that we brought out for these conversations. Ethan stood next to them, quiet as well.

"I don't know. Not yet. For now, we need to hold off on the inquisition. Wait till after Thanksgiving dinner. Maybe there will be an announcement then. I doubt it. But, for now, just keep cool. We will think of something."

I had nothing. It wasn't too hard to sneak out of the camp in the middle of the night. But then what? Miles of the desert all around. We couldn't just hop into Zero's truck, without being seen at some point. We couldn't walk to Utah. That was the reason the fence was only eight feet tall, they knew it was pointless to sneak out. So, I would have to think of an escape plan that could get us to the truck and out, without being seen and that would not get us all killed in the process. For now, I had nothing.

"Fine," Zero said.

We heard tires pull up between the tents and for a brief second, I felt the fight or flight rush of adrenaline. I saw it was a golf cart and two FEMA volunteers. One of them exited the cart with a clipboard in hand. Connected to a hitch on the back of the golf cart was a small wheeled platform and on the platform, was a collection of small rectangle boxes.

"You all in tents thirty-six?" he asked. In the dark, it was difficult to discern facial details.

"Yes, thirty-six and thirty-seven," Alicia said. "What's going on?"

"We have your TV's to install," he said, with a goofy grin.

"Okay. Go for it," Zero said. The man stood still for a second, maybe waiting for a thank you or a tip. When none was forthcoming, he turned around and went back to the cart. Alicia went inside her tent to get the children, who had been inside during our conversation.

Twenty minutes later, we found ourselves seated inside the Welles family tent staring at a thin thirty-inch TV mounted on one of the tent poles to the left of the entrance. Broadcasting on the television was an episode of the show *Friends*, "The one with..." whatever. There was no remote, and we had to walk to the TV to adjust the volume and turn it off. We complained, ever since they were announced, about the TV's and how it was just a distraction to keep us placated. Well, it seemed to work. As we watched, all our cares and worrying were replaced by laughter. After *Friends*, we watched an episode of *How I Met Your Mother*, followed by *Blackish, Modern Family*, and *Joe's Life After*. I knew it was no coincidence they were all sitcoms. Who wants to watch a serious drama in these circumstances? At ten o'clock the TV announced it was time for curfew and the programming would resume at 7 a.m. As I went back to my tent, I couldn't help but feel guilty. Yet, it did feel good to sit down with everyone and just have fun. It was a remarkable thing that such a simple device could make everyone feel better. Ominously, I knew that was exactly the point.

By noon the next day, the mood had changed for the better. Or for worse depending on perspective. Even Zero, who was so adamant about not selling out to our TV providing overlords, was in a cheerful mood after a morning cartoon dose of *Steven Universe*, which was one of our favorite shows throughout our senior year in high school.

As we waited for lunch time, another announcement was made over the invisible loudspeakers. "Good afternoon residents of Zone C," Residents? "As you all know today there will be a Thanksgiving feast at 5 p.m., in every section." There was a slight pause. "To clarify a few things. Everyone will eat at times printed on your I.D. cards. The five o'clock celebration will be a special presentation and announcement, celebrating this American holiday. You can view this presentation at every mess hall or from the comfort of your own tent on the televisions provided. Don't worry if you don't make it down to your mess hall at five, there is plenty of fantastic food for all, during your designated time periods." Another awkward silence. "Thank you. And have a good day."

Zero, who had been sitting on the floor watching *Full House*, with the children, along with Alicia and Kaitlyn, was the first to speak. "What the fuck was that about?"

Alicia punched Zero in the arm and said, "Please watch the language." The kids didn't seem to notice, as the audio from the regularly scheduled program had returned. Drew, Jenna, and Ethan had gone for a walk.

"I think they had second thoughts about having everyone gathered in one place after the brawl in one of the other sections," I said.

"Did that really happen?" Alicia said.

"Who knows," I replied. "Either way, if it did or didn't. I think after the foul mood in the camp over the past week, they didn't want to risk it."

Zero who asked the question in the first place was now laughing with the kids about something Uncle Joey was doing, so I went outside, and Alicia followed. Kaitlyn stayed inside, not watching TV, instead appeared lost in her own thoughts.

"We gonna go?" Alicia said once we were outside in the sun.

"I don't see why, if we can stay here," I said. "I guess once everyone gets back we can discuss it, but I don't see the point." She did not follow up. "Well we have lunch in a half hour, then showers between two and three. So that will keep us busy. You plan on showering, right?" She didn't have to answer; the raised eyebrow was enough. "Right," I said.

"Also plan on doing some laundry while there."

"Good."

At lunch, we all agreed to skip the Thanksgiving festivities. We would head down to the mess hall at our usual dinner time. Lunch was another ham or chicken sandwich depending on preference. The main difference was the smell drifting from the many trailers behind the mess hall: Turkeys in ovens. And the smell was a dose of aromatic nirvana.

The showers in the camp were just off the mess hall on the north side. Made of wood, they reminded me of a dressing room, at a department store. A door, that opened to a two by six area, with a bench and hooks along the wall to hang your clothes. On the left, another entryway to the four by six shower. It was well made and provided decent privacy. Our shower days were Thursday and Sundays, two to three in the afternoon. Some poor souls had 9 p.m. or even worse 6 a.m. shower times. So, we counted ourselves lucky. Usually, there was a line, but we never waited more than fifteen minutes. We estimated about twenty-five people were assigned each hour.

Outside the shower was a FEMA rep who would scan our ID cards and hand out fresh towels. On this day, it was a young woman, who wore a permanent smile like most of the FEMA volunteers. Drew and his entire family were about to enter together.

"What's in the bag?" The young women asked as she was taking the I.D. cards from Drew. Alicia was holding a plastic bag.

"Oh. Just some laundry." The young woman made a crinkle with her brow, like an android hearing something it could not compute. "I plan on just running some water and soap on them, then I will lay them out in the sun." The young woman still looked confused. "Come on, I can't be the first person to do this?"

"Maybe," The young woman said, showing no interest and motioned them into the shower. On the shower door was a sign that read: "Please keep showers under 5 minutes. Respect your fellow human beings."

I had brought a bag of my own. Once Alicia shared her idea of doing laundry in the shower, our group thought it was a great idea and jumped at the opportunity to get our underwear at least somewhat clean. It's one of those issues that no one thinks about when creating a refugee camp.

After showering, we spent the afternoon lounging around in our respective tents. I even took a nap. I did my best to keep my mind blank. Not dwell on the dichotomy of the camp. Twelve days in this camp, and it was evident that the people in charge were doing their best to make everyone as comfortable as possible. The televisions, showers, Thanksgiving dinner and all the other amenities present were devised not of evil intentions, but to provide, as best they could, a comfortable environment for all, in this difficult situation. But, that did not change the fact that we were forced into this camp and held here without a choice. The amenities were no replacement for the lack of freedom or even the lack of knowledge concerning what was happening in the world. By not providing this vital information to the encampment, they were creating a sense of dread. If they were purposely keeping this information from us, then it must not be information they think we can handle. Again, good intentions by those who believe that they know better than us, in positions of power, create a dynamic that could lead to only one result. Blowback. The one-word American military and government officials should be well accustomed to knowing.

I could not keep my mind blank.

CHAPTER TWENTY-THREE

11/28/2024

By 5 p.m., the anticipation was at an all-time high. We had gathered around the TV in the Welles family tent and even went so far as to add one of the cots from my tent, which now was located just below the TV. I sat front and center on this out of place furniture, Kaitlyn to my left and Zero to my right. The rest were seated on the uncomfortable cots as well, Jenna was sitting cross-legged so her legs didn't rest against the metal bar along the edge of the cot and I did the same.

Currently on, some show I had never seen. It was called *Forget About Men*. Must be a newer show. A filmed in front of a studio audience show. Network TV at its finest. We didn't care, we only half-watched.

"Any ideas on what we are about to watch?" Jenna asked.

"*A Charlie Brown Thanksgiving?*" Zero said.

"I can't think of any good Thanksgiving shows," Drew added.

"Probably some special announcement about the upcoming special Christmas dinner," Kaitlyn said. The cynicism was exposed for all to hear. She was beginning to sound like me.

"It's probably just an update on the situation," Ethan said. "We want to let you know all things are going great. We really appreciate your cooperation. We should be thankful we're still alive. Blah. Blah. Blah."

"I hope it's an update on what the hell is going on," Alicia said. "Who attacked us? What are we doing about it? That sort of thing."

"It could be any of that," I added, while not actually adding anything as has been my M.O. this past week. "But, I wouldn't get any hopes up on any real infor-"

"Shh, it's starting," Zero said.

After the credits of the previous show had sped by at a remarkable pace, we were greeted with a blank screen. A flicker showing the N.T.S.C. bars. Then a wood desk framed on each side by a flag. On the left of the screen a United States flag. On the right a blue flag for the President of The United States. Seated at the desk was a man. Pale skin, dark eyes, and gray hair combed slightly to his right, which accentuated the receding hairline. A gray suit, white shirt with a bright red tie.

"Good Evening," The man said. "My fellow Americans on this wonderful celebration of thanks, I want to wish you all a Happy Thanksgiving. This incredibly American holiday is an important institution and one that, even in these trying times, should be celebrated and appreciated." The speaker paused. "So, in that spirit, I would like to give thanks. Thanks to all the hard-working rescue workers. FEMA, the Red Cross, the various state National Guards, and our excellent military personnel. We have the strongest and most powerful military in the world. And even as I speak here, they are out hunting and bringing to justice the perpetrators of this horrendous act. No matter where they hide," Pausing for dramatic effect. "And we will find them. Unfortunately, it is on this issue that I must speak freely. Intelligence has brought to light, that this attack while executed by foreign agents was orchestrated from within our own government." The air just got sucked out of the tent as everyone gasp, including myself. "We have already apprehended many of those who were responsible, and we will surely find the rest." Another pause. "I am sorry to have spoiled your Thanksgiving, but I thought in the interest of transparency, that it best I am as truthful as I can be with each and every one of you. All of us were affected, by this treacherous act. How can we not be? The victims were secretaries, businessmen and women, military and federal workers, moms and dads, friends and neighbors." Another pause. "If you were near the sites of these attacks please allow the military and FEMA workers to do their job. Even so," He appeared to sound off script now, as his cadence had changed from steady and calm to fast and slurry. "This is a strong country, we have always been, we have endured terror before, but nothing on this scale." Another pause. "But we will. This is the United States of America. The home of the free. And we will always be. God bless us all on this Thanksgiving, and God bless the United States of America."

For a few seconds, the camera just stayed on the President, and then cut to black. No one said a thing for at least thirty seconds.

"Who the fuck was that?" Zero asked, breaking the silence. "I thought our president was a woman?"

"Our president was, or is, a woman. President Gillibrand. We re-elected her a few weeks ago," Alicia said.

"What the hell?" Drew said. "I have never seen that guy before in my life."

"Did he even say who he was?" Jenna asked.

"No," Ethan said. "I feel like we missed an episode somewhere."

Yes, that was the feeling. Like we were dropped onto another planet with another United States. It was disorienting. There was also something strange about the whole presentation. Something about the setting, like looking at one of those picture games where you had to guess what was different between the two, even though they looked alike. The oval office wasn't the same oval office.

"That wasn't the oval office," I said.

"What? Where was it?" Zero asked.

"Don't know."

"How do you know?" Jenna asked.

"Cause there was only one window."

"Maybe it was just zoomed in?" Kaitlyn asked.

"No. There was enough space. And on each side of the flags past the curtain, there was a wall, where there should have been a window."

The TV went back to its original scheduled programming, which was an old TV show called *Three's Company*. I stood up and turned down the volume.

I had seen some scary shit in my time, but that presidential address shook me to my core. On the surface, it seemed perfectly fine, but something about the whole thing felt off. The speech was not well written. He, apparently, went off script, yet had to insert the portion about the traitors within the government. It could all be my own paranoia, but I could tell I was not the only one who felt disturbed, the tent had exploded into a vocal debate, about what was really going on.

"Maybe the president died, along with the rest of..." Drew said. "What's it called? The one's who would be called after."

"The line of succession," Alicia said.

"Right. Maybe it's like that show *Battlestar Galactica*. Maybe he was the Secretary of Education or something."

"Maybe," Ethan said. "But, that's not the important part. What about the idea that people in our own government would orchestrate this. That's nuts." He paused. "Why?"

No one had an answer. Maybe for a power grab? Maybe this new president took over via a coup? Maybe the terrorists planted evidence on innocent government officials? Maybe? Maybe? We began to sound like the writers' room of a television show. A whole lot of speculation.

"Look, there is no use to speculate or even worry about what we just saw," I said. "We can't. We have to worry about the here and now. We cannot find answers or have any say either way, even if it is the worst thing imaginable."

This quieted the room. I looked down at my watch. 5:55 p.m., we had been going like this for almost forty-five minutes. Scaring ourselves, with things that have no impact on our lives now. The camp was all that mattered now. I knew that was not entirely accurate, but I had to work on one problem at a time. It was the practical and rational thing to do.

"It's almost six. Let's go get our Thanksgiving dinner and try to enjoy it," I said. They all agreed. As I was heading back to my tent, to grab a jacket, and I asked Kaitlyn to follow me. I found my backpack in a pile of bags in the corner.

"What's up?" Kaitlyn asked as I was reaching into the backpack.

I pulled out a small pair of pliers and pointed to the back of my head. "I need you to remove my staples."

"Me?" she said, and dread overtook her face.

"Please," I said. I sat down on the dirt and motioned for her to come over. She took the wrench and parted the hair on the back of my head.

"You want me to just rip these out?"

"Yes, please."

I heard her sigh and felt a hand steady the back of my head. Then the cold wrench brushed against the back of my skull. Then a slight pinch.

"It's bleeding," she said, as she dropped a staple on the dirt floor.

"Grab one of my shirts." I pointed toward my bag in the corner. She grabbed a shirt, wiped the back of my head and pulled the second staple out.

"Thanks for calming everyone down back there," she said while pulling out the third. "It was like one of those social media news stories that everyone passes around and gets everyone pissed off. But, you eventually realize there is nothing that you can do about it, so all it did was make you mad and ruined your day."

"One problem at a time. Right?" I said.

"Yeah. Get us out of here and then on to Utah, right?" Kaitlyn asked.

"That's still the plan," I said and nodded.

She grabbed my arm and rubbed it softly. "All done."

"Go on, I'm gonna change my shirt and grab a jacket. I will meet you down there."

"Okay," she said and smiled. Then she turned away, and I watched her go. I stripped off my shirt and found a somewhat clean one, grabbed my trusty black sweatshirt, re-applied my beanie to my head, opened the flap to the tent and stared straight into four Army soldiers, all equipped with M4A1 assault rifles.

"Blake Anderson?" The soldier in front asked.

"Yes," I said, doing my best to hide my fear.

"We need you to come with us."

"What for?" I thought about making a run for it, but that would just make me dead quicker.

"Just come with us."

I looked to the west, the direction Kaitlyn went, and I could not see her in the evening light. I couldn't see any of them.

CHAPTER TWENTY-FOUR

11/28/2024

How did they find me? Were they waiting for me, hiding in the shadows, until the rest of the group left? Secret cameras watching? Waiting for their moment? All these questions swirled around my mind as four soldiers walked me through the camp. Two in front. Two behind. No need to ask where they were taking me. But why? Did our questions this past week finally get noticed? Then why just me? The timing is what haunted me. How perfect was it, that they show up when I was alone? Except, I had been walking the camp alone for the past week. They could have grabbed me any of those times. Maybe it was a coincidence. Maybe they came to look for me and it just so happened at the moment it did.

I saw the intake tent up ahead. The answers would be inside. As we approached, I began to sweat profusely, and my heart felt like it was drumming along with a Dead Kennedy's song. At the front of the tent, the flaps opened and I was ushered into the same intake tent we entered when we arrived here, only now it had been turned into some sort of Army headquarters. A large square table, or multiple tables, engulfed the entirety of the room. At the table were a dozen soldiers peering onto computer or laptop screens. As I was lead to the corner of the room and a small plastic chair, I saw on a few of the monitors, images of the camp. Live images, mainly centered on the mess halls. On other screens were spreadsheets and computer code. The spreadsheets I could understand if I had a closer look, the code was a foreign language.

"Sit here," a soldier said and motioned me to the plastic chair in the corner. I sat down and said nothing. The soldier, who appeared to be the highest-ranking member of my escort, went back to the opposite corner of the tent, where a small desk was erected and began talking to the man seated at the desk. The man at the desk nodded and looked over at me. I stared back with a straight face. He walked around the desk and headed in my direction.

He was a large man, at least six-foot-two, with a bald head. A career military man. As he approached I saw the patches on his uniform, and I understood, this was not just a career military man, but one of the important ones. The colonel patch was evident. O-6 pay grade.

"Blake Anderson," he said, as he approached.

"That's me," I said.

"Come over to my desk, we need to have a talk." I got up and began to follow him. "Oh and bring the chair," he said, with a thin smile. "We seem to be running out."

I did as told.

At his desk, he motioned me to sit at the empty space in front of his desk. His desk was clean, except for a stack of Post-It notes and a military-grade protected tablet. As he sat down, he grabbed the tablet and began working it like a monkey playing the piano.

"Aw. Here we go," He finally said, not looking at me, but at the tablet. "Blake Anderson, or should I say, Private Blake Anderson." So, there it is, that's why they grabbed me.

"Not anymore," I said. He ignored me.

"My name is Colonel Miles." He paused, waiting for a response. I gave him none. He looked back at his tablet. "It says here you joined in May of 2021 and were honorably discharged in May of this year." He looked up at me again, as if waiting for a confirmation of the facts. Again, I said nothing. "You were assigned in Syria at a refugee camp in fall of 2021. Then you were assigned special assignments in Afghanistan and Iran. Looks like those were training assignments." Again, he looked up from the tablet at me. I gave him nothing, and he kept reading, only this time to himself. After another thirty seconds, he said: "Sounds like you had a tough time in Syria?"

"We all did," I said.

"That is true. But, I know first-hand how dangerous those camps became. Your Sergeant and many other officers said you were exemplary in your handling of difficult situations."

"I did what I had to."

"That's all we can do." He placed the tablet down on the desk, leaned back in his chair and looked me straight in the eyes. "It also says you killed thirteen civilians, during the last week of your deployment." Was it thirteen? I didn't count. "You did what you had to, to protect the camp. I understand that, and that's why we need you."

"I'm sorry. What?" I said.

"Look. As you may have guessed, the camps are running smoothly now, and we need them to continue to run smoothly. Not many of the soldiers here have any experience with this sort of work."

"It's not what a soldier should be doing."

"You are one hundred percent correct. A soldier is no peace officer.

But, what can we do? The California National Guard is spread thin. The local police have either disappeared or joined with other cities that need help. The County Sheriffs still have jobs elsewhere. FEMA, with its volunteers, can only do so much. The Red Cross has no ability to maintain order in a camp this size. We are needed, and here we are."

"So, you want me to what, re-up?"

"I, technically, don't have to ask, you are still under contract with the Army for three more years." Damn, if he wasn't right. "Your part of the I.R.R. If you were anywhere else in the country you would have already been called." I was caught, nowhere to run. "It just took us awhile to get our databases up and running. We've been slowly going through the list of people in all the camps. But, the last thing we want to do is force people to re-enlist if they don't want to."

"So, I have a choice? Or I don't have a choice?"

"Both, you always have a choice. After reading your file, I figured it was best to approach like this and speak to you, personally."

"Why?"

"You see most of the people in this room," he said, pointing to the large desk in the center of the room. "Most of them have been in the Army for less than a month, some even less than that. Some signed up after the attacks." As in multiple. "We need experienced soldiers. Especially here. Basic training can't come close to training for this situation. But, most importantly, we need people like you, who has served in a refugee camp before and has trained other soldiers."

"I only helped, I wasn't in charge. Trained a bunch of locals, who barely spoke English, and for most of my time with them, I couldn't decipher if they hated me or were grateful."

"It doesn't matter who you trained. We need on the job training for this position. That's why I am speaking to you personally. We need you. Your country needs you."

There it was, your country needs you.

"How long do I have?" He seemed perplexed by my question. "How long before I need to make a decision?"

"I need to know now."

"That is not gonna happen. If I say yes, I need to say goodbye to my friends and let them know what happened. If I say no, I would like to see them before you throw me in the stockade." A smile appeared on the Colonel's face. Yes, we had a choice, but I also knew the consequences.

"I need an answer now, and we can get word to them."

"Sorry, if I don't take your word for it. But, I would prefer to do it myself."

"I understand, but that's not gonna happen." The situation was clear. I either said "yes" and went with them now or I said "no" and went with them to be taken into custody and treated as a prisoner. But, I had one card left to play. They needed me, he made that fact abundantly clear. But, how much? Could I negotiate a one-year term, instead of three? A better bunk? A separate room? Or? "Okay. I will sign up. Right here, right now. If you answer one question honestly. And do one thing for me."

The Colonel leaned forward and said, "Shoot."

"You read my file. You know that while I was, according to others, an exemplary soldier, you also know I was a pain in the ass. I don't take orders as well as I should and am highly opinionated." Colonel Miles leaned back and smiled. "So, if you don't do either of these two things I will say no, and you can throw me in any damn cell you wish."

"Ask."

"I need you to get my friends out of here. They have family in Utah, we were on our way before we ended up here. Let them go."

"You know I can't do that," he said.

"Come on, you can do anything you want."

"I can't let one family go. Then other people will be asking to go as well."

"No one will notice. Believe me. Just send some soldiers to them and bring them here. Tell them they are free to go. Let them leave. Eight fewer mouths to feed."

"What's the question?"

"What?"

"I will think about your request after I hear your question."

"Who attacked us?"

Colonel Miles' mouth twitched and looked to his left, ever so briefly. He doesn't know either. "You know I can't answer that." I opened my mouth to respond when he interrupted. "But, I will make arrangements to have your people set free. They will have to fend for themselves after that, but I will let them go."

"Seriously?" I wasn't expecting this to work. I was prepared to spend however long in a military prison, just because. Just on principle.

"Of course. But, I got to warn you it won't be easy to get to Utah. This country isn't as friendly a place as it used to be."

"I'm sure, but at least they can try."

"So, you'll say yes."

"Yes."

"Excellent." He rose from his chair to shake my hand. I did the same. "Welcome back into the United States Army. Private Anderson."

"Thanks."

"What tents are your friends in?"

"Section CD. Tents thirty-six and thirty-seven."

He wrote it down on one of his Post-It notes.

Within thirty minutes of saying yes, and after a makeshift re-enlistment ceremony, I was in a truck headed to division headquarters. I had found a way out of the camp. Not the way I wanted, but at least my friends will be sent free to go as they please. While I was not looking forward to my time serving my country, a weight was lifted off my shoulders. My friends were free, and I would no longer have to worry and constantly think about our next move. My next move would be whatever orders I am given, and while I would miss my freedom, it will be nice to not have to worry about what's going to happen next.

Maybe when this is all over, I can find them again. In Utah? Maybe. Maybe someplace else. I just hope they understand why I did it, why I left them.

CHAPTER TWENTY-FIVE

11/28/2024 - 12/5/2024

In 2021, I joined the Army, and at the time I thought it was the rational and practical thing to do. It was a month after my mother's funeral. A week after Kaitlyn left for good or, as I now understand it, I left her. I had missed a month and a half of school and didn't want to go back. I didn't want to do anything. I wanted to wallow in my misery. But, I also knew that was suicide for me. Once I went down that path, I may never get back out. Drug addiction was not out of the question. Alcoholism? Yes, sir. I thought I could write a novel, but I knew that would be a disaster of depression. So, what was I to do? The Army would tell me what to do. I would lose myself in the structure. Turn my brain off for a few years. Help my country. It was a rational and practical thing to do. It was a rational and practical thing to do for a mind not thinking clearly.

After one week of basic training, I thought it was a mistake. I have a rebellious streak in me. A need to defy authority or at least question it. I did my best and still was reprimanded many times, for giving the wrong person a wrong look. I fought my instincts and eventually was rewarded with the structure and routine I so desired and more importantly an avenue to get out of my own head. I started to have fun again. Laughing with bunk mates late at night, during our little rebellious acts. It was not easy, but it didn't kill me, and by the time I left basic training I felt alive for the first time in many months.

Then I was assigned to Syria.

Now, in 2024, I was back in the Army, after a six-month reprieve, and as the truck approached the headquarters, I was nervous, yet optimistic. I may not have liked my time in the Army, but I was a good soldier, in fact, you could say I excelled at it. Like a student who finds Chemistry easy, it's just simple Math, yet wants to major in English.

"We're almost there," the young lady driving the truck said. I had been lost in my own head, taking a trip down memory lane, I completely forgot I was in the company of another human being.

"Okay," I said and turned to look at the driver. She had a striking face with sharp edges, black hair and dark skin, wearing the desert camo all the soldiers wore, with her hair pulled back tight against her head. She was small, maybe five-four, yet gave off the impression of strength.

"First day?" she asked.

"No," I said. "Not my first day. My third first day."

"Third deployment?"

"Something like that."

"Yeah. It's been confusing since the attack," she said and made a turn off the main road.

She said no more as we pulled up to a large ranch house, just north of the main road to the camp. The home or as I will now call it, headquarters, was a Spanish style estate that the military had confiscated. It was tucked away from the main road hidden in the desert landscape. As the truck pulled down the long driveway, I began to grow nervous again.

"Here we are," she said, stopping the truck in front of an impressive garage with the three wooden garage doors.

I opened the door and hopped out. "Thanks," I said.

"No problem," she said and gave me another half-smile. "My name is Lena. Wait. I mean Specialist Simpson." She handed out her hand to me leaning over the passenger seat. I took it.

"Nice to meet you, Specialist Simpson," I said. "Blake. Private Anderson." It still sounded strange, yet that was what I was called twenty-four-seven for three years.

"Private Anderson," she said, sitting back up and putting both hands on the wheel. "Better get in there, before they think I kidnapped you."

"That wouldn't be so bad," I said.

She rolled her eyes, and I closed the door. It felt good to flirt, especially with the zero possibility it would go anywhere. The truck pulled away, and I was left alone in the desert in front of a house, that would've been worth a couple million dollars anywhere else in California. Out here in the desert? Who knew what the real estate market was like now that the end of our country had proceeded? Why did I think about real estate?

I approached a wrought iron gate, opened it and entered a front patio area, in front of a large wooden door. The front door was part of a structure of the house that looked like a bastion from a medieval castle. I looked up at the windows on the second floor of the bastion and expected to see archers or at least someone with a French accent telling me to "go away." Instead, nothing, no sentries. Just the evening air and the exterior lights accentuating the curves and features of the home.

I knocked on the front door and waited. Nothing happened. I heard no footsteps or voices. Then again, this house seemed to be built of sturdy material. I knocked again, and this time I didn't wait and just opened the door. Slowly, I peeked inside and saw a man five feet from the entryway seated at a table working on a laptop. The home was dark except for the light from the entryways gaudy chandelier. To his right and behind him was a winding staircase that led to the upstairs of the home.

"Hello," I said as I entered, my voice echoing off the marble floor. The soldier at the desk looked up and looked as though he saw a ghost, then recognition spread across his face. Not recognition of me, but recognition of 'oh yeah, somebody was supposed to arrive this evening.'

"Yes. Yes," he said. "Come in."

I was still wearing my same jeans, black sweatshirt, and beanie and for the first time, I felt subconscious about it. "My name is Blake."

"Right. Sergeant Anderson."

"Sergeant?"

"Yes. Is that not right?" He looked down at his laptop and typed quickly, then paused to read whatever was on the screen. "It says here you are to train the new arrivals on camp procedures and any other training needed."

"I suppose so, but I was just a private before."

"I guess you've been promoted." He looked me over again. "Do you have your bags?"

"No, they are still in my tent."

"Your tent?"

"Yes, in the camp."

"You were in the camp?"

"Yes." Was that not in my file?

"Interesting," he said. "Well Sergeant Anderson, you will, obviously, be given new clothes anyways, so I guess it doesn't matter."

"Nope."

"Okay. Let me give you the tour."

The tour lasted ten seconds inside the house. To sum up; you are not allowed in the house. The house and land have been loaned to the Army, and the homeowners would appreciate it if a bunch of young soldiers didn't destroy it.

"The bigwigs, you know, can stay in the house, but for the rest of us, we are to stay out back in the compound," Specialists Lewis, my tour guide, said. He opened the sliding glass door that led to the back yard, which was what one would expect; pool, built-in barbecue, outdoor TV. But all the amenities were not what caught my attention. Past the iron fence encircling the back yard, stood a large tent community, like the camp that I just left. Soldiers were everywhere. Some were running what appeared to be laps around the camp. Some were waiting in line at the mess hall. It was a section of the camp, but for the Army.

On the left of the camp, was another section, but this did not look like anything at the camp or like anything I had seen before. "What's over there?" I asked as we stepped through the back fence and into the camp.

"That's the prison."

"The prison?"

"Sure," he said and continued his walk to the center row of trailers and trucks that separated the Army billet from the jail. Some trailers were food trailers like I had seen in the camp, but most were portable workstations. Multiple large trailers had satellite dishes on top.

The first trailer we entered, appeared to be the laundry room, where I was measured for my uniform and given Army sweatpants, t-shirt and a sweatshirt to wear. I was told I should change immediately, so I did.

"What size?" The man doing the measurements said while pointing at my boots.

"Ten," I said. He nodded and reached behind to a shoe rack and pulled a pair down for me.

"I should have the rest of your uniform for you later tonight," he said.

"Okay," I said. "Wait, I will also need some underwear." Both men looked at me, the guide and the tailor. "Unless someone wants to go back to my tent in the camp and get my bag."

"No. We will find you some," the tailor said.

Next stop: Procedures and assignments.

My day was to begin at 0700.

0715: Breakfast.

0740: Training exercises, which I was to lead and a procedure document to study.

0930: Study.

1035: Refugee camp scenario training, lecture only. No lab work.

1155: Lunch.

1300: Prison patrol.

1700: Dinner.

1900: Alternating between prison and main camp.

2200: Bed.

Yep, I was back in the Army alright.

I was shown to my tent and was told I was free to check out the compound. I laid down on the oh so familiar cot. I was alone. There was another cot in the tent, but I was the only one assigned to the tent at the time. I would have the whole place to myself. I looked up at the pole next to the opening flap. No television in here. The tent even had the same circular table with the light and heater.

The silence was striking. Nothing but the desert breeze. I sighed and found myself thinking I made a mistake. Some things never change. I looked at the document that was to be my studying for the night. Homeland Refugee Camp Policy and Procedures - United States Army. Dated: October, 2024. Three-hundred plus pages on how to run a refugee camp filled with United States citizens. I'm sure it was thoroughly engrossing, but I put it down on my lap and closed my eyes.

I missed my friends. They were probably on the way to Utah by now. I hope they stopped somewhere to get gas and stayed off the main highways. The children all bundled up in the back seat of Drew's SUV, Kaitlyn between them. Eating chips they found outside a gas station in Barstow. Zero, Jenna, and Ethan arguing over which way they should go. Zero saying he didn't give a fuck, as long as we go. Jenna, trying to get them to listen, but they just talk right over her. Ethan, explaining we should take the side roads and get off I-15. The walkie-talkies. The laughter. The fear. The cool, moist, truck windows. The warmth.

"Sergeant Anderson," a voice said, pulling me out of my dream.

I opened my eyes, another soldier, this one barely eighteen. "Yes," I said.

"Your uniform is ready."

"Thanks...and you are?"

"Private Gooding sir!" he said and went full salute mode.

"Excellent, Private Gooding."

Wearing my new uniform, the next morning at zero seven hundred hours, I found myself a sergeant, staring down five kids who, after the attacks, decided the best thing to do was join the Army. They all just turned eighteen and spent a whole week in Basic before being shipped out here to the high desert of California.

From left to right standing at attention facing me were the following contestants: Jack Jensen, from Tillamook, Oregon, tall, black hair, blue eyes and a permanent smile that made you want to puke. Thomas Grayson, from Des Moines, Iowa, medium build, blonde hair, brown eyes, and the demeanor of a rat in a cage. Noah Thompson, from London, Kentucky, brown hair, brown eyes and an accent that had the stars and bars dripping from every syllable. James Wesley, from Dallas, Texas, built like a Mack truck, black hair, brown eyes, a football player right off the production line. Finally, we had Riley Gooding, from Rexburg, Idaho, scrawny, dirty blonde, and a teacher's pet from the pound.

This was my charge. My squad. Those who I would be responsible for. There was a time when I did not understand the vitriol spewed by those in charge, during basic training. It only took me ten minutes in charge of this lot to understand. Standing in front of a bunch of cocky, eighteen year old's, really turns one into an asshole.

I spent the next week with them from sunrise to sunset. Every morning we re-did basic training; an hour run, an hour on the gun range, which was located at the far edge of the camp. An hour and a half of scenario training. Which was trying to reinforce the idea that you shouldn't shoot those in the camp. Two hours in the afternoon in groups of two, including myself, play-acting at prison guard. After dinner, it was either two hours at the jail or two hours walking the perimeter of the camp. Soon, once I gave the go-ahead, we would spend much of our time at the camp, only on the outside, of course, and a small time guarding the prisoners.

"How long till we can deploy them permanently?" Staff Sergeant Jones asked, one week after I started. The fifth day of December.

"At the camp?" I asked.

"Where the fuck else are we going to send them?"

"I don't know. Don't we have enough soldiers at the camp as it is?"

"Not nearly. We have one hundred thousand people in that camp and barely three-hundred soldiers worth a damn." One hundred thousand minus eight, I thought to myself happily. "So, we need you to get these five ready, before the next babies arrive and we can repeat this useless process."

"Give me another week, and I should get it through their thick skulls, that intimidation is more important in this scenario than action," I said. "Can't have them shooting everyone who looks at them funny."

My Staff Sergeant gave a quick laugh. "True. We've already had multiple flare-ups, and so far, I think we've done a damn fine job. But, it's going to get worse. Not only there but the prisoners as well."

"Where did all the prisoners come from?"

"From the camp. Most were identified as possible disruptors. So to speak. Gang members. Drug addicts. Multiple felony arrests. That sort of thing. They were picked up first, once the database was back up."

"So, they didn't do anything before they got here?"

"No, not all of them anyway, some of them. Some were taken because of what they did in the camp."

"Five hundred out of one hundred thousand isn't so bad."

"Oh, we have a whole list of others, but nowhere to put them. So, we just have the eye in the sky and the surveillance team to track them. We have about one hundred empty cells, strictly for those that act out in camp and after that, I don't know what we can do. Especially, since the camp is just going to get worse."

"Why's that?" I said. I knew why, but I wanted to verify my thinking.

"You were in the camp right?" he asked, and I nodded. "For two weeks? You had three meals a day and two showers?" I nodded in confirmation. "Well, that is about to change. The water supply was temporary, so the showers will soon be over. The food is a donation from the Red Cross and other organizations. And that can't last forever. There is already talk about cutting that back to twice a day."

"It was never meant to be permanent," I said, more to myself than him.

"Damn right, but, unfortunately, no one has any idea what to do. At least that's the impression I get from the Lieutenant." He paused and looked off into the distance, as the sun set and before I was to walk the prison, with my squad. "Just get them ready and yourself as well."

"I will," I said.

"Where are you from Sergeant?" Private Gooding asked while we were walking between a row of prison cells. The cells looked more like large dog crates, with one cot, and a small porta-potty, the kind you would find at a camping store like Bass Pro Shop, nothing more than a bucket with a toilet seat on top, and a tarp for a roof. A six by ten space, fit for a dog and I suppose, now for human beings. I tried to not think about the injustice of this. There was no judge, or jury for these poor souls. I understood the logic behind removing the bad apples from the crate before they destroyed the batch, but this seemed, well, un-American.

"I'm from Rancho Cucamonga," I said.

"Where's that?" The young soldier, Private Gooding said, with the air of a scholar in desert camo.

"Right over those mountains," I said and pointed. The one thing I stressed to these young men in the past week, was, while at the camp or here at the make-shift prison, you were not soldiers. You were guardians. Lethal force was only necessary for extreme circumstances. Use the uniform to intimidate. Never use your weapon. This is all antithetical to a soldier, but it's the only thing that I could add, that was unique and different, from what they learned in the military and read in the verbose procedure document.

"That's right, I heard you were in the camp."

"Yep. I was."

"What was that like?" he asked.

"Like being in a refugee camp, only with sitcoms on TV," I said. Gooding, it seemed, could not decipher if I was joking or not.

"For real," he said, and I just laughed and continued my walk. "There were TV's?"

"Yes, they installed them the day-"

"Blake!" a voice said to my left. A voice I recognized and hoped I had misheard. I turned to the cell where the voice came from and in the early evening light, helped by bulbs overhead, I saw a blonde-haired man lying on the cot. He stood up, and I realized, in horror, that it was, in fact, a voice I knew. The man who was one of my closest friends. A man who should not be here. Zero.

CHAPTER TWENTY-SIX

12/5/2024 - 12/10/2024

No. This wasn't happening. He was supposed to be long gone. They all were. If he was here, did that mean Kaitlyn? Jenna? Drew? Alicia? The Children? Ethan? That can't be. He promised me.

"Blake?" Zero asked, standing at the door to his cage.

"What are you doing here?" I asked.

"What am I doing here? What the fuck are you doing here?" Zero said. Then gave me a look up and down. "You know, besides being in the fucking Army."

I laughed, I couldn't help it. "No, I mean. Why are you here?"

"I went looking for you. We thought they took you."

"What?" I said. This made no sense.

"You disappeared. We all started asking around." All of them? "I eventually got fed up with all their bullshit and got into it with some jock asshole at the main entrance," Zero said. "I got a few punches in, then the next thing I know, there were." He stopped and smiled. "Well, there were some douchebags who look just like you do now, all over the damn place and I was handcuffed, a bag placed over my head, and here I am. I thought they were just gonna execute me. After all the rumors going round. Woke up here a few hours ago."

"You're not supposed to be here," I said.

"I just told you."

"No. I mean you were supposed to be let go. I made a deal."

"A deal? Let go?"

"No one came and talked to any of you?"

"Nope. We just thought you disappeared."

"Motherfucker!"

"Sergeant?" Gooding asked from behind me. I forgot he was still there.

"I need you to go on. I will catch up with you later," I said. Gooding hesitated. "Now Private!" He turned quickly and continued on. I shouldn't leave him alone. We're supposed to be in pairs.

"Sergeant?" Zero said as he gave me a cockeyed look.

"Yeah."

"That's good for you."

"Not so much. Now. I need to get you out of here."

"How?"

"I don't know. But, I will think of something."

"Well, at least I finished what I set out to do." He gave a half-smile. "Found out what happened to your ugly ass."

"Damn, I missed you," I said.

"It's only been a week."

"Seems longer."

"Yep. Everyone's getting anxious. I don't know how much longer I could take it."

"You like it here better?"

"At least here, I know where I stand. Those smiling FEMA people were beginning to freak me the fuck out."

"Yeah," I said. Not much else to say, besides. "I'm sorry."

"Bah. Fuck it. If you thought joining the Army. Again. Was gonna get us out, then that makes sense. But, it makes you wonder who you're dealing with. Fucker's gonna play with you like that."

"I, technically, didn't have a choice. I'm still property of Uncle Sam. For another three years. I told them, if they didn't let you guys out, I would rather be thrown in jail then join up."

"So he fed you some bullshit lie and you signed up."

"Something like that," I said, ashamed at my naivete. My cockiness. They needed me? They only needed another body to do as they say. I calmed myself and asked, "How is everyone?"

"Alright, I guess," Zero said and shrugged. "Oh. Jenna found her dickhead boyfriend, so they've been hanging out. I think Ethan is pissed, but he won't talk about it."

"Aaron?" I asked, even though I already knew.

"Yeah. He's such a douche," Zero said, and we both laughed.

"Look. I'm gonna get you out of here. One way or another," I said.

"How?"

"I don't know. But, we are not staying here any longer than we need to."

"We?"

"Yep. I ain't staying here any longer either. They lied to me. Fuck em."

"That's my Blake."

"**N**ope. Not gonna happen," Sergeant Brown said. The man in charge of the prison.

"Why not? I can vouch for him" I said.

"Vouch for him? What do you think this is? The mafia? He punched a FEMA volunteer, then resisted arrest."

"Come on, you know we all want to punch some of the FEMA workers."

Brown laughed. "That's the truth. But, it doesn't change anything. I don't even have the power to enact such a release, even if I wanted to. Sorry Sergeant. I can't help you."

I spent the next three days doing everything in my power, to try and find a way out for Zero and myself. To the Army, I acted no different than the previous week. I did my training and gave the go-ahead for my squad to be assigned at the camp. I was stuck with them until the new recruits arrived, then they would be passed on to another squad. We were assigned a shift to patrol the perimeter of the camp from 11 p.m. to 4 a.m. It wasn't ideal, but I used the free time during the late afternoon, before I went to bed at 5 p.m., to scout the compound. There was only one problem, even though this version of the Army seemed to be less organized, concerning top-down communication, it was still highly organized. Everything you did was categorized, and surveillance was everywhere. I had no idea how to make an escape.

I spent most of lunch and dinner with Zero, along with fifty other inmates. I got some wide-eyed looks from a few of the soldiers at the compound when I grabbed lunch from the regular side of camp and then walked over to the prison side to sit with Zero. Zero and I would sit and eat, then talk for a good thirty minutes, as the prisoners were given thirty minutes after lunch for exercise. For a prison, it was slack. Then again, these weren't prison guards walking around, but trained, well, sort-of trained, soldiers. The prisoners hardly ever gave much trouble.

It was during this time that Zero updated me on the camp situation. Everyone was making the best of it, but he could tell tension was growing. Kaitlyn was quiet and spent most of her time with the children, Natalie and Jane. Drew, Alicia, and Kaitlyn spent most of the time together in the tent, leaving Ethan, Zero, Jenna, and Aaron, to see them only during the hours for food. Ethan wasn't happy when Jenna and Aaron met again, so Zero spent most of the time with him.

"He, sort of changed," Zero said.

"How?" I asked, sitting at a table in the prison mess hall, on Saturday, the seventh of December.

"Moody as hell. I think we all were, but with him, it was a night and day difference. I knew he always had a crush on her."

"He had a crush on Jenna?" I asked.

"Where the fuck you been?" Zero said. "I mean I know you haven't been around, but yeah, since high school."

After some more discussion on the well-being of my friends, I began to wonder about Zero himself. A few times, I caught him staring off into the distance and then I would say something, and it was like a light switch went on and he was back to being Zero. His incarceration was beginning to take effect on him, and I knew I had to get him out soon.

"I'm still working on getting you out of here," I said. "I just. I just haven't figured it out yet."

"I know."

I got up and prepared to leave, as the bell to end dinner went off and said, "Be aware and ready, it may happen at any time. At any moment."

"Don't you worry about that. You say go, and I'm fucking gone."

By Sunday, the eighth of December, I had begun to get depressed, and the lack of sleep wasn't helping. I would spend my night along with one hundred other soldiers patrolling the edge of camp in the early morning hours. When our shift was done, the morning shift of a hundred soldiers came. Five shifts of one hundred soldiers, with overlap during the lunch and dinner periods. After my shift, I would return to the compound via transport trucks.

I never did see the lovely Specialist Simpson, again. There were times when I did think about her. What was she a specialist in? Driving Ford trucks? In fact, I never saw that truck again. I spent most of my time driven by men, who looked just as happy to be here as I was.

On returning from the camp, we went to the Armory trailer to turn in the M4A1 rifle. Which was like checking out a library book. Every time you checked out the automatic rifle, you were responsible for it, and a GPS system tracked you and the gun. If there was ever a discrepancy, you were in deep shit, to say the least. Why the checking out of weapons, from a central hub? It seemed there was a shortage, so they had to recycle the rifles. Maybe because the National Guard stole their weapons as well. Supposedly, more were coming, but there, again, we ran into some communication issues with Washington or wherever the big bosses were located now. At least we all had our own M17 handguns, which was a SIG Sauer P320 automatic. Again, GPS embedded in the gun, as well as somewhere in our uniform meant you could not be more than ten feet from your weapon at any time without a big red light flashing somewhere at the compound and you were in deep shit. The handgun was either on you or in your locker at the small armory lockers at the end of each row of tents. No weapons allowed in the tents themselves.

After my shift in the morning, I would walk the compound. At ten, would resume the lecture training. Lunch. Range training. Dinner. Then bed. I saw nothing to raise my hopes. Everything was locked down.

Oh, I imagined many ways we could pull it off. But, most of them made me out to be Rambo, and while I counted myself a decent shot, that route would end up with many people dead, including Zero and myself. While I hated the Colonel for lying to me, I had nothing against the men and women wearing the uniform working with me. Would I kill any one of them to save Zero's life? I would think so. Would I kill them to get him out of a prison cell? No. Probably not. I would just have to bide my time. Hope something happened that would provide an opportunity.

On Monday, December ninth, approximately ten in the evening, that opportunity appeared. I was awoken from sleep by a loud siren going off. It reverberated throughout the compound. Then an announcement, "All personnel needs to report to the Transport area. This is an emergency situation. Please see your squad leader and head to the transport area. This is not a drill."

By the time the announcement repeated I was dressed and ready to go. Private's Jensen and Gooding burst into my tent right as I was putting my boots on, over my tired feet.

"What's going on?" Private Gooding asked.

"It's an emergency, Private Gooding," I said, trying to remain calm. This was it. This was my chance. "Something's going down at the camp."

"What?" Private Jensen asked. Fucking moron.

"How the hell do I know? I was sleeping like the rest of you," I said, as I grabbed my tactical helmet and placed it on my head. "Get the rest of the squad and meet me outside as you would be for a shift at the camp, in one minute."

"Yes sir," They said simultaneously and left the tent as quickly as they came in.

Twenty seconds later, all were accounted for just outside my tent. One thing I will say for them, they cared, and they were ready to go.

"First, we go to the central armory. Hopefully, they still have some big guns for us. Then we go." They all stood looking at me wide-eyed. "Let's go."

We turned at a nice trot to the large Armory, which was located right next to the transport area, on the southern side of the house. It was a long concrete driveway probably used for storing an R.V. or a large boat. Outside the central armory, we found a long line of soldiers. But, it went quickly. In an emergency, checking out the weapons was, apparently, unnecessary. I smiled. This was just getting better and better.

After ten minutes in line, I was handed an M4A1 by an old man, I had never seen before. Maybe he didn't know these were all supposed to be checked out. He had the insignia on his shoulder of Captain. I almost laughed. So, this was the captain. I had not met him once since I had arrived.

"What do you need Sergeant, you're holding up the line?" he said, with a distinctly Northeastern accent.

"Do you have any of those stun guns left, I prefer not shooting U.S. citizens?" I said, and the old Captain looked me over.

"Well, you may need to. But, yes, I have a few," he said and handed me one.

"Thanks," I said and grabbed the tiny, small, felt like a toy, stun gun. This was the same model I saw used in the camp by FEMA workers. I had seen them, on the shelves, but never saw anyone check one out before.

I was then rushed outside and met up with my squad. They were in line for one of the transport trucks, that had just returned. All around me the soldiers were talking. Rumors flying.

"Sounds like the whole camp exploded. People rioting," A soldier, I did not know, said, in front of me.

Just as we were about to hop in the back of the truck, I stopped. Private Jensen had already climbed aboard.

"Shit," I said. "I will have to catch up with you there."

"What do you mean?" Private Jensen asked.

"I have to grab something," I said. Jensen, Grayson, and Thompson were now in the truck. "Go on. If we somehow don't meet up. Latch on to one of the squads and tell them what happened. Oh, and try not to shoot someone."

They all looked like I had told them Santa Claus wasn't real. For a second, I did feel sorry, but I had bigger fish to fry. I nodded at the five of them, turned around and ran back to the main compound and headed toward the makeshift prison.

As I came around the main trailers separating the soldiers from the jail, I slowed down to a walk. I had to be careful now. The last thing I needed was someone wondering why I was headed in the wrong direction. I was working on blind hope, that there would be no one manning the GPS tracking post and the fact that one soldier was not on his way to the camp would not be noticed, or even if it was, I had to believe no one would care. They had bigger fish to fry as well.

I arrived at the outer cells and noticed all the prisoners were awake and standing around, talking amongst themselves. One asked me what was going on, I said I don't know. Other's seemed to be worried about their families, since they, rightly, made the connection that an emergency alarm like that meant something was going down at the main camp.

At the center of the prison block, was a small tarp-covered canopy, where Sergeant Brown was stationed. He was the one that monitored the soldiers coming and going. The prison intake. The lunch schedules and most importantly, the locking and unlocking of the doors to each cell.

I made my way north so that I could approach from behind. I saw no other soldiers. All troops in an emergency were to head to the camp. The prisoners were behind bars at this time of night. Nothing to worry about.

I crept up behind the small station and saw multiple monitors set up with night vision so the warden could see all sections of the prison, even at night. Brown sat in a large office chair and was reading a book by the overhanging lights, that wound their way around the canopy's roof. I hesitated. I didn't know how to unlock just one cell so I would need him to cooperate.

I slung the assault rifle off my shoulder and carried it in both hands, left hand on the grip, right hand on the trigger. On my left hip was the stun gun. Right hip, the pistol.

As I crept closer, he heard me and spun around in his chair. "Hey, what are you doing still here? Didn't you hear the announcement?" I stepped into the light, from the evening darkness. "Sergeant Anderson?"

"I need you to open a cell," I said.

"What?"

"You heard me."

"Which one?"

"You know which one."

"You should know I can't do that," he said and rose from his chair. His hands began to move ever so slightly to his hip. I raised the rifle and pointed it right at him.

"You can."

"Maybe. But, I ain't."

"It's just one cell. You open it and were gone. Never to be heard from again. You can tell them what happened. You won't get in trouble."

"True. I won't be the one in trouble."

"I need you to do this now."

"Not gonna happen."

"I will shoot you."

"Will you? Then you would be in a heap of trouble."

"Just do it. Now!" I said, stepping closer to him.

"Not gonna happen. You can do it yourself," Brown said. Then he made a move with his right hand to his pistol. I had expected this. I dropped my left hand off the rifle as soon as I saw the movement, pulled the stun gun from my hip and fired before he could get his gun out of his holster. No sound, just a light yell from Brown as he slumped out of his chair shaking.

"Fuck!" I yelled. I went over to him and grabbed both of his pistols and put them on the table.

"You ass-sshole," he said, with tremors still running through him.

"Tell me how to open the cell."

"F-F-Fuck you."

"Alright then," I said and looked at his central computer. This can't be too difficult, but I just don't have the time. We need to be gone. There was a main system menu: Prisoners, Blocks, Schedule, Army. I clicked on Blocks. Locks or Lights. I clicked on Locks. Unlock Prisoner or Unlock Block. Oh shit. After all this time. I did not know which cell number Zero was in or even which block. I knew where the cell was, but not the details. That's when it dawned on me.

"What are you doing?" Brown said, behind me up on one knee, watching me.

I turned to him and smiled, "What I have to?" His eyes grew wide as I clicked unlock block. I heard a loud clank to the left. Block six was open. Ten Blocks total. I would have to open them all, and I realized that's what I needed to do anyway to secure our escape.

"Stop!" Brown yelled and reached for me. I grabbed the stun gun again and shot him. He went down quick, whimpering and shaking. Block Five. Click. Block Four. Click. Okay, I figured out the pattern. I heard shouting and people running.

"Cell block three it should be," I said aloud. I listened to the unlocking of the cells from the row Zero was imprisoned. I shot Brown one last time with the stun gun, to give me some more breathing room. He called me an asshole again, and I took off running toward Zero's cell.

As I moved down cell block three, prisoners of all shapes and sizes were emerging from their cages. They shied away from me as I approached.

"Zero!" I yelled. From twenty yards down on the left, I heard the response.

"Blake!"

I saw him standing outside his dog crate, with a huge smile on his face.

"You ready?" I said as I approached.

He was still looking around, in a state of shock, as a group of people ran by us, keeping a wide birth of the two of us. "You did this?"

"Of course," I said and handed him the stun gun. "Take this. If anyone gets in our way. Use it." He held it away from his body. "It's just a stun gun."

"Like the ones the FEMA assholes used on me?"

"Yep."

"Nice."

"Now. Can you run?"

"Hell yeah. Ever since I quit smoking a month ago," he said, with that Zero smirk.

"Then let's get the fuck out of here."

We ran. Ran into the desert night.

CHAPTER TWENTY-SEVEN

12/10/2024

"Which way," Zero asked, bent over, hands upon his knees, trying to catch his breath, in the middle of nowhere. After escaping, we ran through the desert for ten minutes straight. Over desert brush, rocks and unidentifiable obstacles. Thankfully, a half-moon overhead projected just enough light to see large objects. We settled at a slow trot, as it was no use escaping only to break an ankle or leg. At first, many prisoners ran with us into the desert, but they weaved their own route, and now it was just the two of us.

"Keep heading the way we're headed," I said, also breathing heavy. That direction, I believed, was southwest. "We should see the camp lights shortly." It was only a ten-minute drive from the Army compound to the main camp, but that was a twisted route via the main road. I figured if we cut through the desert in a straight line we would be there in twenty minutes at this pace.

"As you say, boss," Zero said.

We ran a short distance further when a slight glow began to materialize to our left on the horizon. I grabbed Zero by the shoulder and pointed. Then, as the light grew brighter, we heard, what sounded like firecrackers, popping off, intermittently, in the distance. With the destination in sight, we ran as quickly as we could, our boots kicking up the desert dirt as we went. After five minutes of hard running, the camp appeared below us, just as we crested a small ridge. More gunshots, intermingled with screaming voices, echoing across the desert. As we descended the hill, we found ourselves in the parking lot for the camp. I kneeled behind a car and caught my breath, Zero followed suit.

"Here's the plan, you get to your truck, get it running and ready to go," I said. "I will find the group and bring them to you."

"Umm. I don't have my keys."

"Can you hotwire it?"

"What do you think I am? Some master thief?"

"Damn Zero, we need a vehicle to get out of here," I said. Why didn't I think about keys before now? "Are they in the tent?"

"No. They took them when we arrived."

"Fuck. We need that truck. We're running out of time."

"I got it. I will have the truck ready."

"How?"

"I have a spare key in the wheel well somewhere," he said, and I raised my fist to punch him in the arm. "What? I forgot."

"Okay, whatever, just get it running. Stay back here along this back row. This is-" I looked at the lights surrounding the camp and counted, starting at the east edge of the camp. "Light number ten, count to twenty-four and your car should be somewhere along that row."

"Got it."

"Good luck."

"You too," he said. Then with that wry, Zero smile, turned and ran off into the night.

I began making my way west, hiding behind cars. I snaked my way through the parking lot. I could hear an array of commotion in the camp, but nothing I could see, even though the exterior lights were shining at full power. The lights were supposed to be at half power after ten, but I guess not on this night. At light number fifteen, I saw the entrance gate, that lead onto the auxiliary road that ran along the outside of the camp. I approached the gate and put on my soldier face. Opened the gate and ran across the road to the inner fence and its gate. That gate was open as well, which surprised me, these were usually locked. I entered the camp. I could hear shouting more clearly now. The center of the camp, with all the FEMA trailers and trucks, was to my left. A small glow emanated from the middle of the camp. A fire maybe.

I turned and ran to my right. Past Section BH.

Hurried through section BI.

I saw no other soldiers. A group of people, ran in my direction, toward the fence. They turned and began to climb the fence as I approached them. They stopped dead in their tracks when they saw me in my Army uniform. A man clung to the fence, halfway to the top, like a lizard on a desert wall. I ignored them and ran on.

Section CB.

One more section and I was there. I kept my rifle at the ready as I ran. On my right, I saw some soldiers running the opposite direction on the road between the fences. Probably to stop those trying to escape.

Section CC.

I turned down the mess hall path. Ten rows of CC.

Section CD. Row 3.

I was there. I ran down the row. More people got out of my way. All quickly returning to their tent at my sight. I didn't care.

Tents thirty-six and thirty-seven.

I burst into tent thirty-six… and was immediately punched in the face. My legs buckled.

"Blake!" I heard Jenna yell.

I looked up at Jenna, Aaron, and Ethan. All looking like they saw a ghost, mouths open, eyes wide.

"Sorry man," Aaron said and was trying to help me up. I stood and tried to catch my breath. "I didn't mean… I thought you were…Well, I guess you are."

I tried not to laugh. "I guess we're even now," I said while rubbing my jaw.

Jenna jumped into my arms. Ethan came up and gave me a hug as soon as Jenna pulled away.

"I appreciate the warm welcome, but we have to go now," I said once the air was back in my lungs.

"Go?" Aaron said.

"What's going on?" Ethan asked.

"The camp is falling apart as you can hear," I said. A loud gunshot went off not far from us. "See."

"Fuck me," Ethan said.

"You have one minute, then were gone," I said, when Kaitlyn, Drew, Alicia and the children came into the tent.

"What?" Drew said. I turned around.

"Blake!" Kaitlyn said, and for the second time in twenty seconds, a beautiful woman jumped into my arms.

"Blake, what are you…?" Alicia asked. "What happened?"

"No time to explain."

"At least give us something?" Drew said.

"Joined Army. Broke Zero out of prison. Zero is at the truck. We are leaving in one minute," I said with Kaitlyn still in my arms.

"Well. Okay then," Ethan said.

"Zero is okay?" Drew asked.

"For now," I said. "Look I know everyone has questions, but we have to go."

Everyone began packing bags. No suitcases, backpacks only. Drew's family, along with Kaitlyn went to tent thirty-seven. I found my backpack in the corner. Grabbed some underwear, and threw a pair of dirty pants inside along with a long sleeve t-shirt, and my only coat. I left everything else.

Outside, the sound of gunfire grew louder, as I waited for everyone. It took two minutes, but eventually, they were all outside.

Alicia handed me *The Hobbit* and said, "Don't want to forget this."

"Thanks," I said and slid the backpack off my back and jammed the book inside. I stood up readjusted my rifle and helmet and said, "There is a gate to the west of here. It may be locked, but that's where we're headed. If it's locked, I'll break it. Ethan, Aaron and I up front. Then Jenna, Kaitlyn. The Children, Alicia and Drew at the rear. If you have to carry them," I said, pointing at the crying and scared children. "Carry them. No matter what happens, we must keep going. This place is going to get nasty soon, we need to get out now."

They all looked at me, and I realized how scared they were. I had spent the last two weeks with soldiers. Now, I was back with my friends, and I needed them to understand the stakes, even just a little.

"Let's go," I said, and we headed off.

The chaos had grown in the last five minutes. People running, going in all directions. Rapid gunfire was heard, thankfully it came from the opposite direction we were headed. Ethan, Aaron and I began to get ahead of the rest of the group. So, I slowed down a bit, the rest followed suit.

"We need to pick up the pace," I said.

"I know," Alicia said, but she was struggling with Natalie who was crying intensely and thrashing in her mother's arms.

I stopped and went back to her. Aaron and Ethan stopped as well, but I waved them on. "When you get to the fence wait for us." They turned to run on. "Wait," I yelled, and they turned around. A group of five men ran by us almost knocking Kaitlyn to the ground. "Take this," I said as I handed my handgun to Ethan. "The safety's off," I stated with a smile. Ethan took the gun and ran along with Aaron and Jenna followed. I motioned to Alicia. "Give Natalie to Drew." To Drew. "I will take Jane." Drew handed me Jane. Alicia handed the crying Natalie to Drew. "How you doing?" I said to Jane. She didn't say anything. "You ready to go home?"

"Really?" she asked.

"Yes, but we need to go, so hold on real tight. Okay?"

"Okay."

I ran ahead, Drew behind me. Alicia and Kaitlyn at our sides. Another group almost collided with us and were about to yell something when I pointed my rifle, now held in my left arm, at them, Jane in my right arm. They took off south into the night.

We finally emerged from section CC into the dirt warning track ten yards from the interior fence. Twenty yards to my left I spotted Ethan, Aaron, and Jenna, standing against the fence. They saw us and pointed.

We ran to meet up with them.

Also to the left, forty yards down, I saw two soldiers heading toward the unaware cluster at the fence. I slowed, put Jane down and pointed. "Behind you!"

The soldiers were already aimed at the group at the fence. I pulled my M4A1 level and ran. Ethan turned around with the gun in his hand.

Just as I arrived, I felt a warm mist of moisture spray across my face and heard the automatic rifle. To my right, Ethan, Jenna and Aaron all collapsed.

Ethan had lost the side of his face.

Aaron was gurgling blood from a neck wound.

Jenna was crying, hands over her head, on the ground between them.

"He had a gun," I heard the soldier say.

I closed my eyes. I recognized that voice.

"Sergeant Anderson?"

I turned, they were ten feet in front of me, gun raised and for a split second, the shock of recognition made them lower their weapons just enough. I rose my weapon, aimed and pulled the trigger. Twice in quick succession. I shot both Private Gooding and Private Jensen before they knew what happened.

It was quick. Like most horrible things. I went over to where Gooding and Jensen lay. Jensen was bleeding from the neck, but still alive, blood bubbling around his gasping lips. Gooding was dead from a bullet wound through the forehead, his helmet hung slightly askew on his head. His eyes wide open staring into nothingness.

"Helppmmm," Jensen tried to say. Arms outstretched reaching out to me, grabbing my leg.

"Sorry," I said and shot him in the head.

CHAPTER TWENTY-EIGHT

12/10/2024

I felt nothing. I should have. I didn't.

I grabbed Jensen's weapons. Put the pistol on my left hip, in the band of my pants. Slung the rifle over my left shoulder, turned around and went back to where Jenna and the rest were crying over the bodies of Ethan and Aaron.

Ethan's right side of his face was gone. The bullet entered his left cheek and exploded out the right side of his face. Bone and brain matter littered the chain-link fence behind him.

My best friend, from the age of five, was dead.

Killed by soldiers, I had trained.

I reached up to my face and with my index finger ran it down the side of my cheek and looked at the blood that must be covering my face.

Aaron was dead as well. He bled out from the neck wound.

Jenna was crying in between them. Alicia and Kaitlyn were trying to get her up.

"Jenna, are you hit?" I asked. No response. I knelt next to her and did a cursory pat down to make sure she had not been shot. She had not.

I heard more gunshots to the south. I stood up.

"We have to go," I said. They looked at me like I spoke a foreign language.

"Blake, what did you do?" Kaitlyn asked.

"What I had to. We need to go."

Jenna kept whimpering on the ground, saying, "No... No... No..."

"Kaitlyn, help me get her up." I reached down to Jenna.

"No. Leave me be!" she yelled.

"We need to go!" I yelled right back. I grabbed her by her arm and pulled her up. She just slumped in my arms like a bag of sand.

The children were back in their parent's arms, both parents had a hand on the back of each child's head forcing their faces away from the bodies.

"Kaitlyn, grab her other arm. Help me, or we all end up like this!" I pulled Jenna's left arm around my shoulder. Kaitlyn lifted her right side and put Jenna's right arm around her neck.

We began to move. Leaving the two bodies behind.

Jenna just kept crying in between whispering, "No." But, she slowly began to walk. It took ten minutes, but we eventually reached the gate. It was open. Others in the camp went through just as we arrived, two teenagers who were just as surprised as we were at the gate being open. They went through laughing.

Drew and Alicia walked through, children in hand, followed by Kaitlyn and me, guiding the weeping Jenna. Across the dirt road, we went, to the outer fence and through that open gate. Then just as quickly entered the parking lot.

"Hold up here," I said, helping Jenna to the ground behind a 1990s Plymouth. Hiding in the shadows cast by the cars we all sat down and caught our breath. The children still wrapped around their parents. Kaitlyn had her arm around Jenna. I stood up and looked at the camp. I saw more people trying to climb the fence and into the parking lot.

"Zero should be at his truck about ten rows down," I said, pointing to the east. "Stay low and move quickly between the rows, when I give the go-ahead." I looked at Kaitlyn who now had Jenna's head on her chest, right arm around her. "Kaitlyn, you got Jenna?" Kaitlyn nodded an affirmative. "I will lead." I stood up, keeping my head low. "Let's go."

I ran across the lane. They followed.

Around a 2020 Honda Civic.

A Minivan.

Across another lane.

We kept moving. Zig-zagging our way through the parking lot.

There was a loud crack of gunfire. Everyone jumped. I put my hand up to tell everyone to stop. I looked around the edge of a Toyota truck toward the camp. I saw tents, but no people. I motioned everyone on. To my right, as we crossed another lane of cars, we reached light twenty four, or at least I hoped it was.

"Okay, I'm going to head out and find Zero's truck. It's somewhere in this vicinity. Stay here. Stay quiet." They all nodded. Sitting in the dirt, they all kept their gaze low, not looking at me.

I took off across the lane and began winding my way north through the static automobiles. The further north the less light from the camp. Scanned left, then right, until I spotted the truck and seated in the driver's seat, head on a swivel, was Zero. I smiled and ran back to the group.

"This way. Hurry, we are almost there," I said and, again, they followed without resistance.

When we reached Zero's truck from behind, I knocked on the back of the truck, and Zero nearly jumped out of his seat. He looked at me from the rear-view mirror.

"Fuck yeah!" he said. I knocked out the brake lights in the back of the truck with my rifle, sending shards of broken taillight into the dirt. "Hey!" Zero said. But, I ignored him.

Drew opened the passenger door, and I kept a lookout. First in was Alicia with Jane, followed by Natalie and Kaitlyn. Jenna crawled in, eyes wide, catatonic, as she sat in the front passenger seat.

"Drew, back here with me," I said.

"Wait, where's Ethan?" Zero asked.

"Not coming," Drew said, quietly.

"Why? What happened?"

"He's dead," Jenna said, with an eerie drone.

Zero looked back at me as I was getting into the truck and I just nodded. His face turned down ever so slightly, then turned back around to the job at hand.

Drew hopped into the back of the truck bed. I opened the window at the back of the cab. "Go left around the back of the parking lot. Keep the lights off and go slowly."

"Yes sir," Zero said.

Zero pulled out, and I sat down. I kept an eye toward the camp as Zero crept the truck down the lane, headed north into the desert. I looked over at Drew who was reaching through the small window to pet Natalie's head, where the kids sat between Kaitlyn and Alicia.

"I may need your help," I said.

"With what?" Drew replied.

I held the second automatic rifle at him. His face balked. "Look. We may not need them, but just in case." He took it like it was made of fragile glass. "Just keep it down for now," I said, and Drew nodded.

"Blake were almost to the end of the parking lot," Zero said. "I think. It's getting harder to see."

"Okay once we do, make a right and skirt along the last cars as close as you can."

"Right," Zero replied. His face reflected in the rear-view mirror was concentrating deeply, biting his right lower lip as he drove. He slowed, almost to a stop, and turned right. A bump lifted the car on its left side, and we kept going, slow. Agonizingly slow. Ten minutes had passed before we came to the east end of the parking lot.

"Now what?" Zero asked. I looked toward the front of the camp. I saw multiple cars trying to pass through the front gate. People excited to leave and ignorant enough to follow the road would be caught. The road that leads out of the parking lot and onto the main street that brought us here and would take us back to the 15 freeway. That lone road went inside the camp and through the main entrance, and that was closed by a large gate that now was surrounded by multiple Army transport trucks and theoretically a hundred Army soldiers.

"This a four-wheel drive, right?" I asked.

"You want me to drive into the desert."

"Yep. That's the only way out. Not long, maybe a hundred yards."

"With the lights, off?"

"Yep."

"Alrighty then," Zero said with a terrible Texas accent, "Buckle up everyone, it's gonna get a mighty bumpy out in them there desert."

Drew and I looked at each other. I grabbed, with my left hand, the side of the truck. Drew did the same and grabbed the right.

"We all set?" Zero asked.

"I guess so," Alicia said. I gave thumbs up and off we went into the desert.

Dirt flew into the air as Zero picked up speed. At the first big bump, I had to grab the side of the truck with both hands.

"You alright back there," Zero asked.

"Don't worry about us," I said.

Another significant bump and Drew almost flew out. Zero was picking up more speed.

"Slow down," Alicia yelled.

"I can't we have to keep our momentum, or we can get stuck in the sand," Zero said.

Another bump, a loud scraping sound that emanated underneath the truck and a quick right turn, which almost sent Drew into my lap. But he held on.

"Fuck," Zero said.

Drew trying to right himself stopped and pointed back toward the camp. I saw two pairs of headlights heading down the main road to the south of us. I nodded. The transport vehicles sped by on the road, headed back to the Army compound and over the crest at the top of the valley.

"Zero, turn right and head toward the road," I said.

"Where's the road?"

"Just turn right and if we hit the ridge. Turn right some more."

After more dips and turns and Drew telling me he was going to be sick, we reached the edge of the desert beside the road. My eyesight had adjusted to the darkness, and I could hear everyone breathing heavy.

Zero crept the truck onto the road and made a left.

"Stay slow," I said. "Only if you see another car behind us, do you take off."

"Gotcha," he said.

The road felt smooth as silk after the last half hour.

"Okay I need you to keep an eye on the back," I said to Drew.

"And you?" he asked.

"I got the front," I said, and I stood up with my assault rifle and laid it on the top of the cab, getting an unobstructed view of all that was in front of us.

We drove on, Zero kept the speed at twenty miles per hour, and I kept watch.

We ran into no one. I saw no more military vehicles. Nothing, but the desert road. We all took turns trying to remember which way to the 15, and hopefully not traveling in circles as the roads weaved every which way.

After a right turn and as the road curved to the right the 15 freeway appeared before us on our left. It looked like a black river, still and reflective in the evening light. We were on the side road that ran parallel to the freeway. I could not remember if this was the same path we arrived on, but it didn't matter.

Huge lights suddenly came into focus a half mile down on the freeway underneath an overpass. Ten portable mobile light tower's scattered across the freeway five each on the north and southbound lanes casting their light to the north.

"Zero stop," I said, and he slammed on his brakes. "You see that?"

"Yeah," he said. "What now?"

I looked to my right and saw an industrial building. There was a sign out front that was twenty feet in the air, towering next to the idling truck. It was a dark mass and made me think of the Welles tripods, in *War Of The Worlds*. It read: Solar Energy High Desert, Inc.

"Blake?" Drew asked. He was still sitting in the back looking up at me. I looked down.

I wished we were fighting Martians.

"Just keep moving, slowly," I said. "Until we can find a way around."

We pulled forward. Crawling. We passed a turn off on the right. Everyone seemed to be holding their breath. The only sound was that of wheels on the pavement. The children were awake but in shock. Their worst nightmare roller-coaster had been brought to life.

As we got closer to the lights, I could see they were the same style of lights at the camp.

"Stop," I said. Zero again slammed on the breaks. "It's a barricade. Stopping all southbound traffic."

"What does that mean?" Alicia asked.

"Nothing if there are no soldiers at the barricade or around the off-ramps. This is where we got off to go to the camp. The Summit Inn is a mile up here on the left."

"I don't see anything," Zero said. This was true. I could just make out the barricades from where I stood. I could also see that the road we were on would be lit brightly the further we traveled toward the on-ramp.

"What do we do?" Zero asked as I remained quiet, weighing the options. We had two. North or South. North to Utah or South to Rancho Cucamonga, again. If we could get by the southbound barricades. It would take a while for another vehicle to remove the roadblocks. Then again, they could just follow the path we were about to take. Either way, South was the correct answer. North would be asking for trouble on the 15. South should be empty. Evacuated.

"Okay, I think I got it," I said. "Let's head home."

CHAPTER TWENTY-NINE

12/10/2024

Zero pulled the truck forward.

Twenty-five miles per hour.

Light flooded the road around us.

Zero slammed his foot on the accelerator, and I could hear the engine roar its excitement.

Thirty-five.

Fifty.

Fifty-five.

The truck sped up the side road. We passed the abandoned RV camp. It flashed by in a blink. The road weaved to the right, but Zero had no problem at that speed thanks to the lights on the freeway. A light curve to the left, as we approach the overpass. Then darkness as we pass beyond the freeway lights and we arrive at the overpass. The on-ramp to the southbound lanes is blocked by a concrete barricade.

As expected. What was not expected? The Army truck on top of the overpass. Lights from the truck flash on, as we drive by.

"Go Zero!" I yelled. He stayed on the side road and kept the pace. The Army truck turned left to follow. I pulled Drew down flat in the truck bed.

"I am going to aim for the tires, you aim for the hood!" I said. Drew shook his head. "We have to stop that truck from following!"

I struggled to get up on my knees at the back of the truck. The lights from the trailing vehicle, which had already gained ground, blinded me. But, that was okay, because the lights told me where to aim. I squeezed the trigger and unloaded a shower of bullets on the truck. Hitting where? I did not see. Drew scrambled up next to me and fired. The sound of the rifles, the tires screeching and the engines roaring created an out of body experience like you were watching yourself in a Stallone movie in surround sound.

"Now!" Zero yelled, barely audible to Drew and I. I grabbed Drew by the shoulder, his rifle swung my direction, his face blank and wide-eyed as if in a hypnotic state, and pulled him back down, face first, into the bed of the truck. Zero turned a sharp left into a ditch, ten yards before the side road ended. Drew and I flew three feet into the air, and we grabbed onto each other, hoping not to be thrown into the trench on the side of the freeway. The luggage did the same, and one bag did not make it back, it landed somewhere on the edge of the 15 freeway.

There was a loud crash as Zero struck the chain-link fence that separated the freeway from the road. The fence gave way. I could feel Zero's truck begin to fishtail. So much dirt in the air that I could taste it. A piece of a chain-link fence flew over the truck, scraping the top edge of the truck bed, barely missing me and Drew. Another bump and then a quick right turn. Pavement that caused the tires to screech.

We had made it on the 15 freeway.

I crawled to the back of the truck bed and peered over the tailgate. The Army vehicle sat still on the side road. In the beam of its headlights, I could see smoke.

"We're good!" I yelled. "Zero slow down."

We began to descend the Cajon Pass. Zero stayed in the middle lane riding the brake the entire way. I saw a spider crack in Zero's windshield on the passenger's side.

"You guys okay?" I asked. No verbal answers. A few heads nodded. I slumped down with my back to the cab and exhaled. Drew was sitting now to my left, his body still, eyes opposite of me. The gun, the one I took from Jensen, was at his feet as if he left it there and now was trying to squirm as far away from it as possible.

For the first time since the alarms sounded back at the Army compound, just over an hour ago, I had time to think. Oh, I thought, quite a bit, over the past hour. But, not as Blake. I was thinking and acting as Sergeant Anderson. Was there a difference? I'd like to believe that there was. Who is to say? I acted on my training so we could escape the camp. But, at what cost? At first, everything went so well. I analyzed each situation with clarity and acted accordingly. But, it did not work entirely. Ethan and Aaron were dead. I had made one tragic error. The gun. I offered the gun to Ethan. Why did I? To keep them safe? I analyzed the situation and made a bad calculation. Alicia carrying Jane was slowing the group down. Removed that problem by having Drew carry Jane, and I take Natalie. Why didn't we stay together? I sent them on. Why? We should have stayed together. I don't know. A mistake was made and now, my first friend, the kid who knocked on my door the day after his family moved into the trailer park, the kid who let me come over to his house to play his new XBOX, eat his variety of

Hostess snacks, who told me he had his first crush, at age eight, it was a girl in the sixth grade, and I said I had the same feelings for her and we made a pinky swear that we would accept whoever she liked and let the best man win, neither of us did, this kid, this grown man, who as an adult I never truly got to know, because I spent the last six months wanting to be alone, dealing with my own PTSD, now was dead.

It was my fault.

Why did I kill Jensen so cruelly? I saw him staring at me. Confused. Why had his sergeant shot him in the throat? Ethan had a gun. No guns were allowed in the camp. Was I angry? I didn't feel angry. I felt... nothing.

"You okay?" Drew asked me.

I looked around. We just passed the off-ramp for Highway 138. I could see the outline of a gas station on the north side, surrounded by the San Gabriel Mountains. "I suppose," I said.

Drew nodded and looked away.

"Blake," Zero said, from the front seat.

"What's up?" I said, not turning around.

"Which way?"

"I guess we should get off the freeway before we enter town."

"That's what I'm thinking."

"Get on the 215 and get off at Glen Helen, I believe that we can wind our way into town that way."

"Where are we going?" Alicia asked.

"I guess to my place to pick up some fresh supplies."

"Won't they be looking for you?" Drew asked.

"Yes, they will, and they will be looking for all of us. So we won't stay long. I suppose everyone gave them their correct address when we arrived?" I asked. No answer.

"I didn't," Zero said.

"That's my Zero," I said. "We can hole up at Zero's apartment after we make brief stops at my place, then Drew's."

"Why go back to your place?" Alicia asked.

"I need some tools and supplies. We need to get the GPS devices out of these guns," I said, and Kaitlyn, Alicia, and Zero all turned to look at me.

"What? They are tracking us!" Alicia said.

"You? No. The guns and me? Yes," I said. "Speaking of." I took off my Army supplied uniform jacket. Too bad. It was a good jacket. Infrared reduction. Fire resistance. Then my Army provided boots. Threw off my military tactical helmet, which in all the chaos, I forgot I had on. Stripped off my desert camo pants and pulled the dirty pair of pants from my backpack.

"You taking everything off?" Drew asked.

"No. That's it," I said as I threw the Army pants onto the freeway. All four items, my uniform, littered the road between Highway 138, and the 215 and 15 interchange. I didn't have time to find the GPS signal. Now, I was just in my Army t-shirt and dirty pants. My socks have holes in them.

"What about the guns? Can't we throw them off as well and then they couldn't track us?" Alicia said.

"True, but then we would be unarmed. We spend some time and try to find the GPS devices. If not, then we will ditch them."

Zero pulled off the freeway.

"What's that?" Drew said, his hand pointed toward the southern sky. I followed his raised index finger and saw blinking lights in the night sky. They didn't appear much smaller in size than the stars in the background. It looked like two pairs of eyes hovering in the air slowly moving east. Two pairs of eyes?

"Police drones," I said. "Zero. That overpass up ahead..."

"Yes," Zero replied.

"Park underneath it."

"Okay."

Glen Helen Parkway wound back under the 15 freeway and as it did Zero pulled the truck under the overpass and put the truck in park.

"What's going on?" Alicia asked.

"Police drones," I said.

The police drones, I explained, were equipped with infrared and would be able to spot our heat signatures in the dark. Whether that was true? I had no idea. Like most of my actions the past month, I acted on instinct. On some sliver of knowledge obtained during my twenty-four years of existence. I presented these insights as facts to my friends.

We spent the night under the overpass.

We pulled out as much extra clothing as we could from the suitcases and bags. I put on an extra pair of dirty socks and my heavy-duty brown jacket, which I had stuffed in the bag. Others put on layers as well. Most fell asleep instantly.

I kept watch.

CHAPTER THIRTY

12/11/2024

By mid-morning, the rest of the crew began to stir. I spent the night awake. Not thinking. Not dreaming. Just staring. A zombie on watch.

"Blake," Kaitlyn said. "You've been up all night?"

"Yes," I said. I did not turn around. I did not move.

"We ready?" Zero asked after all the adults were awake. I stood up and took the position as lookout facing forward over the cab, the rifle with me. Drew to watch the back. Same arrangement as last night, only now we needed to keep one eye on the sky.

The drive to my home was slow as molasses. A hundred feet here. Four hundred yards there. The police drones had taken over the duty of patrolling the evacuated areas. We did our best to move when we supposed we were out of range of the cameras. Every time one began to travel overhead, we would tell Zero to stop. Then Drew and I would hop out and hide under the truck. The rest made not a movement inside the cab. Each stop was for thirty seconds, and then the drone was on its way elsewhere. I hoped the truck would appear abandoned on the side of the road. They were just doing a cursory patrol of the area, not looking for anyone in particular. The way I figured it and what I told the group was, we had twenty-four hours at the most to become ghosts. That was how long I calculated it would take for the Army to start looking for us. Well, for me anyway. Then the drones would become real threats. For now, we just needed to avoid drawing attention to ourselves. Again, this was presented as fact to the group.

What would have been a fifteen-minute drive (discounting Friday nights) took three hours in this scenario. It was afternoon when we pulled onto Seagull Dr. The neighborhood looked like we left it. The exception? The spray painted front doors. Every door had a large "X" and a number on top. Most of the homes had the number zero. When we pulled into my driveway, right next to my abandoned car and Kaitlyn's rental, the number above the "X" on my front door was a nine.

Drew and I jumped out of the truck bed, and everyone appeared eager to get inside. Drew was watching Jane and Natalie as Alicia grabbed a bag from the back.

"Leave the bags," I said. "We're not staying long." She did.

They all looked so skinny. Jenna's cheeks were gaunt and dirty. Her jeans were torn at the knees. Natalie's pink jacket was now a pale pink, with brown spots like a spoiled salmon and the bright white puffy ball on the hood, was now a grayish-brown. Alicia's red hair seemed darker and lost all its shine. Drew always had stringy hair, now he appeared to have a black mop on his head, and his clothes hung on him as hand me downs would look from a much larger older brother. Kaitlyn's red converse were faded to a light pink, and the white trim was covered in the desert dirt. She probably weighed a hundred pounds. We were in the camp for just three weeks and two days, yet the changes were evident.

As I approached my front door, I noticed the small piece of wood

The National Guard had used to drill the door shut, since they blew out the deadbolt and door knob, was broken, and the door was open an inch. A stiff southerly breeze would open the door on its own.

Kaitlyn, who was following me, grabbed my arm. I turned and whispered, "Keep everyone out here." I pointed to the broken door so she would understand. The rest were just now coming down the walkway toward the front door. I made eye contact and raised my hand. Palm outward. They all stopped. Jenna in front stopped and tilted her head. The Welles family stood behind her. Kaitlyn stepped back in line with the rest of them.

I slung the rifle off my left shoulder and used it to push the door open. The blinds were all closed, and as the light entered from the open door, I could see dust particles floating in the air.

The house looked as we left it, with a few small items out of step with the room. A box of crackers on the dining table, along with seven plastic bottles of water. A backpack that belonged to no one in our group was laid flat on the red couch. But, it wasn't the dust nor the out of place crackers that put me on edge, it was the smell. A mixture of rotten eggs, spoiled pork, and shit. The smell of death. Of decay. It was a scent I was unfortunate enough to be familiar with.

I entered the living room, rifle at the ready, still in my socks, not too concerned about finding the living, more concerned about who was the culprit behind the smell. No one alive would willingly live in such a place. Keeping to the left. One eye on the kitchen, the other on the opening to the hallway and back rooms. As I came up parallel to the hallway entrance, I side-stepped my way through. The smell was stronger here, making it difficult to breathe. Keeping both the kitchen and hallway in my view. I looked right, then left down the hallway. Slowly I crept down toward the bathroom at the end of the hall. Nothing. The guest bedroom. Nothing. The office, nothing, except it smelled like stale cigarettes mixed with death. Down to the master bedroom. I opened the master bedroom door. The smell overwhelmed me. I turned away from the stench and tried not to vomit on my hallway floor. Took a deep breath and entered my bedroom.

On the bed was a corpse, in an advanced state of decay. A bloated face in a death grin and gray skin peeling away from the cheek bones of a dead man. White liquid oozed around the eyes, ears, and mouth. The eyes appeared brown, but with an egg white coating. Thankfully, my comforter was covering the rest of the body.

I left the room, ran through the house and out the front door. Outside, I sucked in a breath of fresh air. Bent over, my hands on my knees.

"What is it?" Drew asked.

I forgot they were there.

I looked up. "There is a body of a man in my bed."

"What? Who?" Kaitlyn asked.

I shrugged. "I have no idea."

With the door still open the smell began to follow me out into the walkway, and I could see my friends catch a whiff of the decay, as their noses crinkled and their eyes widened.

"What now?" Alicia asked with a hand over her nose.

"We still have to grab some supplies and either find the GPS device in the guns or abandon them?" I said. None of them made a move forward. "And I still need to get a new pair of shoes." I laughed. It was probably inappropriate, and my friends did not seem to think it funny.

Zero and Kaitlyn volunteered. Kaitlyn was to grab whatever was left over in the kitchen. Zero, the camping supplies, and the canned food in the attic. The Welles family and Jenna, waited outside, with an eye on the sky.

I took a deep breath and headed straight to my bedroom. Trying to ignore the body, I opened my closet and found my empty gun safe. It was completely empty. Damn. They took everything. Next to the dresser in the closet, I found my running shoes that had to be at least five years old. But, they would be better for post-apocalyptic survival than the black converse next to them. I ran out of breath and sucked in the rancid air that made me choke. I grabbed some underwear, a jacket, a pair of jeans and another black sweatshirt.

"Blake!" Kaitlyn yelled from somewhere in the house. I gladly left my bedroom with my new clothes and closed the door behind me. Zero was throwing canned food down through the attic opening onto the hallway carpet. Each can landed with a resounding thump.

"What?" I asked as I entered the living room. Kaitlyn was standing in the dining room holding an envelope. She had covered her nose with a kitchen towel that wrapped around her face.

"This was on the kitchen counter," she said.

"What is it?"

"I don't know, but it has your name on it."

I walked over, and she handed it to me. On the envelope were two handwritten names: Blake and William Anderson. A shudder ran from my toes to my fingertips. I dropped my clothes on the floor.

There was a scratch at the back door. Kaitlyn turned and looked.

"What was that?" Zero asked, from the hallway.

"You heard that too?" Kaitlyn asked. Zero nodded and walked past Kaitlyn and me to the back door. Ignoring me and I him. I sat down on the red couch, in a daze. Who could have left this? I, being of absent mind, began putting on my new shoes in a robotic fashion.

"William's your brother, right?" Kaitlyn asked, and I nodded.

"What the hell!" Zero yelled from the kitchen.

I opened the envelope and pulled out a two-page letter. From my right, I saw a dog run into the house. It was a white and black Siberian Husky. It ran right up to Kaitlyn who jumped ten feet at the sight. The dogs tail whirled back and forth, a hundred miles an hour. The dogs face had a black mask around the eyes like a villain from an old Three Musketeers movie.

"He was scratching at the door," Zero said. Kaitlyn bent down with caution to pet the dog as he ran around in a circle in a heightened sense of excitement.

I, meanwhile, found myself attempting to make sense of the letter. Once I saw the handwriting, I knew who had written it.

> Dear Blake and William,
>
> Please forgive me. I know this is the most important thing I needed to say. To say I am sorry. Not that it matters now. If you are reading this (which given the circumstances is highly unlikely), I want you to know I love you both and always will. When I left, those many years ago, I had no inkling that would be the last time I would see you. When I made the arrangement with your mother (It wasn't my idea). My move to Ohio was supposed to help out the family financially, but instead drove a wedge between us. I won't bore you with the details, except to say, again, that I am sorry. I was supposed to be there. To see you grow up. To see Blake graduate High School. To see William, get married. To see your Mother happy. Instead, I am now dying of radiation poisoning.

For the last two years, I have been living in West Hollywood. A week ago, I was on my porch smoking a cigar. Yes, your mom would've forbidden it. I was enjoying myself when I saw it. A sun forming out of nothingness. The warmth went through me, and somehow I survived. At least for a little while. I made the decision to try and find you Blake and hopefully William. But, when I got to this old house, everyone was gone. Already evacuated. I really don't know what else to say. I am in alot of pain now and won't last much longer. I love you both and wish we could've seen each other one last time.

I am sorry.

-John Anderson

P.S. If you could please check the backyard for my dog, Strider, and take care of him, I would appreciate it. He's a good dog. A little stubborn, but loyal.

P.S.S. If you are reading this and are not Blake or William, please leave this letter, but take care of the dog.

Thanks.

I sat stunned.

"Doggie!" Natalie said, from the front door. The Siberian Husky ran over to Natalie and almost bowled her over. Jane was there as well trying to hug the dog as soon as it would stay still.

"Who's?" Alicia asked.

"I don't know, it was outside," Zero said.

"We saw a drone overhead, so we came in," Drew said. His nostrils flared. "Damn it does smell nasty in here, let's open some windows."

Kaitlyn sat down next to me. Jenna was still standing by the front door.

"What's its name, mommy?" Jane asked as both girls had corralled the husky in a group hug, by the front window.

Alicia walked over to the girls and bent down. "I don't know, does he have a collar?"

"How do you know it's a he?" Natalie asked.

"I just do." Alicia grabbed the collar around the dog's neck and examined the tags. "It looks like the dog's name is..."

"Strider," I said.

Alicia looked at me. They all looked at me. "How did you know that?" Alicia asked.

"It's my dad's dog," I said, as I stared at the letter.

"That's your dad in there?" Kaitlyn asked.

"Yep," I said.

My dad. My father. Typical of him to write a letter saying he is sorry. What a crock of shit. He left us. He left me. He's been living forty miles from me for the past six months, and I heard nothing from him. Nothing. He is sorry now? Fuck him. And now he's dead. I could feel it building in my stomach. My father was dead. Lying in my bed. My mother was dead. All that remained were the books she read. My grandparents were dead. While I live in their homestead. My brother was M.I.A. Long gone and far away. My lips began to quiver. My eyes watered. My best friend from childhood? Dead. At my own hands? No. But not without regret with all I could and should have been. A friend until the end? No.

"Look, mommy, he's kissing me," Natalie said as Strider was licking her face, the tail still wagging a hundred miles an hour. The smiles on their faces as the dog licked away was pure joy. The dog had kissed the girls so often you could see lines on their faces where dirt was removed from the cleansing kisses.

I burst at the seams. Crying a deathly wail. My whole body shook. My shaking hands tried to cover my face. Kaitlyn wrapped an arm around me, and still, I wept. I had forgotten how to cry. But, it all came back to me in a giant burst. The girls stopped their assault on the dog and stood up. Drew and Alicia kept quiet, trying unsuccessfully to not stare at this grown man crying with such fervor. Jenna sat down next to me and joined Kaitlyn by embracing me in a hug. I took their warmth and compassion gratefully.

"Oh shit. What happened now?" Zero said as he stood in the kitchen archway holding a large plastic container filled with dog food.

I burst out laughing. A tearful laugh. I couldn't help it. "Nothing," I said or at least tried to say in between laughter and tears.

"What now?" Alicia said.

I calmed myself down to a point where I could speak and stood up. Jenna and Kaitlyn stood up along with me. Catching the eyes of everyone I said, "Now? Now we go."

"What about your dad?" Jenna asked.

"Leave him," I said and saw the eyes of those around me flicker suspiciously. "I think he would be happy to know we found him and left him where he died."

EPILOGUE

12/25/2024

As I sit here now and write this last section, a small candle providing my only light, we are ready to celebrate a makeshift Christmas. Natalie and Jane are asleep in front of a fake Christmas tree. The tree we found in an attic. The presents are wrapped (two tablet's with games preloaded for the kids, and a solar powered charger we discovered in a house in north Fontana, for all of us.) On the couch, Drew and Alicia sleep together, arms around each other, a blanket draped over them. Jenna and Kaitlyn are asleep next to the kids, wrapped in sleeping bags. Strider is asleep as well at the feet of the children. Zero is upstairs, in a second story bedroom on the lookout.

For the past two weeks, we have been house-hopping day to day. We've stayed off the radar of the drones by slowly moving east. Through backyards. Through neighborhoods. Through towns. We have found water. Food. Pet supplies.

This house, which we made into our temporary home for the past three days, is at the northernmost point of San Bernardino, a block away from the road that will take us over the mountains and on our way to Utah. A new suburban development, surrounded by homes built fifty years ago.

We are beginning to look like character's out of an eighties post-apocalyptic movie. Zero started to wear a bandanna around his head, another over his face and an assault rifle slung over his shoulder. (We found and destroyed the GPS tracker embedded in the bolt carrier group.) He moves the vehicles as we traveled east; his truck and Kaitlyn's rental car. Kaitlyn is the nanny of our group, watching after the dog and kids during the day, while the rest of us explore our surroundings and pillage what we need. Drew and Alicia, became our rear guard. Jenna and I, the front scouts. We have run into no one. The Inland Empire is deserted. If there are others out here, we have not seen them. A vast suburbia, ripe for the picking. And pick we do. The truck has been packed to its capacity.

As the first light of morning is approaching, I will finish this portion of the story. We have survived. It will not be an easy trip to Utah, with winter in full swing and an unknown world out there. But, we are ready to go.

If we make it to Utah, I will write that story as well. For now, this is it. I end this as Jane begins to stir and, eventually sits up.

"Is it Christmas?" she asks to no one in particular.

"It is," I say from the small table in the dining room. She turns and looks at me with a broad smile. I smile back. My new family begins to stir, and I feel happier than I have in a long time.

About The Author

Aaron M. Carpenter was a Theatre Arts Major, a Real Estate Tax Searcher, a Data Analyst, owner of a Video Production company and, now, an Author. He lives with his dog, Strider, in West Jordan, Utah.

Made in the USA
Lexington, KY
14 November 2017